Someone Like You

By Elaine Coffman
Published by Fawcett Books:

So This Is Love

Heaven Knows

A Time for Roses

If You Love Me

Escape Not My Love

Someone Like You

Someone Like You

Elaine Coffman

Fawcett Columbine

New York

A Fawcett Columbine Book
Published by Ballantine Books

Published in the United States by Ballantine Books, a division of Random House, Inc., New York, and simultaneously in Canada by Random House of Canada Limited, Toronto.

http://www.randomhouse.com

Library of Congress Catalog Card Number: 97-90246

ISBN 0-449-00007-9

Cover design by Ruth Ross
Cover illustration by Berney Knox

Manufactured in the United States of America

First Edition: September 1997

10 9 8 7 6 5 4 3 2 1

Love and understand the Italians,
for the people are more marvelous
than the land.

—E. M. Forster, *Where Angels Fear to Tread*

For Filiberto Signore

Prologue

Beacon Hill, Boston
Winter, 1871

The crystal goblet had shattered in his hand. Unaccountably. Suddenly. The first thought that had flown through Reed Garrett's mind was that his reflexes had been too fast, because he'd closed his fingers quickly and tightly over the sparkling shards and blood had spewed onto the pristine kitchen tiles.

He wasn't really worried. The cut hurt like blazes, but it didn't seem too deep and he was sure the tendon hadn't been severed. His mother was worried, though. More than worried. When one of the maids had howled at the sight of his blood, his mother had come running–and almost swooned. Quickly, however, she'd gone into action and sent the butler, then the cook, then, alternately, two housemaids to fetch the doctor, a close friend of the family who lived next door in a nearly identical Palladian mansion.

While all the commotion was going on, Reed calmly collected a pan, water, and chunks of ice, and placed them on a chopping table. He'd just thrust his hand into the pan when Dr. John Joseph Ledbetter was ushered into the kitchen, his medical bag in one hand, smelling salts in the other.

"I remember what the sight of blood does to you,

my dear," he said as he winked at Reed, then wafted the salts beneath Leonora's aquiline nose.

"It's not the sight of blood, it's the sight of my *son's* blood," Leonora said, pushing his hand away and placing her fingers on Reed's inky hair. "Now, see to my boy's cut before he bleeds to death and I have to explain to his father how his best friend let it happen."

John smiled. "There's a lot of blood in that water, Leonora, but I doubt your son's going to bleed to death." He gently withdrew Reed's hand and carefully checked it. "It's a nasty wound, but nothing too serious."

Over his mother's heavy sigh, Reed asked, his gray eyes merry, "About three stitches, sir?"

"Precisely." John looked over the top of his glasses. "How did you come to that conclusion?"

Reed merely shrugged his broad shoulders. And John turned to his bag, removing first a linen towel to place a number of items on it. Gently, he swabbed the cut, then began to sew.

Leonora, dabbing at her eyes, flinched when the needle punctured the skin of her precious son, but Reed watched, fascinated, as if the procedure were being done to another. The servants had been rapt at first, all eyes on the drama involving their tall and handsome "Master Reed," but now they were all turning back to their duties.

And duties there were, a score of them, because in just a little over an hour a procession of Boston's finest was due for one of the elegant dinner parties for which Leonora Garrett was hailed. There would be salmon mayonnaise au Gridoni, raised pâté, pigeons and mushrooms, lobster salad, racks of lamb and standing rib, turbot and sole. Many courses. All accompanied by side dishes and wines and topped off with trifles aux cupidons, fruits, nuts, and raisins. A feast fit for kings, as Cook reminded them on every occasion of this kind.

"There," John pronounced. "Sewn up to a fare thee well, and bandaged quite nicely, if I say so myself. Usually I leave that last bit to one of the nurses. They're all much better at it, you know." He chuckled. "Well, I'd better be off, if I'm to be dressed in time for your dinner party." He gave an openly admiring glance to Leonora, who was wearing a splendid yellow silk gown. "Especially if I'm to rise at all to your standard, my dear."

Leonora smiled warmly. "Reed will be all right?" she asked as if her almost grown son weren't there. "No permanent damage?"

"None to worry about." He looked at Reed. "Take care to keep the wound clean and free from infection, son, and you'll be right as can be within two weeks."

Reed rose and thanked him, then watched his mother escort the doctor out through the huge dining room with its massive mahogany table already set for dinner for twenty-four. He sighed. His clothes were splattered with blood and it would be awkward changing into his dinner clothes without help, so he'd best hurry.

His mother, her necklace of yellow and white diamonds seeming to catch and hold and return every ray of light from the foyer's crystal chandelier, stopped him as he reached the staircase.

"Are you really all right, darling?" she asked as she rose on tiptoe and kissed his cheek.

He grinned. "I'm really all right, Mother." Then his expression sobered. "Have you told Father that I've decided against law?"

"No. I was hoping I wouldn't have to . . . hoping that you would change your mind."

"I won't change my mind." He smiled tenderly to soften his words.

"You can't save the world, Reed, no matter how badly you want to."

He looked her in the eye. "I must try. You know I must. It's all that matters to me, Mother."

Basin Street, New Orleans
Autumn, 1871

The city was growing dark. Reflections of yellow lamplight hugged the gutters of the wet street as the carriage made its way slowly through thick, patchy fog. Inside the carriage, Violette Wakefield was finding it difficult to read the newspaper in the dim light, but she was well into an interesting story and wasn't about to give up. A determined woman, Violette shifted her position and held the paper up to the window. Across from Violette, her sister Dahlia sat far forward on the smooth leather seat, the *Daily Picayune* spread over her lap.

Both sisters wore dark, perfectly fitted kidskin gloves to keep their fingers free of ink, and both were utterly absorbed in their reading.

" 'Public calamity . . . sin . . . depravity,' " Violette read, and then quickly turned the page of the *Daily Southern Star* to continue, " 'a vile den of infamy at No. 135 Rampart Street . . . evil consequences . . .

disgusting debauchery . . .' " Suddenly, she let out a horrified gasp.

Dahlia glanced up, giving her sister a stern look to show just how irked she was at being interrupted.

That Dahlia was irritated would not have surprised anyone who knew her and Violette. It was common knowledge back home in Texas that the sisters did not agree on much of anything, and tweaked each other's nerves constantly. Now, though, Dahlia's interest was aroused, so she folded her paper, placed it neatly beside her, and did not bother to hide her curiosity. "What is it?" she asked.

"Listen to this." Violette began to read:

An Inhuman Mother
Who Allows Her Daughters to Lead Lives of Shame

It seems incredible that any mother should be a party to the sale of her own flesh and blood, yet to the shame of the human race, such unnatural mothers do exist. At 91 Conti Street, upon the second floor, Mrs. Harris and her two daughters reside. One daughter, named Hattie, is aged twelve; the other, Lucy, is a child of ten. For some months past, Hattie has led an immoral life of dissipation, her mother being her aide and abettor therein. . . . Two days ago, Lucy joined her sister in sin.

Several people saw the two girls through the window in nature's garb misbehaving themselves with four young men similarly attired. . . . If they are not taken away from their mother and placed in a reformatory, they will be ruined forever, body and soul.

It is obvious that the sordid life witnessed by

young children living in a bordello leads to their corruption and eventual ruin. Steps must be taken to put a stop to the practice of keeping minors in houses of ill fame.

"Indeed," Violette said, and closed the paper with a sickened sigh.

Dahlia unfurled her fan and began to use it furiously, as if to blow away the sordid words her sister had read. "It may not take much to sew the seeds of lustful desire, but I daresay that in this city, sin appears to be in full bloom–and the people seem to sanction it!"

"So it seems."

"I blame it on the heat and humidity. It's a breeding place for more than cockroaches, if you ask me." Dahlia's fan was whirring like the wings of a hummingbird. "I don't know about you, Sister, but I, for one, will be happy to leave this wicked city."

"Sin will always have a large and loyal following, but New Orleans does appear to have one that is larger and more loyal than most. I've been praying since the very second we got here that our stay will be short."

"I think we should make Rachel come with us the moment we find her. She has no business living in such a horrible place. And to think she's raising her daughter here! It's enough to make a body shudder." Dahlia looked out the window. "Oh, I do wish the driver would hurry up. I'm anxious to turn my back on this town before some of its depravity rubs off on me."

"I believe you are sufficiently starched to prevent that," Violette said, amusement in her voice.

"I have a strong constitution, certainly, but I do not like to tempt fate."

Violette and Dahlia had arrived only that afternoon. However, the sisters had not been in the city more than five minutes when they decided it was appropriate that New Orleans had been named for the corrupt regent of France, the Duc d'Orléans. As Dahlia had said, "It most decidedly deserves its reputation for decadence, corruption, and sin. Can you believe the amount of vice here? And prostitution is legal! Did you know that?"

In answer, Violette had given a vigorous nod. She'd never imagined such extravagant wickedness and lapsed morals as she saw on public display in the streets. What had her niece been thinking when she came to reside in this place of gambling, dueling, voodoo, and bawdy houses?

The carriage slowed to a stop and the driver called out, "Twenty-one Basin Street. Are you ladies certain this is the address you want?"

Twenty-one Basin Street was better known as Madame Broussard's Parisian Club. It was not the sort of place that ever enjoyed visits from respectable women, but the sisters couldn't know such a thing, of course. What they did know was that the place—indeed, the entire block—looked thoroughly disreputable.

Violette opened her purse and checked the address on the letter she had tucked away there. "Yes, it's the correct address." She turned to Dahlia and let out a long sigh. "Come, Sister. Let us proceed with haste to see how Rachel is faring."

Dahlia hesitated, looking through the carriage window at the men loitering on the ill-kept sidewalk. She shuddered. "Perhaps Rachel can enlighten us as to the reason she chose this Sodom and Gomorrah. It is little wonder to me that she has fallen so desperately ill. I pray she will listen to reason and quickly return to Texas with us."

From the third-floor window of Twenty-one Basin Street, a young girl watched through parted lace curtains as two women dressed in gray bombazine alighted from a carriage on the street below. The girl's name was Susannah. Her mother, Rachel, had been lying waxen and pale in a vault in St. Louis Cemetery for three days. Susannah Jane Dowell was nine years old. She knew no world but sin.

Chapter 1

Desire, they say, was born amid the fields,
amid the cattle and the unbridled mares.
–TIBULLUS, *Elegies*

Bluebonnet, Texas, 1887

Procreation was all about.

Simply everywhere. In the words Susannah heard, in what she saw–even in her thoughts.

On Sunday the Reverend Pettigrew's sermon was "Be Fruitful and Multiply." On Monday the hens started sitting on their eggs. On Tuesday the barn cat became the proud mother of six blind kittens. On Wednesday there were four new calves in the pasture. This morning the neighbor's stallion kicked down the fence to get at Susannah's mare.

And, to her dismay, procreation–or the lack of it in her life–even crowded into her thoughts. She sighed. She was satisfied with her life in all seasons, save this one. Spring. The promise of spring. The promise that things might be different.

"Bah!" she said. She was becoming soft in the head and foolish. Spring was frivolous and impractical, like a pair of satin dancing shoes. Poor, silly spring. Like the girls in town, with their preening and promenading, more worried about what they were on the outside than what they were within. All their thoughts were centered on finding a husband. So what did they do? They wasted their time adorning themselves so they could engage in empty-headed chatter and flirtation to catch the eye of some lusty fellow. Spring brought many things, but the most important was the promise of work, and there was plenty of that to be done on this farm. The corn was a foot high now, and the weeds were almost as tall.

She picked up her bonnet and was about to go into the kitchen when the happy chirping of a bird distracted her. She looked out her window to see a mockingbird sitting on the fence, singing his heart out. Spring was like that bird, she thought. Happy and singing, building a nest and filling it with hope and promise, much as she had done in the past. But that was a long time ago and she was twenty-five years old now, wiser. She knew there were never any birds in last year's nest.

Out in the field Susannah chopped weeds as if they were the images that had plagued her all morning, consoling herself with thoughts of summer. Once summer came, her thoughts would turn to more productive things than procreation.

A dull ache in her back reminded her to rest a moment. She removed her bonnet, retied the ribbons, and looped them at the crook of her arm. Leaning against the hoe handle, she stared out across the prairie. In the distance, a dust devil dropped out of the sky. She watched it come toward her, snaking its way across the cornfield, rattling the green stalks. Then it was upon her, loosening the braid that hung down her back and blowing grit into her face.

Susannah blinked to clear her eyes. What she saw made her freeze. The dust devil had passed–and left something behind.

A man.

Surely her eyes deceived her. She blinked again. No deception. A man–the likes of which never before had ridden down this road–was sitting atop the biggest red roan Susannah had ever seen.

What a handsome picture he made with the sun sloping down on the right and throwing his thin spectral shadow, tall as a poplar tree, far out across the dusty road. His easy command of his mount, the self-confident tilt of his head, and the beauty of his face and form quite convinced Susannah that he was ready to ride down the primrose path of dalliance. If she knew anything at all, it was men. Men, with their sugared baits and subtle snares, their thoughts on one thing and one thing only: lust.

How fortunate for her that she knew lust for what it was–an iron poker to stir a creeping fire to flame.

As if he could hear what she was thinking, he paused a few yards from her on the other side of the fence. There he sat, right smack in the middle of the road like he owned it. He did not say anything, but he sure did stare.

She stared right back.

His clothes were covered with a layer of fine, powered dust, but that did not detract from him, nor did it hide the fact that his kind did not hail from these parts. Susannah had only to glance at him to be reminded of the finer things of life–of silver-backed brushes, of diamond stickpins and patent-leather shoes–for nothing other than instinct could enable a man to wear clothes so carelessly, to fold such height into a saddle with such lounging grace. His saddle might be worn, but it was hand tooled and finely made. The roan he rode and the dapple-gray packmare he led were finer than any horses in the whole of west Texas. She could not have been more surprised if he had been riding over a red velvet carpet wearing evening clothes and a black silk hat. She had never seen a man like him pass through this part of Texas. He must have made a wrong turn somewhere, she thought, repressing a grin.

Stuck out like a dog with two tails, he did.

Not wanting any part of him to touch her, she stepped out of his shadow and into the warmth of full sunlight. If she had been a brazen sort, she might have stared a bit longer. But she had stared overlong as it was. He was handsome as the devil, she would hand him that.

Not one to waste time, she put her bonnet on and returned to her hoeing. That kind of treatment would be enough to send an ordinary man on his way, but as she had surmised, this was no ordinary man.

She chopped furiously for a few moments, acutely aware that he had not moved. She kept on chopping, until she could feel the heat of a blister rising next to the callus on her palm. How many blisters would it take, she wondered, before he lost interest and went on his way?

She dared not look at him, but she knew the exact moment he urged his horse forward and rode through the open gate onto her property. She paused and gave him a hard, unwelcoming stare.

When that didn't seem to affect him, she returned to her work. A second later, he drew rein and pulled to a stop right in front of her. Heaven help her, but she had to look.

He smiled, tipped his hat, ever so politely, and said, "Good morning."

She gave him her back.

"Good morning," he said more loudly.

"Morning," she said, giving him a quick glance.

He seemed ready to sit there until he turned to stone. Unable to send him on his way, she had no choice but to leave herself. She turned and began to make her way between the cornstalks.

The moment she did, she heard the horse's heavy breathing coming close behind her. Just as she made the decision to run, the horse and rider cut in front of her, blocking her path.

"A moment of your time," he said in tones that were as articulate as they were unfamiliar.

She stood there blinking against the sun's brightness and taking in the sight of him, as if by doing so she might learn something about him or why he was here. He had a black, flat-brimmed hat on his head and wore a collarless shirt that fit tight at his throat. Now that he was close enough, she could see his black coat was made of fine broadcloth. His pants, of the same color, hugged his legs with nary a wrinkle.

She squinted and looked straight at him. Heaven was reflected in that face, but she was not tempted. He was just a man, and there were plenty of them in town. But as the thought formed, her heart pounded steadily, as if contradictory words might spill out: *but none like you, love. None like you.*

Her face was hot and sweating. The dust devil had left her hair hanging wild and unbraided down her back. A gnat ball buzzed about her head. The dress she wore was old and shapeless. Not that she cared, for Susannah might be young and her body innocent, but she knew men. No matter who they were or where they were, men were all the same. That was something neither distance nor time could change.

"You are trespassing," she said.

He crossed his arms over the saddle horn and leaned toward her. He took a deep breath as if he were inhaling the freshness of the cornfield. " 'Her presence fills with perfume all the field,' " he said, a teasing smile playing about his mouth.

That went over like a prickly pear, she thought. He was wasting his time and hers and she was determined to let him know it. "Don't tell me you rode all the way over here just to spout a line of poetry." Her voice was flat.

"You don't like poetry?"

"I don't have much time for poetry, and I have even less time for people with nothing better to do than to waste mine."

A breeze stirred. It blew a long strand of her hair across her face. She propped the hoe against her hip, then gathered her hair into a large skein and pulled it over her shoulder. Hurriedly she began to braid it.

" 'Amarantha sweet and fair, ah, braid no more that shining hair.' "

Just the sound of his voice made her heart vibrate like a plucked banjo string, and that angered her. She wanted to remain impersonal and uninterested. She did not want to feel anything. Not for this man. Not for any man. It took nothing more than his presence to bring back the memories of too many things, things she wanted to forget–a warm, sultry evening; the aroma of an opium pipe; the soft, throaty laughter of a woman; the guttural grunt of an impassioned man; real silk stockings and feather boas; the fragrant smells of Creole cooking; and the shame of too much knowledge.

Ride away and give me peace.

As she had learned to do long ago, she banished the unwelcome thoughts and quickly finished braiding her hair. "What are you, a traveling poet?" she asked, and tossed the fat braid over her shoulder.

He chuckled. "Hardly that."

In spite of his smile, she remained impassive. "What do you want?"

He removed his hat and wiped the sweat from his forehead. Like his clothes, his hair was black, but his eyes were as gray as goose down. "As I said, a moment of your time. Nothing more."

"You've taken up more than a moment of my time already."

He didn't know it, of course, but Susannah wasn't a woman to be swayed by poetry any more than she was swayed by jet-black hair and goose-gray eyes–no matter how soft those eyes were. Without a thread of kindness running through her voice, she said, "I've work to do, so state your business and be on your way."

He nodded, putting his hat back on. "Short and sweet and to the point. All right. How far is it to town?"

"You just passed a sign that told you."

He raised his brows. "Then I must have missed it. What's the matter? Don't *you* know how far it is either?"

She pursed her lips. "Five miles." When he made no move to leave, she added, "Straight down that road." She pointed the way so there was no doubt.

He glanced innocently in the direction she had indicated, but remained where he was. "I'm looking for work."

"Then maybe you'll find what you're looking for in town."

"I was hoping to work on a farm."

"Ask the sheriff. He usually knows who's hiring in these parts."

"I was hoping to work on *this* farm."

Her heart pounded. Her palms grew moist. She put both hands around the hoe handle–just in case–and then she stared him in the eye. "And why *this* farm?"

He smiled as if he knew every little thought that was going through her mind. "I noticed your fences could use some work, your pastures, too. Seems as though you could use an extra hand. I'm sure a woman living alone might find it helpful to have a man around."

Her heartbeat escalated. She tightened her hands around the hoe. A woman could not be too careful. "What makes you think I live alone?"

"You don't wear a wedding ring."

"Lots of people can't afford a ring."

"A man who married a woman who looks like you do would manage to come up with a ring."

She chose to ignore that, but she did loosen her grip on the hoe handle. "We don't need any help, and if we did, it wouldn't be you. We don't hire drifters," she said. For pure spite she added, "And we don't hire troubadours, actors, or poets."

He smiled in a slow, relaxed way and said, "Well now, if you gave me a job, I wouldn't be a drifter, would I?"

"No, maybe not, but you'd still be a troubadour, and I've developed a sudden aversion to those. Now, why don't you go try your charm on someone else, someone who might be interested or flattered?"

He tilted his head to one side and looked at her oddly. "I wonder," he drawled, "if it's poetry you hold in such contempt, or is it men?"

He got her with that one, but she wouldn't let him know it. Without a word, she turned and walked off. Let him come after her. She didn't care if he ran her down this time.

She did not hear him coming behind her, so after a few minutes she slowed her gait, but she did not stop. She would walk to the back of the cornfield. By the time she reached it, he would be gone.

Reed Garrett watched her stomp off, unable to understand her hostility, yet in spite of it, there was something about her that he admired. Perhaps it was her open honesty. She did not care for him and she didn't mind showing it.

He gathered the reins in his hand. Well, there was always next time.

He guided his horse into a turn, then suddenly glanced back at the woman and shrugged. *Why not?* he asked himself, and without understanding what prompted him to do so, he rode across the field to where she had begun again to chop weeds.

She looked up in surprise. She was a simple beauty blooming with rustic health, Reed thought. With a change of clothes, she would be a daughter of the gods, for she was divinely tall and fair.

"Why are you staring? Have you nothing better to do?"

Reed frowned. She was far too young and far too lovely to be so bitter. Her behavior–everything about her, really–reached out to him by some mysterious faculty of suggestion. How odd to have just come upon her and yet to feel as if he could read her face–and if not that, then most certainly her voice.

"I was thinking–"

She cut him off. "Go do your thinking someplace else, troubadour."

Reed wondered how such loveliness could be so cold and dour. Well, he wasn't so hard up for a pretty face or a job that he had to beg for work. He would, as she suggested, ride on and try someplace else. Any woman who went to that much trouble to be inhospitable ought to be left alone.

He gave her a brief nod, bringing his fingers up to the brim of his hat. "Good day to you, then."

He turned and rode back the way he had come, then kicked his horse into a gallop, leaving the farm and the caustic woman behind. The sun to his back, he rode westward, heading toward the town of Bluebonnet. The smell of life was all about him, for the fields and roadside were bursting with bloom. Little did it matter that it was mostly prickly pear, fire-wheel, and evening primrose, not to mention the dazzling color of bluebonnets that stretched as far as the eye could see. This was a flat, dry part of the world, and he had thought it rather bleak when he'd first encountered it, but one had only to scratch the surface a bit to see its real beauty.

He thought again of the woman. He didn't even know her name.

Reed passed a few cowhands working cattle. He nodded in their direction. None of them said anything; they merely watched him.

After riding about a mile or so, Reed crossed a narrow creek. Just as he reached the other side, he was set upon by four or five wild and rowdy cowboys looking for a diversion–which, apparently, he was. He recognized them as the men he'd passed a ways back.

Before he had time to react, one of them roped him and pulled him from his horse. They dragged him through the water for some distance before turning toward land. Reed wasn't certain if they intended to drown him or hang him.

Once he felt the earth beneath him again, Reed struggled to his feet. He saw there were five riders in all. It was obvious which one was the leader. The sorrel the cowboy rode was tall and a bit thin legged, but Reed figured it was a good and solid mount with a saddle not quite as fine as Reed's McLellan, but one any man would be happy to own.

The other three riders lined up abreast of the leader like aides-de-camp. They didn't concern Reed too much, but the leader certainly was worthy of concern, with his dark, maliciously ardent eyes. The fifth man held the rope. He kept the tension tight as he rode up to the water's edge.

"Get his horses," the leader said, and one of the three men rode after Reed's mount and packhorse. When he caught them, he led them back to where the others waited.

The leader looked over the roan and the gray. "You steal these horses?"

"I bought them."

"Don't see such fine horseflesh around here too often."

"I didn't buy them here."

"Where'd you get them?"

"In Maryland."

"You a Yankee?"

"I was too young to fight in that war."

"You from up North?"

Reed nodded.

"Where?"

"Boston."

The leader glanced at the man holding the rope. "He's a Yankee and these horses are stolen. Tie him up." He turned his horse and rode off, calling back to the others to bring along Reed's horses.

Reed fought against the ropes as he watched the cowhands take possession of everything he owned: his horses, his McLellan saddle, his Colt revolver, his hunting rifle, a fine Sharps Creedmore that was worth a pretty penny.

When the one holding the rope reached for Reed's hat, it was too much, and Reed took a swing at him.

That was when the rope tightened about his chest and he was jerked from his feet. He could feel his body flying across the ground. He clenched his jaw and tried to shut out the pain as he wondered if they would drag him behind that horse until he was dead.

A moment later, his head smashed against something hard, and everything in his world went cold and black.

Chapter 2

Something flapped nearby and Reed opened his eyes. A blackbird flew off.

It was early morning and the sky was beginning to lighten from a rosy pink to a pale yellow. In the distance a mourning dove called, only to be drowned out by the long shriek of a train whistle coming from far off. His head felt as if it had been split with a broadax. His stomach churned and he thought he was going to be sick. He closed his eyes.

When he opened them again, he saw pinpricks of sunlight floating before him. Great white puffs of clouds drifted overhead and he thought back to when he was a boy and how the maids would hang the laundry on the lines on a day such as this. But it hurt his eyes to stare at the whiteness of the clouds, so he closed them again.

Reed awoke. A sharp pain shot through his skull, and he felt as if his eyeballs were going to pop out. He put his hand to his head and felt a large lump, then saw blood on his fingers when he pulled them away. He tried to sit up, but the swirling in his head prevented him. He lay back down and closed his eyes, waiting for the dizziness to pass. He must have drifted off, for when he opened his eyes again, he could tell by the angle of the sun that it was late afternoon. He had no way of knowing just how long he had been out, but he did know two things: one, that he was so hungry his ribs were knocking together, and two, that everything he owned was gone.

He tried to stand, but fell back to the ground.

He made it to his feet on the second try, then stood there for a moment, his legs weak and rubbery. When he felt stronger, he started walking, having no idea where he was headed. His head throbbed with each wobbly step, but he managed to make his way across a field, his gaze locked on the angled roof of a farmhouse that seemed to rise up suddenly out of the horizon.

He walked in the direction of the house, trudging over hard-baked earth, stumbling occasionally over a clump of dry grass. The smell of something cooking made his mouth water, and he wondered if there would be any charity for him behind the walls of that home. He couldn't guess what time it was and reached for his watch, then remembered it had been taken from him, along with his money. He thought it might be getting close to six when he recalled that in Boston they always dined at seven.

How far away that all seemed to him now, and yet invariably his thoughts went back across the ruins of time and he found himself at the Cabots' ball, walking down the red carpet that had just been rolled out by the footmen, then stepping into a crimson-walled drawing room, and after that, into a ballroom where the luster of many candles reflected off the polished parquetry floor.

Wax candles. Women laughing as they spun around the room in dresses with wide tulle skirts.

The warm gaze of his mother, wrapped in deep blue velvet and wearing the family diamonds. The emotion was rich and ineffably tender.

He retreated from those feelings and was swept with a new and deeper sort of weariness. He felt as if he had been struggling for hours to climb a steep precipice, and just when he had reached the top, he was plunged over the side into an abyss. The memory passed with the tinkling of a sheep bell, and Reed saw the fine drawing rooms of Boston disappear, only to face the reality of stubborn hot sun and parched earth and a stomach that would not be quieted.

By the time he reached the farmhouse, his stomach was rumbling loudly, and his mouth was watering at the thought of getting something to eat. He could not remember when he had eaten last or when he had been so hungry.

Beneath the sparse shade of a mesquite tree, he paused and stood looking at the farmhouse before his hunger drove him on and he crossed the cleanly swept yard, scattering a few clucking chickens. He walked around the corner of the house–and stopped short, staring down the gleaming barrel of a rifle.

"Take another step and I'll blow a hole through you."

The voice belonged to a thin young boy who eyed him nervously. The lad didn't look a day over twelve or thirteen. But he had a rifle in his hands, and that made him formidable.

Reed tried diplomacy. "Pardon me, but I was ...dering . . ."

... boy waved the rifle barrel at him. "Take your ... elsewhere. We don't cotton to strangers ..."

"I'll be on my way, then, but I would like a drink from your well."

"Mister, the only thing you can have is a bullet hole through your middle, unless you start walking." He waved the rifle again.

"Thanks for your hospitality," Reed said.

He walked along the wall of the house until he reached the corner, where he turned and spied a pie cooling on the windowsill. His belly rumbled. He paused and looked behind him. The boy was nowhere in sight, so Reed put his hands into his pocket and fished around, thankful that the old knife he inherited from his grandfather wasn't valuable enough for those cowhands to steal. He opened the knife and cut himself a healthy slice of pie.

He took a bite and almost choked.

He had never tasted anything so wretched. The pie looked okay. He tried another bite and spit it out. He had never suspected anyone could do such a horrible thing to a pie. Hungry as he was, Reed couldn't bring himself to take another bite. He was ravenous, but he wasn't stupid. A man could die from eating the likes of that pie. No wonder that young boy was so skinny. Reed put the slice back on the plate and put the whole thing on the window ledge where he'd found it.

He crossed the farmyard and stopped by the well. He drew a bucket of water, then took a tin cup from a peg, dipped it into the bucket, and was about to take a drink when he heard a terrible racket. For a moment he thought a coyote had gotten into the henhouse, but then he saw a woman running toward him, a rake in her hand, both of her chins flapping as she went. For a split second he was transfixed by what he saw. Reed had seen homely women before, but he had never seen anyone so downright ugly. Every place he looked, she overflowed–save her head, where her mouse-brown hair was so sparse, it looked as if someone had taken pity on her and tried to draw some on with pen and ink. Surely she had been standing behind the door when the good Lord handed out looks.

It suddenly occurred to him the woman was dangerously close to clobbering him with that rake. Cup still in hand, Reed took off running.

Hard as it was to admit, Reed found himself chased off by a woman who looked awful enough to have been the mother of that pie. He ran through the garden, leaping over tomato plants and trailing vines of squash, not stopping until he came upon a milk cow grazing placidly in a pasture some distance away.

When Reed stopped to catch his breath, he realized the woman had vanished and he was still clutching the cup. He looked from the cup in his hand to the cow and decided he would put both to good use.

He had never milked a cow before, but he'd seen it done many times. How difficult could it be? Besides, Reed was starving and in no position to let an opportunity pass. After his previous encounter, he was glad to settle for a little fresh milk. Anything would be better than that pie.

Even starving.

He slipped his belt off and looped it around the cow's neck to lead her to the gate, where he could tie her. He had almost reached the fence when he saw two men riding toward him. Before he could say "Howdy," they roped him and yanked him from his feet. This was becoming a habit.

Winded, Reed lay on the ground and looked up

at the two men standing over him. One of them was the boy who'd chased him off with the rifle. The other man, Reed supposed, was the father.

"We have every right to hang a cattle thief," the man said. "But I think I'll haul you into town and let the sheriff deal with your thieving hide."

"I'm no cattle thief."

"And I suppose that ain't your belt what's looped around my cow's neck?"

"I wasn't going to steal anything but a cup of milk," Reed said in his defense, but the man poked a kerchief in his mouth and tied his hands behind his back.

Once they arrived in town, Reed was yanked off the horse. He stumbled and fell.

"Keep your gun pointed at his head," the man said to his son. "If he tries to get up, shoot him."

"Okay, Pa," the boy said as he looked at Reed nervously.

Reed figured the slightest movement might cause the lad to shoot, so he lay in the dirt among horse droppings and waited. The sight of him lying there drew the eye of a few curious bystanders who paused to speculate on just what he must have done.

A door opened. Reed heard footsteps crossing the boarded walk, then a voice. "You did the right thing, Hiram. It's better to bring someone in and let the law take care of it instead of taking matters into your own hands."

"See the man, Mommy! He's lying in the dirt!"

"Hush up, Sara Jane."

"Lookey at that," a male voice said. "A grown man playing in the dirt."

Several people snickered.

"Haul that poor bastard to his feet and let's have a look-see."

When he was yanked to his feet, he saw a man close to fifty, so fat his belt hung under his belly. His face was pumpkin round and a bit red, but his eyes looked kinder than those of his accuser, the man named Hiram. A tin star was pinned to his vest. The man pushed his hat onto the back of his head and gave Reed the once-over.

"What's this I hear about you stealing?"

"A thief!" someone shouted.

"Lynch him," another yelled.

"He looks like he'd slit your throat for two bits," a woman said.

"I say stretch him up right now!" another called out.

"The sheriff will take care of that," another woman said.

Listening to the shouts and comments as a crowd began to gather, Reed felt sweat run down the curve of his spine, and his wrists ached where the leather thongs were tied too tight. He gazed around at the inhospitable crowd and wondered just how it was that his life had deteriorated so that he'd been brought this low.

"Will y'all shut up just a damn minute and let me find out what's going on here?" the sheriff said.

Someone grabbed at Reed.

The sheriff slapped his hand away. "Dab-nab it! Royce, will you get your hands off him, before I shave your mustache and stuff it up your nose?" The sheriff hitched his britches up. "All right now. We've got a man accused of stealing, but there ain't gonna be no hanging. He'll get his chance before a judge, but first off, I've got some questions to ask, and I'd appreciate it if everyone here would go on home or at least stand back and be quiet."

No one made a move to leave.

That seemed to please the sheriff. "Now that we've got a little law and order here, let us proceed."

"Just string him up and be done with it," a boy yelled.

"I'm not stringing up anybody."

"Lock him up, then," a man on crutches shouted.

"I don't know that he's done anything wrong, and if y'all don't get quiet, I'm not ever going to find out. I can't lock up a man that hasn't been charged, and I can't charge him with anything until I find out, exactly, what it was that he did. If I think he's guilty of the crime he's charged with, then I'll lock him up. If not, I'll let him go. Now, has anyone else got something to say? Because the next person who yells out is going to get locked up without an investigation. Do I make myself clear?"

No one said a word. As far as threats went, that one worked pretty well, but Reed was reminded that nothing had gone right since he came to this godforsaken place. He could not help wondering what would happen to him next.

Chapter 3

"She's lying again," Aunt Violette said. Then she handed her small brown dog of dubious lineage a treat. Buckwheat looked at the treat and left it lying on the floor, because at about that time, Aunt Dahlia's cat, Parsnip, sashayed into the room. With true dog fervor, Buckwheat gave chase. He went after Parsnip in a barking fury, which made Parsnip arch her back, hiss, and turn tail and run.

Susannah looked at them and shook her head. Parsnip was a finicky Persian. She and Buckwheat had been going at it like this for more than six years. One would think they'd have learned to coexist by now.

As if reading Susannah's thoughts, Aunt Violette said, "They will never get along."

True to her nature, Dahlia said, "They might have, if that hound of yours had any breeding. What can you expect from a mutt?"

"Nothing much, except the knowledge that he will get the best of a pedigreed cat every time."

Violette Bradford Wakefield was Susannah's sixty-six-year-old great-aunt, the widow of John Jacob Wakefield, who was killed in the Civil War. Her sister, Dahlia Bradford, was a sixty-four-year-old spinster who recently had developed a fondness for fibbing, even, as Violette said, "when the truth would sound better."

Violette looked at Dahlia as if she was trying to

remember something, then said, "What were we talking about before we got onto dogs and cats?"

Dahlia shrugged.

"I remember," Susannah said. "Aunt Dahlia said Reverend Pettigrew winked at her on Sunday and you said–"

"–she was telling a fib," Violette finished.

Aunt Dahlia clasped her hands behind her and straightened her back. "The Lord knows–"

"–you are telling a fib," Violette insisted.

Dahlia ignored her and went on. "The Lord knows I am telling the truth. I may be old, but I'm not blind. I know when a man winks at me, and I'm telling you the Reverend Pettigrew winked at me when he ate dinner with us last Sunday, shame on him. And that is the gospel."

"Oh, fiddlesticks! Reverend Pettigrew has one glass eye, and the other one had something in it. If you call all that blinking he did a wink, then he winked at all of us," Violette said. "He blinked constantly for a good half hour."

"I could see sin in his eye," Dahlia said.

"Heaven forbid! What you saw was hunger. The poor man undoubtedly was ravenous."

"Say what you will. He may have only one eye, but it's a fast one. I know he winked at me."

"How do you know?" Aunt Vi asked, her face glowing with amusement.

Dahlia's mouth thinned slightly. "I know those kinds of things."

"What kinds of things?" Violette asked.

"The kinds of things that go on between men and women."

Violette glanced at Susannah, who fought back a

smile. "And how, pray tell, would you know? You have never been married."

Aunt Dahlia looked as if she was trying to settle on an expression. "I have good ears."

"Good ears? Dally, have you taken complete leave of your senses? The things that go on between a man and a woman involve quite a few parts of the body, but believe me, the ears aren't among them."

"I may have never married, but I spent twenty-five years sleeping in the room next to you and John. As far as men and women are concerned, that makes me some sort of an expert."

"An expert? Rubbish. That makes you an eaves-dropper and nothing more."

Buckwheat and Parsnip made another dash through the parlor on their way to the staircase. A free-for-all erupted when they reached the second floor.

Aunt Dahlia rose, made a faint twittering sound, cast her sister a sour look, and departed, calling her cat as she went.

"Here, Parsnip. . . . Here kitty, kitty, kitty. . . . Here, Parsnip. . . ."

Parsnip let out a loud shriek. Seconds later, a few tufts of white fur came floating into the parlor.

Aunt Vi looked up and smiled. "Maybe we should start collecting cat fur instead of goose down. We could stuff it in a pillow and give it to Dally for Christmas."

Susannah laughed. "I think that's a perfect idea, Aunt Vi."

"It's a beautiful day for our ride into town," Violette said with genuine delight.

"It's going to rain," said Dahlia.

"Rain? Why, there isn't a cloud in the sky," Violette said.

Dahlia raised limpid eyes and sighed forlornly. "It's going to rain, just the same. I can tell by the way my hip's been hurting. Mark my word, it's going to rain."

"Then let's worry about the rain when it starts. I say there is no need to put a damper on such a fine day."

Dahlia gave a grunt of disagreement but said nothing more.

Susannah looked at her aunts. It was obvious they were sisters, but where Violette was all softness and curves, Dahlia was all sinew and sharp angles. It was as if the contours of their bodies had dictated their dispositions.

"I hear Mr. Poindexter has received a shipment of fine linen cloth," Susannah said.

"That last length of broadcloth we bought from Poindexter's store wasn't fit for flour sacks," Dahlia reminded them, since she took it as her duty to never let anyone forget an unfortunate situation. "Remember that bolt of calico from the year before?" she asked with her jaw thrust out. "Wore out in six months. I told you we shouldn't have bought it."

"Yes, I remember, Aunt," Susannah said.

"Speaking of which, I just remembered something," Violette said. "I need new knitting needles."

"We don't need frivolities, we need staples. Tea, oats, baking powder, and flour come to mind," Dahlia said.

"I have all that written down," Susannah said. She brought the reins down with a gentle slap on the mare's broad back and urged her into a trot.

The sun was beginning to burn down upon them by the time they drove into Bluebonnet. Seeing a heavily loaded wagon taking the corner too fast, Susannah had to yank the reins to keep from being hit. The mercantile was just a couple of blocks away, but a shifting crowd of people, their attention riveted on something she could not see, began spilling into the street. It looked as if every person in the county had come to town this morning with the sole purpose of standing in the street.

"What on earth is going on?" Dahlia asked. "It looks like the Fourth of July."

"I have no idea, Aunt," Susannah said. "Perhaps we will find out what's happening if we can make it to the mercantile."

They drove past the long, sagging porch of the Peach Orchard Hotel, the blacksmith's shop, the funeral parlor, and the mail hack parked in front of Western Union. They were passing by the druggist when Susannah realized the crowd had grown and moved out so much that it truly blocked the street now.

"Looks like this is as far as we can go," she said. She could not believe the number of people milling around in front of them.

"What do you make of it?" Violette asked.

"I don't know." Really curious, Susannah stood on tiptoe to see if she could get a better view. She couldn't, so she climbed up on the wagon seat. But she still wasn't tall enough to see what was going on. Whatever it was, the crowd seemed emotionally charged as if they were waiting for something to happen.

"Can you see anything?" Dahlia asked.

Susannah climbed down. "Nothing to give a clue as to what's holding their attention. They are gathered in front of the sheriff's office, but that's about it."

"Well, move closer!" Dahlia said, exasperation evident in her voice.

"I can't, Aunt, unless you want me to run someone down."

Obviously trying to ease things a bit, Violette asked no one in particular, "Has there been a murder? Was someone shot?"

Susannah shrugged. "I don't know, but it looks like the whole county has turned out." She glanced across the street. "Well, almost the whole county," she amended, seeing Otis Crowder and Lee Roy Harper passed out on their backs in front of the Roadrunner Saloon, their snores sounding remarkably like the organ at the First Methodist Church.

Dahlia scooted forward in her seat. "Maybe there's been a bank robbery."

Violette shook her head and gave a snort. "I doubt there's enough money left in the bank to buy a lollipop, let alone tempt a serious bank robber. That drought we had last summer nearly did everyone in."

"See if you can get a little closer," Dahlia urged, "so we can find what the ruckus is all about."

Susannah eased the mare forward; they inched their way past a row of horses, tails switching, tied to a hitching post. She drew the mare up next to the crowd.

Everyone seemed to be talking at once. Susannah could see the sheriff trying to establish order. He didn't seem to be having much luck. Sheriff Jonah Carter had been a colonel in the Confederate army and he liked everything to be orderly, even crowds. Suddenly, he drew his pistol and fired three shots in the air.

"Dab-nab it! When I say I want a little peace and quiet, I mean I want a little peace and quiet. The next man who so much as mumbles will find himself locked up for a week. Do I make myself clear?"

The talking died away and Jonah turned and looked at Hiram Bixby, who stood between his wife, Mabel, and a man who looked as if he'd been through plenty. "All right now. Tell me what went on," he said.

"I caught this here man stealing."

As Hiram started speaking, there was a sudden break in the gathering and Susannah could see at last what was going on. Her glance swept the crowd and lighted upon the stranger. She inhaled sharply. At first, she didn't recognize him, for his clothes were showing the effects of being dragged through the brush and his face was bruised and scratched.

Susannah held her breath, remembering the strange accent, the casual elegance of his appearance, the air of refinement that marked him as different. She wondered what he had done, and the thought that she had been alone out in the cornfield with him sent a cold shiver down her spine.

Jonah held up his hand to gain everyone's attention. "Tell me your name, mister."

"Reed Garrett."

"And where do you hail from, Mr. Garrett?" the sheriff asked.

Reed drew the back of his hand across his bleeding lip. "Different places. Nowhere in particular."

"You're a drifter, then?"

"When the work plays out, I move on. If that's what you mean by drifter, then I suppose I am one."

The crowd began to whisper among themselves. Things of interest didn't come to Bluebonnet very often, and when they did, the spectacle drew a lot of curious bystanders. Susannah and her aunts remained in their buggy, their attention focused on what was happening.

The crowd seemed to be getting a little more on edge, ready to be both judge and jury. Someone threw a rock. Susannah knew how unpredictable crowds were. She had heard stories about a couple of lynchings right here in Bluebonnet. Of course, that had been during the war and the men they lynched were suspected of being Union spies–which, it was discovered later, they were not. The possibility that it could happen again hit her squarely. She felt nothing for this stranger, true, but the thought of anyone being hanged by an unruly crowd sickened her. Quivers of anxiety rushed over her.

Jonah turned to Hiram and asked, "Just what crime did Mr. Garrett commit?"

"I told you I caught him stealing," Hiram said with much exasperation in his voice.

"Well, what in tarnation did he steal?"

"I caught him stealing my milk cow. That was after he stole a pie."

"He stole a pie?" Jonah asked.

"Yes sir, a cow and a pie my wife baked. Mabel had just put it on the windowsill to cool when this man came along and took it."

A rumble of laughter erupted from the townsfolk.

"Well now, what do you have to say to those charges, Mr. Garrett?"

"I didn't steal a pie."

"You didn't?" Jonah scratched his head. "Hiram says you stole a pie. You say you didn't. Now, one of you is lying and it's my job to find out which one."

"Perhaps we are both telling the truth. I didn't steal a pie, but I did take one slice."

"You ate one slice?"

"No, I only took a bite; then I put it back."

"You took a bite and put the slice back with the rest of the pie?"

"Yes."

"That's mighty strange, don't you think? I mean, why did you steal the pie in the first place?" Jonah asked.

"I was hungry."

"You were hungry, so you took a piece of pie?"

"Yes."

"Then you took a bite and put it back?"

"That's right."

"You couldn't have been too hungry if it took only a bite to fill you up. That is mighty strange behavior for a hungry man, don't you think?"

"I said I was hungry. I was not desperate. Only a desperate man could eat a pie that tasted that bad."

This time the crowd loudly erupted with laughter. Men were guffawing and slapping one another on the back. Women were laughing and shaking their heads in agreement, as if they knew exactly what point Reed Garrett was making, and they did, for everyone in the county knew that Mabel Bixby couldn't boil an egg. It was reported that licking your fingers after touching something Mabel had cooked could lay you up for a week.

Susannah was relieved when she heard the laughter. She felt her body relax and she leaned back, about to make a comment to her aunts, when Violette spoke up.

"I hear Mabel's coffee is strong enough to raise a blood blister on a rawhide boot."

Susannah waited for Dahlia to contradict, but heard not a word. It was the first time she could remember her aunts agreeing on something.

When the laughter died down, Sheriff Carter confronted Reed. "What's this about you stealing a cow?"

"I wasn't stealing that cow."

"All right. If you weren't stealing the cow, what were you doing with it, taking it for a walk?"

Everyone laughed.

Except Reed Garrett, who said, "I was going to get myself a cup of milk."

"What did you want a cup of milk for?"

"Maybe he was baking something," someone shouted and members of the crowd laughed again.

As Susannah looked at Reed, she noticed his feet were placed well apart, as if he was ready to hold his ground. In spite of his standing quite still, there was nothing about him that spoke of fear. His face was expressionless and the narrowed eyes moved from time to time to stare dispassionately across the throng. Susannah had a feeling he was judging the temperament of the bystanders.

The sheriff looked at Reed, waiting for his answer.

"I told you. I was hungry."

"And since you didn't eat the pie, you thought you'd try a little milk," Jonah said.

"That's right."

That answer caused a stir of conversation by the bystanders. "If you don't have a horse and you can't even buy a cup of milk, what are you doing here in Bluebonnet, destitute and down on your luck? Were you expecting a handout?"

"No, and I wasn't destitute when I arrived. I had money and two horses, but I was robbed and dragged behind a horse until I lost consciousness. When I came to, my horses, saddles, guns, and my money were gone."

Jonah didn't seem to believe Reed–or to disbelieve him. When he opened his mouth to say something, the thundering sound of approaching horses caused everyone to turn and look up the street. The mounts of half a dozen hands from the Double T Ranch were kicking up a cloud of fine, powdery dust that settled on everyone.

Susannah coughed a few times to clear the dust from her throat, then busied herself with brushing off her skirts. When she finished, she saw that Reed Garrett was watching the ranch hands with an angry look and clenched fists.

"That's one of my horses and that's my saddle," he said, and nodded at a large red roan.

"Curly," the sheriff called out to the man on the roan. "Where'd you get that horse you're riding?"

"From the remuda at the Double T."

"And the saddle?" the sheriff asked.

"Belongs to the Double T."

"Well, where in tarnation did the Double T get them?"

Curly was flummoxed. He took off his hat and rubbed his bandanna over his bald spot. "I don't rightly know," he said. "Just found the horse in the remuda this morning when I went out to catch myself a mount, and the saddle was in the tack house."

"I'm going to have to ask you boys to come over here," Jonah said. "We've got a little problem that needs clearing up."

"Old man Trahern ain't gonna like this," Curly said, and guided the roan through the parted crowd to where the sheriff stood.

"Old man Trahern doesn't run things in Bluebonnet." Jonah turned toward Reed. "Is this one of the men who took your belongings?"

Reed shook his head. "No, he wasn't with them."

"Are you certain?"

"Yes."

"And yet you say this is your horse and saddle?"

"That's right."

"Do you see any of the men who robbed you in this group?" Jonah waved his hand in the direction of the hands from the Double T.

"No. None of these men robbed me."

"Of course, you can prove this horse is yours," Jonah said. "Do you have a bill of sale?"

"I did, but it was taken with my money and other belongings."

"So you have nothing to prove the horse is yours."

"Nothing except my word."

Some people in the crowd began expressing doubts, but Susannah saw a glimmer of admiration in the sheriff's eyes. What did Jonah Carter see that she and the others didn't?

She noticed that as the stranger spoke, he looked

about, his features twisted in obvious frustration. He glanced around at the people who had gathered to watch. His hard gaze swept the crowd until it came to rest on her.

She shifted her position on the hard wagon seat. She could not help feeling a bit fidgety beneath his scrutiny, and she wondered if he remembered her. She needn't have wondered. Before she knew what he was about, Reed nodded toward Susannah accusingly. "Ask that woman over there. She can verify what I say."

"Me?" Susannah asked.

The sheriff nodded and folded his arms across his vast middle, which served as an indication that he would wait all day if necessary.

Susannah considered Reed warily. He might wear his clothes elegantly and have impeccable manners. He might speak eloquently and with the airs of a person of a wealthy class; but his face, hard and tanned as if carved from stone, was closed and remote. Beneath the dark brows, gray eyes stared at her and Susannah shivered.

When Susannah didn't say anything, Sheriff Carter asked, "Is that right, Miss Susannah? Do you know what he's talking about?"

Before she could answer, Reed said, "She saw me on that horse. She was working in the cornfield when I rode by. I stopped and asked her for directions."

Susannah blinked, but didn't open her mouth. She couldn't. The words were frozen in her throat, not that it would have mattered. She was certain her heart was pounding so loud, it would have drowned out anything she said.

"Miss Susannah? Can you vouch for what this here fella is saying?"

Once again, every eye in town was turned toward her. Normally, that would have been enough to send her shrinking away, but without knowing why, she suddenly felt brave–and ready to come to the stranger's defense. "Yes, he stopped on the road where it passes by our farm. He was riding that roan just as he said."

"And the saddle? Did you see it?"

"Yes, Sheriff. It's the same saddle I saw today!"

"Anything else?"

"He was leading a fine-looking dapple-gray packhorse as well."

A buzz of conversation went through the crowd.

Susannah saw the gleam of victory in Reed's eyes. "He was looking for work," she said, then gave him a hard stare.

He returned her stare and that prompted Susannah to speak with a tone that sounded smug even to her. "I did not hire him."

Apparently Dahlia had been silent as long as she could. "If you ask me, she showed uncommonly good sense in not hiring anyone who looks like he does."

Violette made a disbelieving sound. "And what, pray tell, is wrong with the way he looks?"

"Too handsome," she said, matter-of-factly. "A handsome man is good for nothing except giving a woman ideas she's better off without."

"What ideas would that be?" Violette asked.

"That is not something I care to discuss right here on the main street of town, within earshot of half the community."

"That means she doesn't know," Violette said.

As Susannah watched, Violette looked at Reed Garrett with keen interest–which quickly turned to deep speculation.

"Looks like you've gone and found yourself a witness," Sheriff Carter said.

"I'm thankful for that," Reed said. "Does that mean I get my horse and saddle back?"

Sheriff Carter looked down at the ground and pondered the question for a minute. He kicked a dirt clod one way and then back the other. "I guess I can't see any reason why not," he replied. "Miss Susannah's word is good enough for me."

He turned to Curly. "Hand over the man's horse."

"Tate ain't gonna like this any more than his old man," Curly said.

"Well, you tell Tate to come on into town because I've got some things to ask him. I'm not through with this. Not by any means. I want to know how this man's horse and saddle ended up on the Double T, and while I'm at it, I'd like to know what Tate knows about this man's other belongings."

"I'll tell him."

"And you can also tell him if he wants to get mad at anybody, he can get mad at me."

Curly handed the reins to the sheriff. "I'll see that he gets the message," he said.

The sheriff watched Curly walk off and join his friends. He turned to Reed and offered him the reins. Realizing that Reed was still tied, the sheriff turned to Hiram Bixby, who stood nearby, looking sheepish, and said, "I guess you'd better untie him, Hiram."

"What about my cow?"

"You've got your cow and your pie," Jonah said.

"But he was stealing my cow."

"I don't recollect ever hearing of any thief that rustled cattle on foot or by looping a belt around the neck of the creature. If part of this stranger's story is true, then I reckon all of it is."

Hiram didn't say anything, but he did untie Reed.

"Thanks," Reed said, and began rubbing his sore wrists.

Susannah was wondering if that was going to be all there was to this incident when Jonah said, "Folks around Bluebonnet don't cotton to aimless, drifting strangers in town." He paused and hooked his thumbs through his belt loops, doing his best to look wise. "Course, I might be persuaded to release you—seeing as how you've gone and got yourself a witness and all, if you give me your word that you'll get out of town and stay out. Bluebonnet is a peaceful enough place and everyone here wants to keep it that way."

"I'll be happy to leave, but not without all of my belongings."

Jonah stroked his chin, then nodded. "Sounds fair enough to me. You've got your horse and saddle now, so you can be on your way."

Evidently that didn't sound too fair to Reed, for he was quite adamant when he said, "I won't leave until I have everything that belongs to me, and that includes my money, hat, guns, and pack, as well as my other horse."

"I'd like to remind you that you don't have a place to stay, and the town of Bluebonnet has a law against vagrants. You'll have to be moving on, son. With or without all of your belongings."

"Excuse me, Sheriff," Violette called out.

"Have your say, Violette. Lord knows everyone else in this blasted town has spoken his piece."

"I wanted to tell you Mr. Garrett has a place to stay. I hired him to work for me when he stopped by our farm."

Once again people in the crowd broke into discussion.

"Your niece said she sent him on his way," Jonah said.

Violette glanced at Susannah in a mildly sheepish way. "Yes, so she did, but you see, I hired him after she sent him packing."

"Hired?" boomed Susannah. "Him? Aunt Vi, what are you saying? Why . . . I . . . You can't mean . . . This is too much."

Violette patted Susannah's hand. "Now, dear," she said, attempting to sound severe, "that's really unlike you to–"

Dahlia spoke up. "Violette Wakefield–"

"Just a moment, Dally." She turned back to Susannah. "I'm sure you couldn't possibly have an objection to hiring a nice man like Mr. Garrett."

Dahlia tried again. "Vi, you can't–"

"Hold your horses, Dally." She turned back to Susannah. "As I was saying, I am certain you couldn't have any objection to Mr. Garrett's coming to work, especially considering how much it will benefit all of us to have a strong back to help with things. We have been discussing hiring someone to work full time."

"We've been talking about hiring Jester Buford," Susannah said, "not some stranger."

"Well, after he's been working for us a spell, he won't be a stranger."

Susannah opened her mouth, but Violette spoke too quickly. "Well, go on, Dally. You wanted to say something?"

"I have been *trying*," shouted Dahlia, "but you keep interrupting me."

"I am not interrupting you now, so have your say."

"I would rather be mad," she said forlornly.

By this point Jonah was looking a bit put out, and as he always did when he was a bit put out, he took out his pouch of tobacco and rolled one of his enormous cigarettes.

For the first time in her life, Susannah wished she smoked.

"I'll be leaving you ladies to work out your differences," Jonah said. "I've got a mountain of things to do." He turned back to the crowd. "All right, folks. Break it up. Show's over. You're blocking the way, and there are folks waiting to get past. Come on, now. Get on with what you were doing."

Completely flabbergasted at her aunt's out-and-out lie, Susannah continued to sputter and stammer until Dahlia took up the cause once again.

"You don't mean to sit there and tell me that you hired that . . . that reprobate!" Dahlia whispered to her sister. "I won't tolerate it, you hear? I simply won't tolerate it."

"I'm afraid you'll have to," Violette whispered back, adamant. "I've already hired him."

"Then unhire him!" Dahlia said. "I won't set foot on the farm until you do."

"Suit yourself," Violette said. "The farm is, after all, mine."

"I only hope," Dahlia went on to say, raising her eyes piously toward heaven, "that you never find yourself unwanted by your own flesh and blood, cast out among the heathen swine. Life is hard enough without a woman's own sister tossing her out on her ear."

Susannah opened her mouth. "But–"

"I won't be swayed," Violette said, holding up her hand for emphasis. "Not by anyone."

"But why?" Susannah asked.

"I have my reasons," Violette replied. "Perhaps you will understand one day."

"I will never understand," Dahlia said quickly.

"Oh fiddle, Dally Bradford. Sometimes I think you are the most irritating woman. The two of you will simply have to trust me on this. Now take me to the mercantile so I can get my knitting needles."

"So you can stab us with them," Dahlia said so sourly that Susannah was instantly humored. Her spirits may have lifted, but she was still shocked. Once she and her aunts were inside the mercantile, Susannah glanced out the window and noticed that Reed Garrett was leading his roan toward the parked wagon. After tying his horse, he leaned against the wagon and crossed his legs at the ankles.

Let him wait! Served him right if he had to stand there a year and a day. Susannah began to order the things on her list. When they returned to the wagon, Reed jumped to their assistance, grabbing parcels right and left, then loading them.

"Why, thank you, Mr. Garrett," Violette said. "I do believe I'm going to like having you around."

"I won't." Dahlia snatched her parcels from Reed. "I can carry my own, thank you. I've been doing it for almost sixty years."

"You've been in a bad mood for sixty years, too, but that's nothing to crow about."

Dahlia was outraged. "Honestly, Violette, I think you would like a case of the plague if it had a handsome countenance."

Violette ignored her and held out her hand. "I'm Violette Wakefield. This is my niece, Susannah Jane Dowell. The sourpuss is my sister, Dahlia Bradford."

"Pleased to meet you," Reed said. "I guess you heard that my name is Reed Garrett."

Violette laughed. "The whole town heard," she said as she climbed into the wagon, then patted Susannah on the knee. "I think it will be quite nice having a man living on the farm again," she said cheerfully. "Don't you agree?"

Susannah shook her head. "I don't know. I have a very uneasy feeling about this." She neither looked at Reed nor bothered to lower her tone.

"Well, come along, Mr. Garrett," Violette said. "We'd best be heading home before we get into mischief. We need to have you settled in before dark."

Reed adjusted his saddle, letting the stirrups out. Curly was a bandy-legged fellow, and he'd hitched the stirrups up as far as they'd go. When he finished, he heaved himself into the saddle.

As they headed out of town, Reed rode behind the wagon, giving the three women time to discuss him in depth. His ears certainly were burning. Not that he could blame them. Women living alone couldn't be too careful. He was mighty beholden to them for all they had done.

His gaze went to the back of the one called Dahlia. Thin nosed and hard headed, she was going to be difficult to win over. Her sister, Violette, had a face as warm and open as a sunflower. He knew she was as wise as she was considerate, the milk of human kindness flowing through her veins. The one they called Susannah–well, she was hard to get a handle on. Studying her rigid posture, obstinacy was a word that sprang to mind. Did she ever laugh?

He rode along, listening to the soft murmur of the women's voices, the creak of a wagon wheel, the hollow ring of hooves striking hard ground, and the distant rumble of thunder.

He looked up at the sky and saw nothing but blue dotted with an occasional white puffy cloud. That blow he'd taken must have rattled his brains, because, he realized, that wasn't thunder he heard. It was his stomach rumbling.

After a while, when it seemed the ladies had tired themselves out talking about him, he urged his mount forward until he was riding next to them. Dahlia gave him an unwelcome look. Violette smiled warmly. Susannah stared right through him as if he were as thin as air. He smiled inwardly at that thought. If he didn't eat, and eat soon, he just might be.

Chapter 4

The drifter was riding on the side closest to Aunt Violette, which did not bother Susannah in the least. It simply made it easier to ignore him, but he did not take much notice, since it was Aunt Violette to whom he directed all his conversation.

Susannah found that irritating. How dare he ignore the fact that she was ignoring him. When she ignored someone, she wanted them to be aware of it; otherwise, what was the point in going to all that trouble?

"Thank you for coming to my aid back there," he said.

"Thank you for the bald-faced lie, you mean," Dahlia said.

Aunt Violette ignored her sister–something she did regularly–telling Reed, "The offer was sincere."

Upon hearing those words, Dahlia gasped and fell back against the wagon seat, fanning herself furiously. The sudden movement jolted her straw hat, which slid down over her eyes.

"Is she all right?" Reed asked.

Violette nodded. "She'll outlive all of us."

Susannah wasn't really listening to any of this. She was still stuck a few words back. Sincere? What was Aunt Violette thinking? She really meant to hire this man? A man who looked like him? What would they do with him? Hang him up for an ornament? He probably didn't know the first thing about farming–or anything else, for that matter. Well, she would take that back. He probably knew a lot about preying on innocent young ladies. She would bet her Sunday-go-to-meeting dress that he was, just as she'd first suspected, one of those traveling men who went around the country taking advantage of unsuspecting women, leaving a string of broken hearts and a few babies behind.

A traveling man. Not much to recommend him as far as she could see, but the farm was, as Aunt Violette said, hers, and that meant she was free to do as she pleased, although that was a right she rarely exercised. So why did she choose to exercise it now?

"You're really offering me a job?" Reed asked, his odd Yankee accent sounding horribly foreign to Susannah.

"Like I said, the offer was sincere. You've got a job if you want it," Aunt Violette said.

Susannah groaned.

His gaze swept past her aunts as he looked her directly in the eye. Susannah felt uncomfortable at his boldness. He continued to stare for a moment, then turned to Violette. "I'm mighty beholden to you for a job, ma'am. I don't mind telling you I need work."

Susannah snorted.

He looked right at her and said, "I am beholden to all of you for this job. I hope that I can find some way to express my gratitude."

Dahlia had her hat perched in its proper spot. "We appreciate your gratitude, Mr. Garrett, but bear in mind one thing. We are giving you a job, and that's all we're giving you."

He smiled.

Susannah did not know why he bothered her. He

was pleasant enough and not bad looking. His manners were beyond reproach. It occurred to her that that might be what annoyed her. Two and two didn't add up. He passed himself off as one thing, but everything about him said he was something else. Fact was, not in any shape, form, or fashion was he like any other hired hand she'd ever seen. Naturally that made her suspicious, and if there was anything Susannah wasn't when she was suspicious, it was friendly.

"Just how long are you planning on staying?" she asked.

"For as long as your aunt needs me, which I hope will be until the end of the season. At any rate, I don't plan on leaving here until I get back everything that belongs to me."

Dahlia stopped fanning herself long enough to say, "He'll cause trouble. I know it. I knew he was a troublemaker the moment I saw him."

"Are you a troublemaker, Mr. Garrett?" Violette asked.

Susannah knew Violette was being facetious, but that didn't stop her from wanting to clap her hand over her aunt's overactive mouth.

"I guess you could say I avoid trouble, but I don't run from it. I'm not like those hands from the Double T, if that's what you're asking. A man can use his brains or his brawn to get what he wants. I prefer the former."

"An educated troublemaker! Lord help us!" Dahlia said, and began fanning herself in earnest. When that proved ineffectual, she gave a fairly credible imitation of a swoon.

She was ignored, of course, and Susannah felt a

twinge of pity for her eccentric old aunt. No one ever took the time to scratch Dally's exterior to see the sterling qualities beneath–tarnished though they might be.

"If getting your belongings back is the only thing keeping you here, you might as well leave right now," Susannah said. "Old Thad Trahern, who owns the Double T, thinks he runs things in these parts, and that usually means Double T hands take what they want and–"

Violette interrupted. "That's not entirely true, Susannah. They don't always get what they want. If you'll remember, Thad's son, Tate, has been wanting you for years."

Dahlia made a remarkable recovery in time to add, "And he isn't any closer to getting her now than he was eight years ago."

Reed, leaning low over the saddle, watched Susannah. His arms rested on the saddle horn.

Susannah wanted to look away but felt as if she were being hypnotized and drawn into those dark gray eyes of his. She felt paralyzed, unable to break away–either from him or the rampant rush of feeling he inspired.

Violette spoke up, easing things a bit. "You're welcome to tie your horse behind the wagon and ride with us."

"I'll just follow along right here, if you don't mind," he said.

"Suit yourself," Violette said. "You're welcome to ride wherever you like."

Susannah didn't wait for any more polite conversation. She slapped the horse with the reins harder than usual, and that caused the gentle mare to leap forward. The sudden motion sent Susannah's bonnet flying off her head, but she paid it no mind. She would rather make another bonnet than stop the wagon and go back and retrieve it with Reed watching.

A few moments later Reed rode up beside Susannah, holding something out to her. "Your hat, ma'am."

She snatched it from his hand and wedged it beneath her skirts. "Mr. Garrett, you may dispense with the attempt at sounding southern–badly done, I have to tell you. I am certain that in whatever part of the North you hail from it isn't customary to say 'ma'am.' For all your Yankee cleverness, it seems you haven't realized that while southern women are gentle and accommodating, they are neither weak nor gullible." She slapped the mare again, and the wagon pulled ahead, removing Reed Garrett from her sight. But it did not leave behind the sound of his laughter, which seemed to follow for far too long.

Violette took Reed's hand as she alighted from the wagon and said to Susannah, "I'll show Mr. Garrett the place out back. Why don't you and Dally go over to the house and round up a few things to make Reed comfortable? He'll need linens and such."

Violette hadn't known Reed long, but she was considered a good judge of men and horseflesh. She was willing to wager that he wanted to ask a favor of her but was hesitant to do so in front of her sister and niece. Her heart went out to him. He was down on his luck and it touched her. "Before they go on up to the house, is there anything you can think of that you'll be needing, anything I didn't mention?" she asked quietly in the kindest tone she could muster, knowing that he would accept kindness but not pity.

He shrugged, his glance darting to Dahlia and Susannah. Violette could almost see the knot of embarrassment she knew was forming in his throat. "It's all right, Mr. Garrett, you are among friends, and I can assure you that anything you get, you will work for. It isn't charity."

"Thank you. If you wouldn't mind . . . if it isn't too much trouble, I'd sure be appreciative of a little something to eat."

Violette slapped her forehead. Poor man. She hadn't meant to strip him of all his dignity. "Lord save me for an idiot! Of course you would. And didn't I sit there big as a bump on a pickle and hear you tell the sheriff you took a bite of that pie because you were hungry? Please forgive my oversight, Mr. Garrett." She turned to Susannah. "Will you–"

Susannah looked completely ashamed of herself, and Vi was happy to see her niece hadn't lost her kind streak after all. "I'll bring some of that fried chicken and a couple of roasting ears. I think there are a few leftover biscuits, too."

"I'd appreciate it," he said. "I'm sorry to put you to all that trouble."

Susannah nodded. "It's no trouble, Mr. Garrett, I assure you. There is nothing embarrassing about being hungry. It is an honest feeling and a saintly one."

Susannah gave Violette a knowing smile, then took Dahlia's arm, and started toward the house.

"I really am sorry to put you to so much trouble," Reed said.

"It's our pleasure, believe me. I apologize for Dahlia. Sometimes my sister is such a fusspot. She's an old maid, you know."

Reed chuckled. "You aren't sizing me up for the job of changing her station in life, are you?"

"I offered you a job to help you out. I didn't bring you here to torture you, Mr. Garrett."

"You don't think my staying here will be a problem with any of the folks in town, do you?"

Violette was liking him better and better. "No one in town will–well, there is one person who might mind, but he's no one to worry about."

"Who might that be?"

"A fellow by the name of Tate Trahern. I believe you heard the sheriff and me mention him. He's old Thad Trahern's son and the only heir to the Double T, which is the largest ranch in these parts. As I said before, Tate has been sweet on Susannah for as long as I can remember, not that it's done him any good. Susannah doesn't pay him any mind."

He looked in the direction Susannah and Dahlia had taken. "She doesn't appear to pay anyone any mind."

Violette followed his gaze, but Susannah was already in the house. "It is difficult to keep a cracked kettle from leaking now and then," she murmured.

Puzzled, he finally said, "Well, I hate to think I'm the cause of anyone being angry at her."

"Tate won't stay mad at Susannah for long. She's the only thing he's ever wanted that he can't have. He won't risk making her mad at him. And if he does, he can just take himself off and scratch his mad place."

"You're a nice person, Mrs. Wakefield."

"So are you, Mr. Garrett. You aren't married, are you?"

"No. Why? Are you interested?"

She laughed. "I would be, Mr. Garrett, if I was thirty years younger."

Over the next week Reed learned many things, not the least of which were that Dahlia and Violette seemed to live to disagree, and that their parents must have loved flowers, or, at least, horticultural names.

The plow horse was Rosebud; the milk cow, Peony; the pet goose, Daffodil, or as Susannah had told him, "more appropriately called Daffy."

When he had asked why, Susannah merely smiled and said, "You'll find out soon enough."

But it was the name bestowed on the fat old sow with thirteen piglets that brought the biggest smile to his lips. Who would ever think of giving a pig such a dignified name as Miss Lavender?

Reed was in the barn loft, storing hay that had been curing in the pasture, and, as if she knew he was thinking about her, Miss Lavender let out a loud squeal, followed by several grunts issued in rapid succession. Hearing the ruckus, he moved to the door where the pulley hung. He looked outside. Miss Lavender had quieted down somewhat, but he didn't know for how long, since Dahlia's cat, Parsnip, was watching her from a fence post not too many feet away. Tormenting Miss Lavender was a favorite pastime of Parsnip's.

The back door slammed, and Reed looked up to watch the leisurely progress of Violette and Dahlia down the back steps. They ambled along the path arm in arm, making a stop here and there to admire a butterfly or smell the fragrance of the snowy white blooms of the rosebushes that wound through the rails of the picket fence. Their tall frames seemed somehow regal to Reed. As he watched them, their silver heads bent in conversation like conspirators, he wondered what they were talking about. At these rare moments when they'd called a truce, they seemed as happy as a pair of nesting birds. How alike they were. How different.

Violette was as cheerful and sunny as Dahlia was gloomy and somber. And yet, in spite of their differences, their disagreements, there were times when they would disappear together, often to go walking, arm in arm, as they were now. Were they remembering the way things used to be? Reminiscing about the past? He couldn't help but think that they must have been quite the rage in their day, beauties, both of them, and wondered why Dahlia had never married. As the two sisters passed beneath the open doorway where he stood, he saw that both had tucked white roses in the buttonholes of their dresses.

He was distracted for a moment by the flapping of wings. He looked out just in time to see Daffy scurrying across the barnyard in hot pursuit of Susannah's aunts. Unable to run very fast, Daffy flapped her wings to help her along and was gaining momentum when she miscalculated and slammed into the picket fence that ran around the perimeter of the backyard. Feathers flew everywhere.

Daffodil honked once and picked herself up. She waddled around a bit in a dazed, drunken manner. Watching Daffy stumble over her own webbed feet, Reed remembered Susannah's words and chuckled.

The soft, muffled whinny of a horse drew his attention, and he watched as Susannah came riding across the pasture on Rosebud's gleaming sorrel back. She was riding astride, with no saddle, her long, slender legs gleaming white in the sunlight where her dress had blown back. Her hair hugged her head, but curled about her face. Reed figured she had been down to the creek to swim and wash her hair, especially when she dismounted and carried a small bundle into the house.

Long after she had disappeared inside, he kept seeing those long, slim legs–something he had no business thinking about. He grabbed the pitchfork from its resting place against the wall and returned to his haying. There was no room for a woman in his life. Hard work would drive that need away.

He had not been working overly long when he thought he heard someone call his name. He paused and listened.

"Mr. Garrett, are you in here?"

It was Violette. "Up in the loft," he called, "storing hay."

"Come on down," she said. "I've brought you a big glass of lemonade."

"Be right there," Reed said.

She inhaled deeply and her eyes seemed to brighten. "Ah, I remember the times we used to play in the loft when we were children. What a delight that was. I don't think there is anything that smells better than hay when it's just come in from the field . . . or anything that makes me recall more pleasant memories." She allowed her gaze to fall upon the ladder that went up the wall to the loft for just a moment before moving over to him. "How I wish these old legs of mine could carry me up the rungs of that ladder just one more time," she said, then paused, reflective. "You know, it isn't so much the things that happen to you when you grow old that I mind, but the things that you can no longer do."

He was moved by the depth he saw in this woman, the understanding, the wisdom. She reminded him a great deal of his own mother, and the pain of their separation, the knowledge that he could never go home again was as hurtful as it had been the day he first left Boston. He had to remind himself that the past had no place in his life now.

"I have a feeling you've stored up a lot of memories, just like I'm storing that hay," Reed said, not knowing what possessed him to make such a remark.

"Yes," she said, "it is sweet to remember. You know, looking back now, it seems as though all my recollections are set to music, even those that were hard to bear. At this point in my life, memories are my fondest possession."

"Life has been good to you."

"Oh yes, I've had a good time of it, and few regrets. How fortunate I am to have the memories, to be able to live the good times twice."

From somewhere outside the barn came the sound of Susannah's voice. She was calling Miss Lavender with a musical lilt to the sweet promise of tasty slops.

In response, Miss Lavender went into an oinking frenzy.

Susannah's laughter was seductive as hell. It made

him want to go to her, to see if the promise in her laugh was, in fact, reality.

He stared toward the open door, envisioning how she must look at this moment. He wondered during their first meeting if she ever laughed, now he'd learned she did, but would she do so in his presence? Would he see her eyes light up at the sight of him? What good times would Susannah remember when she was Violette's age?

Violette broke into his trance of preoccupation with Susannah. "You are wondering about her memories?"

"Perceptive, aren't you?"

"It's an old woman's advantage. Tell me, what were you thinking of in regard to my niece?"

"As you guessed, I was thinking about her memories–or lack of them, as it would appear. Although I've only been here a short while, she doesn't seem to have much of a life, aside from this farm and the two of you."

An expression of deep and profound sadness crept over Violette's face, but it lingered for only a moment until she was able to push it away. "I knew it! I knew it! I knew it! I had you pegged right. I knew you were a sensitive man the moment I laid eyes on you."

"What makes you say that?"

"You're not the first man to notice my niece by any means, but you are the first to see past the external beauty. I think you are more attracted to what's inside that girl. Most men look at her and see a pretty ball to play with. You see a ball of yarn that must be untangled. Something similar about you . . . like calling to like mayhap."

"Pain identifies pain. Suffering begets suffering. Suffice it to say, it is something I have a grasp of."

"You and Susannah have much in common, I suspect. You have the touch of the healer in you, young man. It's a shame you weren't a doctor." She suddenly looked down at her watch pinned to her bosom. "Goodness me! It's almost four o'clock and I've got vegetables to gather. I have enjoyed our visit, Mr. Garrett."

"Please, call me Reed."

"If you call me Violette."

"Very well."

"Good. Perhaps, when you have been here longer, we can talk more of these things."

"Perhaps," he said, "but right now, I'd better get this work done." He picked up the pitchfork and turned toward the ladder.

She watched him go. "Work is a great calmative, is it not? An opiate for the mind, a healer of the body."

"It is also a way to escape."

"And it consumes you."

"Always."

Violette turned and left the barn, saying softly, "I think you are a man who had much to leave behind."

From the ladder Reed looked toward the door, but there was no trace of Violette in the doorway, nothing at all of her, save the resonance of her words.

"How wise you are, old woman. How wise and how right," he said. Then he lost himself in his chores, easing for a time the burden of memories.

Chapter 5

Reed knew that if Susannah had suspected he was down at the creek fishing, she wouldn't have come for a swim. But she didn't know, and by the time she discovered it, she had already stumbled on him sitting quietly on the bank, cork bobbing in the water, his thoughts a thousand miles off.

He had been sitting there for at least an hour, listening to the sound of insects, the occasional bleat of a sheep or the bawl of a calf. It was a tranquil spring afternoon, hotter than it had been during the past few days. He heard a splash and looked toward a thick stand of weeds that grew along the creek. A green frog cut a V in the water, disturbing its glassy surface as it swam toward the other side. A few seedpods left over from last fall floated out of the weeds.

Susannah suddenly rounded the bend in the path and saw him. She was surprised, jerked to a halt, and exclaimed, "Oh my goodness! It's you!"

Reed could tell that her heart was galloping. Why was she so uncomfortable around him? He could never remember any other woman being so uneasy in his presence.

His gaze dropped to the bundle she held clutched tightly against her chest. "Going swimming?"

"No . . . I mean, I'm not . . . that is–" She stopped and took a breath. "I was . . . but I'm not now."

"You seem to be having some difficulty. Did

you come down here to go swimming or not? Which is it?"

"I was, but I've changed my mind."

"You changed your mind because I'm here?"

"Can you think of a better reason?"

He shrugged. "Don't let me stop you. I'm as harmless as a fly."

"I can't believe anyone was ever stupid enough to fall for that."

He laughed. "Oh, you'd be surprised."

"I doubt it."

There was something about the way she said that that made him wonder, something that went beyond mere cynicism. Had she fallen for a similar line herself? Had she been seduced by some cowboy who drifted into her life and then drifted out again?

"Well, now that you're here, you might as well join me," he said.

"I didn't bring a fishing pole. I didn't know you like to come down here."

"I've only been a couple of times. If you want to fish, I can cut another sycamore sapling for a pole."

"What are you using for bait?"

"Frogs mostly. I also found a couple of hellgrammites under some rocks I turned over."

"Have you caught anything?"

"Two sun perch about the size of my hand. I threw them back."

He got a nibble and yanked the pole. The hook shot out of the water, naked as a needle. "They get my bait every time."

He put a frog on the hook and swung it out where the creek made a wide turn. The water was deeper there. Maybe the fish would be bigger. He wasn't certain, since he didn't know the first thing about fishing.

He watched the frog float on top of the water; then it went below the surface. He felt a tug on the line. It pulled tight. The end of the sycamore sapling bent over into a U. The fish kept on going. It must have been a big one, and Reed was afraid it would snap the sapling in two. He wasn't about to lose this fish–not in front of Susannah–so he stood up.

"Where are you going?"

"After this fish." He waded out into the water. "I'm not–" He stepped into a deep hole, swallowed a mouthful of water, and sank. Water rushed over his head and into his nose, but he held on to the pole. He surfaced, took a gulp of air, and found his footing. The line went slack and he thought he'd lost it, but it went tight again and Reed kept just enough pressure on to feel those moments when he needed to pull in and when he needed to give a little slack. He followed that damn fish all over the place, thrashing about in deep water over his head and floundering in the weeds along the creek bank. He was thinking he would never land this fish when the line snagged on a log in the shallows. He saw the fish flip in the weeds.

"Holy moley!" he heard Susannah shout. "It's a big one. A bass! I don't remember ever seeing anyone catch a bass in here."

He took a dive toward the fish, but it flipped just before he caught it. "You still haven't seen anyone catch one," he said between pants and gasps.

He saw the fish in the weeds and took another dive. He caught it this time and felt his hands close around cold, smooth flesh. The fish thrashed and he felt the spines of its fins brush against his arm. The fish wiggled free. He dived for it again and came up with his arms full of flapping fish, weeds, gravel, and creek mud. But he had his fish, and he threw it toward the bank before it could get away.

He heard a yelp and then a squeal and looked up in time to see the big white-bellied bass hit Susannah square in the chest. She caught the fish with a loud "Oooof!" then took a few steps back, trying to keep her balance. She still held the fish, but when she looked down and saw it, eye to eye, she made a sound of disgust and dropped it.

He stumbled toward her, fighting against the pull of bottom mud until he was on the bank. He stopped a few feet from Susannah, panting hard, water running from his soaked clothes. The fish was flopping around, bits of grass and sand clinging to it, but it was far from the water now. He was too tuckered out to do much more than stand there, wet and winded as a blown horse, looking at her. She still had a surprised expression on her face, and the front of her dress was all wet. He remembered her going eye to eye with that fish and began to laugh.

Surprised at first, she suddenly started laughing, too. "I wish you could see yourself," she said in short gasps. "You're a holy mess. Your hair is plastered to your face in front. In the back it's sticking up like the feathers in a war bonnet."

He looked her over. "You're not so tidy yourself."

She glanced down at her wet dress and laughed harder. When she got control of herself, she asked, "You didn't exactly handle that fishing pole like you'd done much fishing."

"I haven't."

"What made you decide to come down here, then?"

Reed shrugged and began dusting the grit and gravel off his soaked clothes, then went to pick up his catch. "It's Sunday, my day off. There wasn't much to do, and I found myself thinking about a fish dinner." He paused a moment, looking at the fish. He wasn't sure where he should pick it up, so he just reached for the tail. It flipped out of his hand. "Slippery little devils, aren't they?"

"Pick it up by the gills."

Reed didn't move. He knew what the gills were, but he wasn't certain how you picked a fish up by them. Susannah must have sensed that, for she walked over to the fish and picked it up by inserting three fingers into its gills. She held the fish aloft. It hung down past her elbow.

"It's a big one, the biggest I've ever seen."

"I thought you said you'd never seen anybody catch one before."

"Not in this creek, but I've seen them caught out of ponds."

"Looks like I finally found something us Yankees can excel at."

She ignored that comment and said, "Here, hold the fish while I take that piece of cord off my bundle of clothes. We can run it through his gills and stake him in the water."

He took the fish from her, inserting his fingers into the gills just as she had done. "What for?"

"So he won't die."

"You want to keep it alive?"

"Of course, but if it were me, I'd throw it back."

"Is that what you want me to do?"

She shrugged. "It's your fish."

"I thought we'd eat it."

"You can if you like."

"Then why go to all the trouble of keeping it alive if we're just going to eat it?"

"So it will stay fresh. Of course, you Yankees may prefer to eat fish that has been dead for several hours."

"Some Yankees know how to fish. Boston is, after all, a seaport. I just don't happen to be one of them."

"Why not?"

"I never went fishing, so I never learned how."

"You really never fished before?"

"No."

"Truly?"

"Honest to God."

"Why didn't your father take you?"

"He didn't know how to fish."

"Why?"

"I guess his father didn't know how either. My family isn't the fishing type."

"What do you mean? I didn't know you had to be a type to fish."

"We liked fish, but our cook bought it at the market, then prepared it."

"You had a cook?"

He thought of the delicious boiled shad dinners, of the cook's tendency to burn the roe. "We had a cook–and a butler, nine maids, a groom, a driver, three gardeners, plus a few others."

"Your folks were rich?"

"They were . . . genteel."

"They were rich."

He thought of blue china flowerpots filled with spiky palms standing in front of French windows, of drawing rooms and heavy damask drapes, chintz poufs, velvet-covered tables laden with china, silver, and crystal. "Yes, I suppose you would say so."

"And you gave all of that up so you could catch your own fish dinner?"

"It would appear that I did."

"Why?"

He held the fish up. "Are you going to get that string? He looks like he's about to draw his last gasping breath."

"Oh, I almost forgot." She ran toward the bundle she had dropped and quickly removed the length of twine she had tied it with. When she'd finished and returned the fish to the water, she said to Reed, "If you could put a stake into the shallow water there, I will tie this twine around it so the fish won't get away."

He did as she asked, then sat down and pulled off his boots. He poured the water out of them and set them aside to dry. "A fish that big will make a lot of chowder."

"Is that what they eat where you're from?"

"Yes, it's a popular dish in Boston. You don't eat it here?"

"No. We don't have fish very often, and when we do, it's always fried." She wrinkled her nose. "You don't like the food we cook?"

He paused before answering, delighted by the sprinkling of freckles across her nose that were the same golden color as her eyes. "I like your food, but there are times when I miss some of the things I grew up with. Fish chowder is one of them."

She looked as though she remembered something from her past, food perhaps. He was dying from curiosity, but he was afraid to ask, afraid he'd scare her away, so he said quickly, "I can make fish chowder. I wrote my mother and she sent me the recipe. It's the only thing I know how to cook."

When Susannah said nothing, he turned and picked up his pole, then dug around in his pocket. He pulled out a small frog. "I guess I lost all the others when I went in the water."

"That one looks dead."

"It is, but maybe the fish won't mind." He baited the hook and cast it into the creek.

"I bet you won't catch another bass. It will be a perch or an old mud cat, more than likely."

"It doesn't matter. Catching is half the fun. Why don't you come over here and sit down so I can talk to you without getting a crick in my neck, or would you rather stand there like a statue?"

"I . . ."

"I'm harmless. I just want some companionship, a little conversation. If you're uneasy, you can cross over to the other side. That log over there is sturdy enough for you to walk on. I crossed over it myself, not long ago."

He knew she rarely talked to a man other than to make a few comments about the weather or livestock prices, but he also knew he was different from anyone who had come to Bluebonnet, and he was from Massachusetts, a place she had only heard about. He guessed she might be intrigued, thinking he had seen much of the world. She was a curious person, full of questions.

"I suppose I could . . . for a little while."

She crossed over the log and took a place on the

other side of the creek, sitting on a tree stump and tucking her skirts about her. He liked the way splashes of sunlight leaked through the foliage to paint her with dapples of lemon light. Nearby a bird on skinny stick-like legs hopped along a branch of a dead tree.

They sat in companionable silence, regarding each other.

A breeze stirred, rustling the green, waxy leaves of a cottonwood tree overhead. The sun struck Susannah full in the face and made her eyes appear as warm and buttery as freshly pulled taffy. Her face and arms were tanned, but Reed knew that without clothes, the rest of her would be milky white. His gaze went back to her eyes. He liked her eyes and their long, soft lashes. He liked the fullness of her mouth, the heart shape of her face, the high cheekbones. Hell, he liked everything he saw.

Susannah broke the spell.

"Tell me about Boston . . . about your home."

"Boston's a busy seaport, built around a harbor, so there are a multitude of ships coming and going, bringing people and goods from everywhere. It is much larger than any of the towns near here, and quite different. In the West things are spread out. In Boston we are a bit more cramped. The streets are crooked and narrow–some of them twist and change guises as they meander along. The houses are mostly brick or frame; the streets are cobbled. There is a lot of America's history there."

"I remember studying the Revolution in school."

"The Tea Party?"

She shrugged, turning her head to one side. "That, yes. And about Paul Revere . . ."

"And his midnight ride."

She nodded. "You have snow there?"

"Every winter. Sometimes the drifts come up so high, they cover the windows. Have you ever seen snow?"

She shook her head. "Not like that. Twice, since I came to live with my aunts, we had snow. Once it was very light. It barely covered the ground. The second time it was a real honest-to-goodness blizzard with a foot or two of snow. It was so beautiful. My aunts made snow ice cream for me."

"Snow ice cream?"

"Snow, vanilla, milk, and sugar. It was wonderful. I cried for days when the snow melted, knowing I'd never have snow ice cream again."

"When did you come here to live with your aunts?"

"They are actually my great-aunts."

She had smoothly avoided his question. "I suppose it was hard to find yourself suddenly without parents."

"Yes, I've missed a lot of the normal things in life, things most people take for granted. I not only had no parents to grow up with, but I had no brothers or sisters either. I always envied people with large families."

"You were spared the fights."

"What I wouldn't have given for a busted lip or a bruise–anything that would have shown that I belonged."

"At least you had your aunts."

"Oh, yes, and I am truly thankful for them. But they're old, you know, and set in their ways. If there had been just one other child about. . . . You know, I used to have dreams about growing up in a large family." The enthusiasm seemed to drain from her face. "I soon learned no one is interested in dreams. Reality is the stuff of life here. Work, weather, sickness, religion–these are the things they understand. So, I let my dreams go and I watched them drift away like clouds driven by the wind."

"Where did you live before you came here?"

She licked her lips as if her mouth had suddenly gone dry. "Louisiana."

"New Orleans?"

"Yes."

"I was in New Orleans a couple of times. Now, down there they really know how to cook fish. Do you remember much about it? Do you recall the place where you lived?"

Suddenly she grabbed up her bundle and sprang to her feet. She hurried across the log so fast, her feet barely skimmed its rough surface. As her feet touched dry ground, she turned angrily toward him. "Yes, I remember. I remember more than I'd like. Just once I'd like to forget, but there is always someone . . . someone like you, who won't let me."

He came to his feet, tempering his next words, speaking softly, doing his best to be gentle. "What's the matter? If I said something wrong, I apologize. I didn't mean to cause you to dig up old and painful memories."

"How do you know I was digging up old and painful memories? Maybe I don't like prying men who stick their noses in other people's business."

She started walking home. She heard him call her name and started running. The sound of his voice faded away behind her, but even then Susannah did not stop until she reached the sanctuary of the back porch.

The sky was turning black and clouds were churning. Gusts of wind stirred up sand and bits of debris so that, even safe in the recesses of the porch, she had to shield her eyes. It was going to be nasty weather, a real summer storm. Already, large, scattered raindrops were pelting the ground, leaving behind the sweet smell that comes only when rain first begins to hit dry dirt.

A brilliant bolt of lightning flashed, then ripped across the sky, but she didn't hear a sound. The sky was turning darker and the clouds were in turmoil. Hail began to come down in marble-size pellets. The yard was dusted with white.

For a long time she stood on the porch and watched the storm and listened to the *ping, ping, ping* on the roof. She thought about the fish and wondered how Reed was faring. Then she reminded herself harshly that she didn't care.

That night the thunderstorm grew worse, with fierce, howling winds that uprooted trees and knocked down fences. When Susannah walked into the kitchen early the next morning to get the stove going, she found the kitchen flooded.

She stood in the doorway for a few minutes, just looking around the room, taking in the state of things. "Well," she told herself, "this kitchen isn't going to mop itself," so she removed her shoes and waded into the room to start the cleanup, holding her skirts aloft.

There was a gaping hole in the ceiling where she could see clear through the roof to the blue sky overhead. She was thankful the storm had blown on through, but mighty put out that it had taken part of the roof with it.

"Would you look at that," Violette said, coming into the kitchen behind her, the strings to her dressing gown trailing into the water.

"You better hitch up your nightie, Aunt Vi."

Violette hitched without missing a step. "Is anything ruined?"

"I don't know. I just came down."

Everything was wet, Susannah noted, but nothing was damaged beyond repair, save the peach pie that was sitting on the table and the salt and pepper in the shakers. The curtains and tablecloth would have to be washed, along with everything else in the kitchen, and the floor would probably buckle and there would be watermarks on the walls, but it could have been worse. "Nothing too important is ruined, but there's a lot of washing and cleaning to be done." She glanced up at the roof. "Of course, I don't know what we'll do about that."

"We'll get Reed in here, that's what we'll do."

Reed . . . Her aunt said that as if she had suddenly glimpsed the Messiah. Next she supposed she would be hearing that Reed could walk on water. Him! The one who didn't even know how to fish. But then she remembered he had caught the biggest fish she'd seen in these parts. Luck. That's all it was. Pure-d luck.

She remembered, too, the softness in his voice, the downy grayness of his eyes. He was a man of contradictions. Hard as nails one minute, soft as a gosling the next. He troubled her and filled her thoughts, and that made her irritable.

"I'm mighty glad we have him. I'm certain Reed will have that hole patched in no time."

Susannah crossed her arms in front of her and looked at her aunt. "Reed Garrett isn't the answer to all our problems. I doubt he can fix a roof. And the last thing we need is someone up there who doesn't know the first thing about what he's doing."

"That's what I say," Aunt Dahlia agreed, coming into the room. "Have you looked at his hands? Sissy hands if I ever saw them. Soft as a baby's bottom and just as clean. They aren't the hands of a laborer, I'll tell you that."

"If that reasoning were true, then I'd be a carpenter," Aunt Violette said, holding up her hands. Then turning to Susannah, she said, "Why don't you get dressed and go find Reed. Tell him to come over as soon as he finishes feeding the stock."

Susannah knew that tone of voice and knew, too, that it wouldn't do any good to offer any resistance. Aunt Violette was an easygoing sort, but when her mind was made up, it stayed that way.

Susannah went to find Reed, which she did, delivering Aunt Violette's message, as requested.

He came to survey the damage an hour later. After looking inside the kitchen, he put a ladder against the house and climbed onto the roof. She could hear him tromping around up there like a wounded buffalo.

A few minutes later, he poked his head through the hole and called down to Susannah. "Can you hear me?"

"They can hear you in Fort Worth. Do you need something?"

"No, just wanted to let you know that I don't think it's too bad. Nothing structural, just some shingles that need replacing. Once that's done, I can patch up the ceiling in the kitchen."

Susannah stood in the kitchen below looking up at him. His head was upside down. She found it annoying that he was so nice looking even upside down. "How long do you think it will take?"

"If I can get the materials, not more than two or three days."

Susannah nodded. "I guess you'd better drive the wagon into town and get the supplies right away, in case we're due for any more rain." She made a point to turn around as soon as she'd spoken. It wouldn't do for him to think she wanted to look at him any longer than necessary.

She heard his clomping footsteps on the roof, then the sound of him going down the ladder, and breathed a sigh of relief. Now that he was gone, she could get her mind on something constructive, like cleaning up this mess.

She waded over to the back door and opened it, letting in the warm spring air and the fresh smell that came with it. She inhaled a lungful and found her spirits lifting. The most important thing now was to get the water off the floor, so she hitched her skirts up over her knees and, armed with a broom, she began sweeping the water out the back door. When she finished, she took the mop and bucket and began the arduous task of mopping up what the broom had left behind.

The bucket was half full of water when Susannah heard someone knock on the door. She turned around and saw Reed standing there looking better than a blue-ribbon bull. She was about to ask him what he wanted, when she realized he was looking at her rather strangely and hadn't said a word. She wanted to ask him just what he was gaping at when she remembered her skirts. She yanked them down.

"I'm sorry. . . . The door was open. . . . I had no idea–"

She cut him off. "What do you want?"

"Do you need anything from town?"

"A new roof."

"Got that on order," he said in remarkably good humor, then turned away.

She walked to the back door and watched him. She wondered what he was so chipper about. Maybe it was the fish chowder. She opened the screen door and called out. "How was your fish chowder?"

"I didn't have any."

"What did you do with the fish?"

"I threw it back."

"Why?"

"Because some golden-eyed girl asked me to."

"You go around doing everything a woman asks you to do?"

He climbed into the wagon and picked up the reins. "Yes. Genteel cowards run in my family."

Chapter 6

The sun was beating down on him all the way into town. A snake doctor landed on the back of his hand, and Reed waved his arm to make it fly away.

A puff of wind, faint and fragrant, carrying the scent of peach blossoms . . . He imagined Susannah standing in a shower of petals with her back against a tree . . . the first glimmerings of desire . . . a face he could not forget. Her memory was enslaving, like a charm, the whispered promise of more to come.

Susannah racing up the path from the creek . . . birds fluttering and chirping on the wire fence along the side of the road . . . the sound of her voice . . . the sun beating down on the road that stretched ahead and turned it to the color of burnished gold . . . Susannah's eyes . . .

He remembered yesterday down at the creek. She had been so lovely. The way she looked when she came face-to-face with that fish.

Why couldn't he stop thinking about her?

Susannah standing in the kitchen, barefoot . . . Susannah riding up from the creek with her skirts hitched up and her long white legs gleaming . . . the musical sound of her laughter . . . the earthy color of her hair . . . the empty place in her bed at night . . . the empty place in his bed every night.

He was glad to see he was on the outskirts of town. Now he could get his mind on something else.

He quickly found everything he needed at Peterson's Hardware Store, loaded up and was ready to go. He was starting to head off when he spotted the UNITED STATES POST OFFICE sign on the Buck and Smith General Store.

He remembered the letter in his pocket, the one he'd written to his family, and pulled to a stop.

Susannah was in the kitchen ironing curtains when he knocked on the back door. She knew it was Reed because she'd seen him through the window as he passed by in the wagon. "Come in," she called out.

She had been thinking about him while she ironed. Well, not him precisely, but rather she was making a mental list of things for him to do–aside from his regular chores. So far the list included painting the fence, chopping wood, and putting new wire on the chicken house and a new seal on the pump.

The door opened slowly, and Reed poked his head through. "Pardon the intrusion. I wanted to let you know I'd be working on the roof. There might be a shingle or two falling down, so it would be best if you and your aunts didn't come out the back door until I finish."

Susannah nodded. "I'll tell them. Thank you." She picked up the iron and pressed the ruffle around the bottom of the curtain, mindful that Reed Garrett was still standing in the door looking at her. When he made no move to leave, she put the iron down again.

"Is there something else, Mr. Garrett?"

"No, I don't suppose there is. I'll be getting on to work, then."

"Fine," she said, not bothering to watch as he shut the door behind him.

The moment he shut the door, she put the iron down and took a deep breath. She didn't know why he disturbed her, but he did. She wanted to dislike him and tried very hard to give him that impression, but in truth she could not find one thing about him that wasn't likable. It wasn't him personally that she had a problem with. It was simply the fact that he was a man. She didn't just fear Reed Garrett. She feared all men.

She picked up the iron and listened to him climbing up the ladder, knowing the exact moment when he began removing the old shingles.

She told herself that anyone who found pleasure in listening to a man throw shingles into a wagon bed ought to be locked up. She pushed him out of her mind and began ironing furiously. She swore not to think about him again, then carried the iron to the stove to heat it. While she waited, she washed the enamel pan sitting in the sink–the one she had used to gather eggs this morning. That done, she thought about him again.

She found herself wishing her life had been a normal one. What would it be like, she wondered, to love someone like him? How would it feel to let her fear go, to reach out and accept the friendship, and more, that she knew he offered? How would he react if he knew the truth about her?

An hour later, her ironing finished, she thought about carrying him a bucket of cool water. Not because she was thinking about him, mind you. This would be an act of pure benevolence. What he was doing was hot work–tedious and slow. More than once she had heard his sudden exclamation and surmised he must have hit something, most likely his finger. She bit her lip. The last thing in the world she wanted was for Reed Garrett to think she gave him special notice.

She removed her apron and hung it on the peg. Just as she turned to leave the room, she saw the water pail on the cabinet next to the stove. She paused a moment and eyed the pail, her mind at war over what to do.

Give him a drink. . . .

Go on with your chores. . . .

Over and over the two choices reverberated through her head. All right, she thought, she would take him some water. After all, giving a body a drink of water didn't exactly indicate any special interest. She would do the same for a stray dog.

She was about to pick up the pail when suddenly the hammering stopped and she heard an outburst that sent chills down to the very center of her righteous core.

"Good God almighty! Dammit to hell! Son of a bitch! Shit, damn, hell, piss!"

Her horrified eyes on the ceiling above her, she listened with disgust as he went stomping around the roof, flinging out the same oaths–and a few even more profane ones–over and over as loud as he could.

Without wasting a moment, Susannah grabbed her broomstick and headed out the back door. By the time she cleared the porch, she saw that creature with the devil's own vocabulary walking toward the well.

He was drawing up a bucket of water when she came up behind him and let him have it.

Whack! Whack! Whack!

"This is a farm run by decent Christian women. We don't allow any filthy talk around here." She whacked him again for good measure.

He jumped a country mile and turned in midair, saying as he came down, "What in God's name . . . ? "

She whacked him again. "You leave the good Lord's name out of this."

He had the grace to look ashamed. "Beg your pardon. I hit my thumb, hit it hard . . . with the hammer. I'm afraid I let my temper get the best of me."

She barely glanced at the thumb he was holding up, choosing instead to give him a look that said she wasn't the least bit sorry for him. "And God was to blame, of course, for your being foolish enough to whack your own thumb."

"I don't suppose I was thinking much about blaming anyone at the time."

Her muscles rigid, her gaze locked on him, she said, "You will have a heap of explaining to do come Judgment Day."

"I don't doubt that for a minute, but perhaps the good Lord will be merciful and take into consideration the punishment I've already received from the working end of that broom," he said, nodding at the broom she still clutched in her hands.

She relaxed her grip on the broom and slowly lowered it to the ground. "I won't tolerate any more outbursts like that."

"Then you will be happy to hear that was just about the extent of my wickedness," he said loudly.

"Will you lower your voice? I don't want to disturb my aunts. You obviously never heard of stately quiet."

"You can have stately quiet when you're dead."

She made a disbelieving sound and turned away.

"Don't you want to look after my thumb?"

She paused, glanced over her shoulder at the thumb he was holding out in front of him. "Suck on it," she said with as much venom as she could muster.

He laughed. "I've already tried that. It didn't help."

"Douse it with a little water and get back to work," she said as she started walking back to the house. "Honest hard work will take your mind off your thumb, as well as your obvious need for profanity."

She marched up the back steps and opened the door, deposited the broom in its proper place, then loudly closed the door behind her.

"What was all that ruckus?" Aunt Dahlia asked as she hurried into the kitchen.

Susannah did her best to look casually indifferent. "Nothing to worry about, Aunt. It was just that hired hand making a fool of himself and making light of the Lord's name."

Dahlia gasped. "The devil you say!" She went to the kitchen window and peered out. The action caused her gold-rimmed glasses to slide down her nose. She promptly pushed them back up, then moved in closer for a better look. "Why, that heathen! I knew him for a sinner the moment I saw him." She narrowed her eyes, as if that made her short-sighted vision more acute, and looked at him again. "The devil in disguise, that's what he is. Right here in Bluebonnet, right here on our farm. Why, it's enough to make an angel cry."

She glanced back at Susannah. "Tell me, what did he say?"

"Suffice it to say that he has a large vocabulary of curse words."

"Which ones?"

"I am not about to repeat them, Aunt. Nor would you want to hear them."

"Well, of course I would–just to verify what a heathen he really is, of course."

Susannah smiled. "Of course," she said. She crossed the room to stand by her aunt, and the two of them resumed their spying on the heathen through the window. They watched him turn away from the well and walk across the yard toward the house.

"Just look at the way he walks," Dahlia said. "Now, I ask you, have you ever seen a God-fearing man walk with such . . . such pride? Proud as a peacock, if you ask me." She nodded her head, apparently satisfied with that comment and added, "Pride before destruction, as the Good Book says." She nodded her satisfaction again, and two fat sausage curls fell down across her eyes. She pushed the curls back and patted them into their proper place.

Susannah was still looking at the way he walked, which was, as Aunt Dahlia said, prideful, when she began to notice something else. Of course, she knew now he'd enjoyed a life of some wealth and privilege. Still, he had presented himself to them as simply a down-on-his-luck drifter going through life the same way he moved from job to job. He did not have that lock-hipped way of walking that characterized a man who had spent a lot of time in the saddle. The more she watched, the more she was convinced there wasn't a cowboy bone in his body. Maybe he hadn't left Boston very long ago. Maybe he'd been chased out of Boston. Stood to reason. Him, with his Satan black hair and the devil's own gray eyes.

"He's a devil, I tell you," Dahlia said. "A real bête noire. Why, just look at him, all black and fierce. He's enough to frighten a decent woman out of her wits."

Susannah looked at him again and thought that for once she agreed with something Aunt Dahlia said. As she turned away from the window, she couldn't help wondering if he would prove to be her own personal bête noire as well. She decided then and there that she would be on the lookout for any clues he might give as to who he was and why he was here.

Violette came bouncing into the kitchen amid a profusion of lavender ruffles, her white hair looking like a cotton ball perched atop her head. But it was the two red dots of rouge on her cheeks that made Susannah bite her lip to keep from smiling.

"Lovely, lovely day, isn't it? I can't remember when I've seen one finer. I woke up this morning thinking–" Violette stopped in midsentence and looked at Susannah and Dahlia. "Has someone died?"

"No, Aunt, why would you think that?" asked Susannah.

"You look like you're in mourning. Is anything wrong?"

"Nothing is wrong," Dahlia replied. "We were merely observing that heathen you hired to work here."

Violette walked to the window and peeked out. "He looks pretty good to me," she said matter-of-factly. "Nothing I can see that would sour a woman's stomach." She studied Reed a bit longer. "Makes me wish I was twenty-five again."

"Violette Wakefield! I told you the man is a heathen. Why, Susannah heard him saying the vilest of curse words. Things were going quite nicely around here, but now that he's got God all stirred up, no telling what will happen."

Violette leaned closer to the window, trying to get a better look. "I don't rightly know, but man was made in God's image. If God looks like that–" She paused. "Maybe we shouldn't criticize."

"Hogwash! I was made in God's image. Do you think God looks like me?"

Violette turned to stare at her sister. "Lord, I hope not."

Susannah stifled a laugh and said, "Somehow, I don't picture him with sausage curls."

Violette looked in Reed's direction once more. "A man like that, he could tell you to go to hell and you'd look forward to the trip."

Susannah smiled. Aunt Vi had misbuttoned her dress again, and the hem on one side was a good three inches longer than on the other. "Were you looking for me?" she asked, hoping to get the conversation off Reed Garrett and onto something else.

"Yes, I was. I heard the two of you talking, so I thought I'd come on down and tell you that the new dress I am sewing for you is coming along beautifully. Perhaps you can wear it to the church picnic at the end of the month." She waved her hand back and forth like a fan to cool the heat from her round face. Susannah noticed that the buttons at her sleeves were undone, so the cuffs flapped back and forth with each movement of her hand as if they didn't know which way to go–something that seemed to fit perfectly with Violette's rather absentminded manner.

Susannah looked from one aunt to the other, marveling at how two sisters could be so different. Aunt Dahlia being perfection personified, she was beautifully and impeccably groomed, without a hair out of place. She never went out without her bonnet, her parasol, and her white cotton gloves. There was always a spray of artificial violets with a sachet pinned to the collar of her dress. Her collars were always white and so were her cuffs. Once, when Violette had asked her why she always dressed up so, Dahlia had replied, "If I should have the misfortune to die away from home, I don't want there to be any doubt whatsoever in the mind of the person who finds me that I was a lady of the most refined and genteel sort."

Worrying about what happened after you were dead wasn't exactly high on Violette's list of things to be concerned with, so she went about her daily living looking, as Dahlia said, as though she dressed in the dark.

Dahlia's face, although pleasant to look at, didn't have the soft fullness Violette's had. She was shaped rather straight, like a floor lamp. Since she had been blond in her youth, one would have expected her to turn gray as she aged, but the color of her hair seemed to have taken a wrong turn and wandered off somewhere in between the two.

In Dahlia's opinion, everything was either right or wrong. With nothing in between. She was a woman of little patience, impatience being a hazard of perfection. And yet her eyes were as innocent and untouched as they must have been when she was a baby. For some reason Susannah could never imagine her being grubby or dirty, even as a child.

When she was younger, Susannah thought of her aunts as vegetables. Aunt Dahlia was a carrot; Aunt Violette, a cauliflower.

"Good heavens! I seem to have misplaced my sewing scissors," Aunt Violette said. "Have either of you seen them?"

"They are on that length of ribbon pinned to your bosom, Aunt," Susannah said.

Violette looked down. "My, my, however did they get there?"

"You put them there," Dahlia said.

Violette looked at them as if they were a living, breathing thing. "Well, come along, then," she said to the scissors. "We've a lot of sewing to do."

"She is such an absentminded darling," Susannah said, gazing fondly at her aunt who was marching out of the kitchen.

Dahlia shook her head with disgust. "We were always such an intellectual family, although Violette seems to be doing all she can to change that." Susannah laughed. For the moment things were back as they had been before he came.

Chapter 7

West Texas, with its greasewood, flash floods, and scanty rain, took up a chunk of the state. It was big, empty country with little water, few roads, few people, and even fewer towns. It had a lot of stretches of desert and semiarid land, for it was an extension of the Chihuahuan Desert that originated in Mexico.

By the time the desert reached Bluebonnet it had begun to play out, leaving the Chisos, Davis, and Guadalupe Mountains behind to become a place without trees, hills, rocks, firewood, or water. From there, the dry, desert terrain became sandy, fertile soil covered by a huge expanse of wind-fluttered grass, so flat that people swore they could see for a hundred miles.

Most of those who did the swearing were ranchers, but there were a few people who worked small farms. Like Susannah and her aunts, the other farmers raised mostly cotton, along with a little corn, oats, grain sorghum, and winter wheat, while running only a few head of cattle. For them the rich west Texas soil was a farmer's dream–when there was enough rain.

Last year had been a dry one, the flat grassland baked hard by a steady prairie wind. It was difficult sometimes to remember that beneath the parched grass lay fertile ground. But anyone who had lived around Bluebonnet for long knew that could change any moment, violent weather being one of the grassland's specialties.

The winter before last was the coldest Susannah could ever remember, with the temperature dipping down to thirteen degrees below zero. The year before that, they found twenty mourning doves in the backyard, killed by biscuit-size hailstones.

It was in the midst of her thinking about the phenomenal weather that another thunderstorm blew in. Typical, Susannah thought. Just typical. She was returning from a trip to town. She had driven the buggy through the gate and was heading for the barn when the wind began to get stronger, whipping the few sparse trees and sending anything that wasn't fastened down hurtling through the air.

She had almost reached the barn when a jagged bolt of lightning struck frighteningly close. It was followed by a tremendous crack of thunder that left Susannah's ears ringing. The explosive sound frightened the buggy horse and caused Rosebud, the docile mare, to rear. Then she bolted into a dead run. Dashing wildly, Rosebud veered off the road, heading straight for the fence.

Susannah saw what was coming and tried frantically to stop the mare, but no amount of pulling back on the reins would curb the frightened animal. A second later Susannah screamed as Rosebud hit the barbed-wire fence and the buggy flipped over onto its side.

Susannah was thrown clear. The fall knocked the wind out of her, and for a moment all she could do was lie there, stunned, trying to breathe. When she had recovered, she managed to climb to her feet. She put her hand on the wheel of the overturned buggy for balance until the dizziness had passed. At that moment, she heard Rosebud, and when she looked, she saw that the mare hadn't fared well.

By the time Susannah reached her, Rosebud was bleeding profusely from a deep cut on her chest and several smaller cuts on her front legs, which were still tangled in the wire. Susannah approached her slowly, talking softly, then took her by the curb piece to prevent her from moving and cutting herself more deeply.

It took some time, but Susannah did manage to get her untangled from the wire. Blood was everywhere, and Susannah prayed that the mare wouldn't bleed to death before she could lead her back to the barn.

Lucky for both of them, Reed had been digging post holes for a new fence and saw the accident. He had dropped the post-hole digger and come running. It wasn't until he rushed up to her and grabbed her, asking, "What happened? Where are you hurt?" that Susannah realized she was covered with blood, most of which belonged to Rosebud.

She put her hand to her head and felt a small wound there. Reed looked at it. "I think we can wait to attend to that Susannah, but Rosebud has to be looked after right away. You go on into the house."

"No, I want to help. She's lost so much blood."

"Come on, then."

Still in a daze, Susannah followed him as he led the mare into the barn and stood with her back against the corner of a stall so she would be out of his way. She watched Reed as he talked to the mare in a soothing voice. With a confident air, he ran his hands over her, checking the savage cut across her chest. "These are deep. She's losing a lot of blood. They'll need stitching, and fast."

He turned to Susannah. "If you're going to stay, I'll put you to work. Hold her steady and keep her calm. I'll be back in a minute."

Susannah went over and took hold the halter. "Where are you going?" she asked.

"To get something to sew her with. She's losing too much blood."

He was back very soon and said, "Get me a bucket of water and some coal tar from the tack room."

Scarcely aware of what she was doing, Susannah brought the things he needed, then held the mare steady, calming her with softly spoken words and strokes to her head. Her attention was riveted on Reed as she watched him bathe the lacerations, his hands moving over the wounds with assurance. When he began to stitch the cuts, he was as competent as any physician she had ever seen. In fact, better. She had never seen such small, neat stitches.

She couldn't help wondering where he'd acquired that skill. "You do that like you've done it before."

He seemed amused. "Anyone who has spent much time around livestock has done this a few times."

That was true, of course, but still, there was something about his professional manner, his competence and ease, that made him seem much more experienced than the average rancher or farmer. She found herself watching his hands. It was distracting, for she could not help imagining how those same hands might feel if they were touching her with such gentle thoroughness. The thought was frightening, yet she could not put it out of her mind.

She watched him cover the neat stitches with coal tar.

"What are you doing that for?"

"It will keep the blowflies off the cut so they can't lay eggs. The last thing we need is for this cut to fill up with worms."

She understood that. In the summertime blowflies were a terrible nuisance. The least cut or scratch on any of the livestock would become infested with worms if exposed to open air.

"You are very good at this. Have you ever had to sew up a person?"

He turned his head so swiftly to look at her that Susannah was caught off guard. The look in his eyes was fierce. For a moment she tried to think if she had said something to offend him.

"Why would you ask me a thing like that?"

She shrugged. "I was just wondering, that's all. It seems that with the traveling you must have done, you might have encountered a situation where someone needed similar attention."

"Why would you be wondering about something like that?"

"I was just curious to know if there was any difference between sewing up an animal and a human being."

He turned back to the mare. "Flesh is flesh whether it's human or animal. There isn't much difference between the two–although animals are generally better patients."

She thought of Aunt Dahlia as a patient and

smiled, but said nothing, content for now merely to watch. The scare was over and Rosebud looked as if she would be all right.

Suddenly, Susannah realized that Reed was not wearing a shirt. She knew he'd been digging holes, and she had seen his shirt hanging on a nearby fence post. He sure was lanky, she thought. He had a hollow belly that seemed to skip his waist as it blended downward into slim hips. His arms were taut, his chest smoothly muscled and tanned, as if he went without a shirt quite often.

He was so sure of himself, so capable. She had watched him that day in town when the crowd was riled up and seemingly eager to turn itself into a lynch mob. He had stood up for himself with confidence and dignity. He wasn't loud or tough, but he wasn't the kind to back down either. He was a man to be admired, and it occurred to her then that she did admire him. She admired him for his masculine qualities, true, but it was his gentleness more than his strength that captured her attention and drew her to him. And those hands . . . She found herself thinking, *If I had someone like you, I could overcome all the pain and shame of my past. I could raise a family and lead a normal life . . .*

If I had someone like you.

Chapter 8

As he did every Saturday afternoon, Reed rode into Bluebonnet.

About the only thing he saw there on this particular day was a street full of horse droppings, which told him things had been more active than usual. It was still a bit early for the ranch hands to hit town, yet most of the law-abiding folks had already concluded their business and left. Bluebonnet wasn't a place for women and children on Saturday after the ranch hands got paid.

On the edge of town he passed by the Missionary Baptist Church. Next to it was the Reverend Elijah Wheeler's house. A big chinaberry tree stood in the front yard with two swings hanging from its sturdy branches. He rode on by the Boot and Saddle Shop, the blacksmith's, and the Texas Barber Shop all lined up, their window panes blazing in the sun like mirrors.

A mule was tied in front of the Boot and Saddle Shop. As Reed passed, the mule started braying and sat back on his haunches. He snapped the reins and took off down the street, bucking and braying. A man ran out of the barber shop, shaving cream over his face, the barber's drape still around his shoulders. He lit out down the street, chasing the mule and hollering for him to stop. A few people came out of the buildings along the street to see what all the commotion was about. For a moment it looked as if things were starting to pick up, but then the fellow with the shaving cream caught his mule and, after a scolding, led him back. Dogs stopped barking and the townfolk returned to their stores. All was quiet once again.

It had been over a month since the last rain, and in the intense heat, it didn't take long for things to dry out. The street was packed hard and dry. It drummed solid beneath his horse's hooves. Right now the place looked as dead as a graveyard, with only two horses tied at the hitching post in front of the saloon, tails switching. The long shadows of late afternoon stretched across the street like a barrier warning the unsuspecting away.

Reed rode past the shadows and up to the Buck and Smith General Store, dismounted, and went up the steps, his boots knocking loudly on the boardwalk. A bulletin board next to the window was covered with wanted posters, snuff signs, funeral handbills, and a notice that the Widow Peabody's farm was to be sold at auction.

He opened the door with the glass panels that said SAM SMITH, PROPRIETOR in gold letters, and stepped inside.

The mingled smells of green coffee, burlap, tobacco, harness leather, cheese, glazed calico, and asafetida surrounded him, but Reed didn't pay that much mind. He hadn't come into town to shop. He walked back to the post office and exchanged a few pleasantries with Daisy Hitchcock, a young blonde who was substituting for the sick postmaster.

Daisy had talked with Reed on many a Saturday afternoon over the last several months. "You mailing a letter to your folks as usual?" she asked.

Reed nodded and handed her the envelope. "I guess it's starting to become quite a habit, isn't it?"

Daisy took the letter. "It's a nice habit, writing your folks like you do. We've got a lot of cowboys around here, but none of them are as good about writing home as you are. You must have mighty nice folks."

"I do. They're the best any man could have."

"I heard a sermon just last Sunday. It was about honoring your father and mother so that–"

"–your days will be long upon the earth." At her wide-eyed stare, he added, "We have churches in Boston, too."

"Oh," she said, and her face colored. She hastily scanned the envelope. "You sure do write fancy. Does everyone in Boston write as fancy as you do?"

"Well, I never thought much about it one way or the other, but I'd say a good many of them have handwriting that's not too different from mine."

"You must have had a lot of book learning to write like that. Nobody around Bluebonnet can write as fine as this. Heck! Nobody even comes close, not even Judge McCarthy, and he's had the most book learning of anyone in town. He went to college." She paused and gave Reed a curious stare.

Reed knew what was coming next.

"Have you been to college?"

He thought he had mentioned once that he had studied at Edinburgh, but he was not certain. That was the trouble with not always telling the truth. You couldn't remember what lies you'd told or what truths you'd left only partially told. Thankfully he was spared answering when the bell over the door tinkled. Both Reed and Daisy glanced toward the door as a man walked in.

He was dressed in typical cowboy garb, although it was obvious his clothes were of a finer cut and cloth. He was wearing a pair of expensive chaps, and the spurs on his boots rang as they struck the wooden floor. This caused everyone to stop what they were doing and turn to look.

"Afternoon, Tate," Mr. Smith said as he walked toward his customer with a bolt of linen clutched in his arms.

Tate nodded stiffly. "Afternoon."

Reed recognized the bastard right off as the leader of the bunch who robbed him that day. He turned to Daisy and whispered, "Who is that?"

"It's Tate Trahern. His pa owns the Double T."

Reed sized up the man who Violette had told him had tried to court Susannah. He didn't like him for that reason alone–not to mention what Tate had done to him after pulling him off his horse and stealing everything he owned. If his father owned the Double T, he didn't have to resort to stealing. It was now plain to Reed that Tate had robbed and roughed him up merely for amusement. Reed did not like the idea of being anyone's entertainment.

Tate got angry just watching that slow-ass Sam Smith. It took him a solid week to put down the bolt of cloth he was holding before he could turn and ask, "What can I do for you, Tate?"

Tate didn't say anything. He knew Sam didn't expect to be treated with respect, respect being something Tate didn't have for anyone.

Taking his own sweet time, Tate pushed his hat back off his forehead with one finger and sauntered over to the case where firearms and boxes of bullets were displayed.

Sam stroked his beard thoughtfully, then followed him. "Looking for anything in particular?"

"No. Give me a couple of boxes of shotgun shells," he said, his gaze scanning the store, going over the half dozen or so people there, pausing to stare at Daisy. He saw a stranger talking to her, and he felt his anger rise. What in the hell was she doing talking to that drifter?

As Tate looked at the drifter, he thought there was something familiar about him. Suddenly he remembered where he had seen that face before. Reed Garrett. He had known that name since the day Curly came back without the big red roan and the saddle.

He wondered if Garrett recognized him–not that he cared. There wasn't anything that drifter could do to him. He gave Reed a quick, dismissing look, and said to Sam, "You got any of those new shotguns?"

"I've ordered a couple of the bolt-action ones. Newest thing on the market."

"What about the magazine-loading kind?"

Sam scratched his head. "Don't reckon I've heard anything about those. Magazine loading, you say?"

Tate didn't answer. He was watching Daisy. He liked to make her fidget.

Daisy looked away from Tate and waved the envelope Reed had handed her a few minutes before. "I'll get this letter off to Boston as soon as the stage comes through," she said nervously. "Will there be anything else?"

Reed looked from Daisy to Tate and back to Daisy, but made no comment other than to say, "I guess that'll be all for this trip."

"See you next week, then," she said. In an instant she disappeared behind the curtain that covered the door to the stockroom.

Tate ignored Reed and turned back to the counter. He heard Garrett walking a few feet behind him, but he kept on looking at the items on display until he heard the door open, then close.

Reed had barely left the store when Tate picked up the boxes of shells. "Put them on our account," he said as he shoved the shells into his pockets and walked to the back of the store.

"Will do," Sam said.

Tate paused a few feet from the curtained doorway. "Daisy, don't go making yourself scarce. I saw you talking to Garrett."

Daisy poked her head through the curtain and walked out to where Tate stood. "Hi, Tate. What brings you to town? It's a little early for you to be coming in to get drunk, and I know you didn't come in just for those shotgun shells."

"Does a man need a reason to come to town to see his girl?"

"Am I your girl, Tate?"

"I said you were, didn't I? That makes it so, doesn't it?"

"I guess it does." Daisy fluttered her eyelashes and smiled. "I didn't expect you till later. I can't leave now. We won't be closing up here until six o'clock."

"I can wait. Tell me why you were acting so friendly to that drifter."

Daisy paled. "I wasn't so friendly, Tate. You know I don't have eyes for anyone but you."

"Yeah? Well, you better make sure it stays that way."

"I reckon I'll be sweet on you for as long as you're sweet on me, Tate."

"You didn't answer my question, Daisy. How come you and that drifter looked like you two was all wrapped up in each other?"

"Wasn't nothing like that, Tate, I swear. It's just that he comes in here almost every Saturday to mail letters, so we've gotten to the point of passing a few words, that's all."

"Letters? He comes in here to mail letters?"

"That's what I said, and I didn't stutter."

"You honestly expect me to believe he comes in here to mail letters like some old lady?"

"Believe what you like, but it's the truth. He comes in here every Saturday. Ask Mr. Smith if you don't believe me."

"Who would a drifter have to mail letters to?"

"Even drifters have families, Tate."

"He writes to his family?"

"Yes. His name's Reed Garrett and his parents live in Boston. Golly, I'd never sent a letter all the way to Boston before he came. Sending those letters that far sure does make this job a lot more interesting. Why, I feel like I've traveled someplace myself."

Tate wasn't listening. "Let me see that letter he just mailed."

"I can't do that, Tate."

"You're my girl, aren't you?"

"You know I am."

"Then give me the letter. I'll give it back. I only want to look at it."

Daisy glanced toward the front of the store, where Mr. Smith was grinding up a pound of coffee for Mrs. McCormick. "I can't, Tate. You know I can't. I could lose my job if Mr. Smith found out."

Tate went on pressing her, confident he could bring her around. Daisy always liked to put up a show of resistance, but in the end she always gave in.

"Please don't push me, Tate."

He frowned, unable to figure out what was going on. "You getting sweet on that Garrett?"

"You know I care for you, but my pa is sick and we don't know when he can go back to work. Right now, I'm the only one working. My whole family is depending on me. You know that. I can't afford to lose this job, Tate. I just can't."

Tate hooked his hand around the back of Daisy's head.

"Tate, what on earth . . ."

He pulled her head forward and kissed her. "I sure have missed you," he whispered. "I hardly worked, thinking about you."

"Thinking what?"

"The same thing I'm thinking right now–how purty you are."

"I still can't give you that letter, Tate. No matter what."

"Okay, we'll let it ride for now," he whispered, touching her face and nose and cheek and ear. Daisy leaned into his hand, kissing his palm. He pulled her closer. Their mouths touched.

She pulled back. "Tate, please . . ."

"Don't you worry. Old Sam Smith is too near blind to see anything happening this far away."

"I pray you're right, Tate. I surely do."

"I'm always right. I'll see you at six," he said and left the store.

An hour later Tate was standing in front of the saloon smoking a cheroot, a piece of whittling in his hand, a pile of shavings at his feet. His hat was pulled low over his eyes as he watched Reed Garret mount his roan.

Bastard. Tate didn't know why he hated that drifter from Boston, but he did. As he watched him ride slowly out of town, he was thinking that if that Yankee knew what was good for him, he'd never set foot on Double T land.

On his way back home, Reed took a shortcut across the Double T.

He wasn't certain if he did it because it was a quicker route or out of spite. Regardless that he had gotten his roan and saddle back, he was still chapped over the loss of his pistols, not to mention the gray mare.

He had no more than finished wondering if he'd ever see the things that were stolen from him again, when he came upon a group of Double T cowboys. They were swimming in the river, stripped down to their bare skin. They were having such a good time, they didn't even notice him. Reed looked around and saw shirts, socks, boots, and britches tossed in a pile, even a pair of string drawers. He felt his insides grow warm at the thought of finding something that belonged to him.

He left his horse hidden in the trees a few yards off and made his way toward the river to the place where their clothes lay scattered. As soon as he was close enough, he spied his own gun belt with the ivory-handled Colt he had owned for more than three years.

He dropped down low and crawled on his belly. Grasshoppers scattered as he began to propel himself by his elbows through a stand of grass until he was closer to the river. Frogs jumped ahead of him. Overhead, honeybees swarmed around a black honeycomb. But he kept on crawling until he reached the spot where his gun belt lay next to some cowhand's clothes. Quietly he lifted the gun belt and looped it around his neck, arranging it so that the pistol rested on his back. Then he turned to crawl away. Suddenly he paused and looked back at the cowhands' clothes. He gathered up the bundle and made his way to where their horses waited. Quickly he tied it to one of the saddles and slapped the horse's rump.

He didn't wait to watch the horse run off but made his way back to where his own horse waited. A moment later he put his spurs to the roan's sides and galloped away.

When he reached home, he stopped in front of the barn and unsaddled his horse. He was just about to lead him into the paddock when he heard someone walk up behind him. He drew his pistol and turned around, pointing the Colt straight at Violette Wakefield. "Good God above, don't you know better than to sneak up on a man like that?" he said, sheathing the gun.

"I do now," Violette said, her questioning eyes resting on the pistol. "Is that a new gun?"

"No. It's one I've had for a few years."

"I've never noticed it before."

"I haven't had it on since I came here."

"Why are you wearing it now?"

"Because I couldn't wear it before, since I didn't

have it. It was stolen along with my other things. I got it back today."

Violette's eyes sparkled with interest. "Today, you say. Well, bless my bones, don't stand there with your teeth in your mouth looking at me. Tell me what happened. I want to know how you got your Colt back, my boy, and don't leave anything out."

Reed laughed. "I thought you were absentminded."

Violette gave him a wry smile. "Only when I want to be," she said. "I'll walk with you to the paddock, and you can tell me all about it."

"It isn't a very interesting story. In fact, it's rather boring," he said, and went on to explain.

When he finished, Violette slapped him on the back. "It's just as Dahlia said–you're a man who uses his brain instead of brawn. I like that. An ordinary man would have wanted to prove himself and ridden in there with a challenge, guns blazing. I like your way better."

Reed chuckled. "I don't know. Where I come from we would call it stupid to go in with guns blazing."

"That's more in line with my way of thinking, too. It is infinitely better to gain what you want without doubling a fist."

"You live longer, too."

Chapter 9

Over the weeks that followed, there were instances when Reed saw glimpses of something in Susannah he could not understand. One time in particular would stand out forever in his mind.

Reed decided to breed the two youngest of the five mares Susannah and her aunts owned. Since they didn't have a stud, Reed did some work for Judge McCarthy, asking that in exchange he be allowed the use of the judge's fine-blooded stud, Texas Flyer. Judge McCarthy was so impressed with Reed's work that he told him to take Flyer and keep him at the Wakefield place for a couple of weeks. Texas Flyer was too valuable an animal to pasture breed by allowing him to roam around loose with the two mares.

Juan Flores, the cowhand who worked for the judge, came with Flyer, since the temperamental stud was accustomed to him. It was early one morning that Juan led Flyer into the paddock where Reed waited with one of the mares, a sleek black they called Black-Eyed Susan.

The moment Flyer caught the scent of Black-Eyed Susan he began snorting and prancing, tossing his head and making it difficult for Juan to hold him. Reed saw Juan's predicament, so he left Black-Eyed Susan where she was tied and went to help Juan with Flyer. For several minutes the two of them struggled to control the huge stallion.

At last they brought Flyer to within five feet of the mare, but Reed held Flyer back, refusing to allow him to mount the mare until he calmed down. "This horse of yours needs to learn some manners. I've never seen a stud behave so poorly."

"Sí, señor. I tell the judge this all the time, but he does not listen. Flyer, he is too aggressive. He is no gentleman, that one. Juan is afraid he might savage one of the mares."

"That's what I'm afraid of, too," Reed said while using all the strength he had to hold Flyer back.

Finally the temperamental stallion began to quiet. Reed led him closer.

Flyer began to act up again.

Reed pulled him back to their original position.

Over and over they repeated this pattern. Eventually, Flyer seemed to understand that he was allowed close to the mare only when he behaved. Thus motivated, he remained calm long enough that he was allowed to approach the mare.

Flyer had just mounted Black-Eyed Susan when Reed heard someone approach. Glancing over his shoulder, he saw Susannah step through the barn door and out into the paddock.

"I've been looking for you. Aunt Violette wanted you to–" Susannah gasped. She did not move, and her face seemed to pale. Reed couldn't help noticing how beautiful her eyes were, large and fixed upon the two horses that were breeding. He cursed softly to himself, knowing this was no place for a woman to be and certainly not for a woman who had no knowledge of things of this sort.

Susannah spun around and went off at a run. He knew how horrified and embarrassed she must be.

He couldn't let her go without at least trying to say something to ease her discomfort.

Reed handed Flyer's lead rope to Juan. "Take him to the barn and rub him down. I'll be back in a minute."

Juan nodded. "Sí, Señor Reed. I will take him back pronto."

Reed went looking for Susannah.

He came upon her sunbonnet. It was lying brim down in the grass. He remembered seeing her in it, remembered how it veiled her features so that only the tip of her nose showed from the side. How like the blinders the plow horse wore . . . and so reflective of her approach to life . . .

He paused for a moment, just long enough to bend over and pick up the bonnet. He pulled its streamers through his fingers. Was her losing it an omen?

He found her at the edge of a small meadow on the other side of the garden. She was sitting in a swing that her aunts had made for her when she first came to live with them. He saw her there, her silhouette in sharp detail against the vivid green of summer grass.

He did not understand why he felt compelled to ease the discomfort she obviously felt. Perhaps it would have been best to let her deal with it in her own way and then to act as if nothing had happened.

He couldn't do that. A latent sort of tenderness burned within him, a tenderness that made him want to reach out to her, this creature who was like a flower that never bloomed, a promise that was never allowed to go beyond the tight confines of a bud. He stepped closer, and she lifted her head and stared at him, her expression hard and accusing.

"What do you want?" she asked.

"I'm sorry about what happened. Although it was a perfectly natural thing that we were doing and nothing to be embarrassed about, I know you must have been shocked by what you saw."

She leaped from the swing almost as if she'd been shot. Then she walked a few steps away and turned, giving him her back. He could see her arms hugging her waist as if she were trying to give herself comfort. He stepped behind her and tried to console her by putting his arm on her shoulder.

She whirled around, almost throwing his hand off her shoulder, looking as if the very act of him touching her was loathsome. Her violent reaction caught him off guard.

"Keep your hands off me!"

"I was just trying to–"

"I know what you were trying to do."

"I only wanted you to understand that it was a perfectly natural–"

She scoffed at that. "Don't bother. Believe me when I say there is nothing, absolutely nothing that you could tell me that I don't know already. I know you. I know men. And I know just how natural it is to turn a trick."

Shocked, Reed could only stare at her, unable to think of anything to say.

As quickly as it had come, the wild expression in her eyes began to fade. When she spoke again, her voice was subdued, almost gentle. "Now you know," she said, the anger, the venom gone. Her voice became even lower, softer, as if she was trying to tell him she was sorry. "Now you know I am not what I seem."

"What is–"

"You don't understand. No one understands." She shook her head and tears welled up in her eyes. "There is nothing you can do. Just leave me alone."

He reached a hand toward her–a gesture of friendship, nothing more–but the wary, almost frightened look came back into her eyes.

"Stay away from me," she said, "far, far away. I'm warning you."

Without another word, she hurried off in the direction of the house, leaving Reed to stare after her. He looked back at the swing where she had been only moments ago. He stood watching it move slowly back and forth until it grew still. He turned away and noticed her unsullied bonnet still in his hands.

That night Reed lay in bed, unable to sleep, thoughts of what had transpired earlier weighing heavily on his mind. He was still stunned by Susannah's outburst and her choice of words. Not only was it not in line with the woman he had come to know, but try as he might, Reed could not understand how a seemingly sheltered and virginal woman would know the phrase "turn a trick." He was determined to find out.

He rolled over with a sigh and closed his eyes. It seemed he had just found another reason to stay.

Chapter 10

As was their custom, Susannah and her aunts moved to the parlor when the evening meal was finished.

The windows were open. Outside it was very still. Nothing stirred. The scent of honeysuckle drifted into the room from the flower bed beneath the window. The peace of the countryside enveloped the room, where silence prevailed, save for the steady ticking of the clock on the mantle.

Susannah was thinking about the baskets, brimming with berries, in the kitchen. She wondered if it would be cool enough to start cooking them down to make jelly at six o'clock in the morning. Or should she get up earlier?

Sitting across from her, Dahlia was stitching together the perfectly cut squares of a quilt top that she held firmly in her pink hands. Even the bluebonnets pinned to the lace at her throat were still as fresh looking as they had been this morning.

Susannah looked from Aunt Dally to Aunt Vi and smiled. There were blossoms in Aunt Vi's hair, and the wilted zinnia she had picked before breakfast was still pinned to her bodice. Two bright red dots of color on her face stood out like markers announcing–to anyone who might have trouble knowing–the exact location of her cheeks.

Today she had on two different earrings: a tiny gold stud in the left ear, a dangling creation of black jet in the other. From beneath the hem of her dress her bare toes peeked out, and Susannah found herself wondering if her aunt would remember where she'd left her shoes. Dear, dear Aunt Vi. It was such a treat to wake up each morning and rush down the stairs, as she had done when she was a child, to wait and see what impulse Aunt Violette had given in to that day.

This morning it had been the petticoat, for she had come down to breakfast wearing it on top of her dress. As she said, "What's the point in having a beautiful red petticoat if you're going to hide it beneath a dress? You ought to put it out where folks can see it. Not much joy in having something wonderful if you can't share it. Besides, I think it makes me look like I have on a whole different outfit."

Susannah nodded in agreement. Aunt Vi was right. It did look different. In fact, Susannah couldn't think of a time when a red taffeta petticoat worn over a blue dress wouldn't look different. It was one of the things Susannah found so endearing about her, this giving in to impulse. Truly Aunt Vi lived a life in which innovation, inventiveness, and creativity were allowed free rein.

Violette was sorting through a bowl of last year's rose hips. She took another sip of port and turned to her sister. "The trouble with you, Dally, is you are far too serious. You are one of those people who lives sensibly and sanely and has nothing to show for it."

Dahlia looked completely flabbergasted. "Nothing to show for it? I don't know how you can say that, Sister. Why, this house is full of my collectibles."

"Tangibles," Aunt Violette scoffed. "I'm talking

about memories, opportunities taken, and you speak of material goods."

"If you are referring to Elijah Ashcraft . . ."

"I said opportunities taken, not opportunities missed."

"You always thought I should have married Elijah," Dahlia said, sounding bitter.

"No, I believe you are the one who's always thought so. I have always thought you should have followed your heart."

Dahlia blew out her wrinkled cheeks in indignation. She patted one of the two matching silver combs that held back her hair. "Don't feel sorry for me," she said in her huffiest tone. "Just because my name begins with Miss, don't go thinking that means anything. I haven't missed as much as you think I have."

Susannah paused, her needle in midair, and watched Dahlia adjust her posture to sit more primly on the edge of her chair, the epitome of one who has taken umbrage and is determined to enjoy it to the fullest. Susannah thought about what her aunts were saying.

Aunt Dahlia always did what was expected, Aunt Vi almost never did. Life was very strange. Her aunts were all she had, and both of them were quite dear to her. But Susannah could not help wondering sometimes if Aunt Vi was not right. In the end, what was important? What really made a difference?

Of the two, who would be more remembered? The one with no more substance than vapor?

Or the one who caught sunlight and turned it into a rainbow?

Although they were both getting on in years, Aunt Dally seemed to be growing old, while the word that came to mind when Susannah thought of Aunt Violette was . . . well, ripening.

Violette polished off the last drop of port, then put the glass on the round table beside her. She glanced around the room and sighed.

Susannah had seen her do this enough to know it meant Aunt Vi was ready to have some conversation.

"Did you hear that poor Mr. Smithers lost his memory again?" she asked. "He mounted a horse and forgot how to ride and fell off?"

"I heard about it at church yesterday," Susannah said. "Everyone there was talking about it. Poor Mr. Smithers. He was lucky he didn't break something."

"He did. He fell off his horse and broke his arm," Dahlia said.

Susannah stared at her aunt. "Where did you hear that?"

"At church yesterday."

"Aunt Dahlia, I was with you at church yesterday when Mrs. Appleby and Miss Sally Mayfield told you about Mr. Smithers. All they said was he fell off his horse. They didn't mention his breaking his arm."

"Broke his leg, too," Dahlia said. "In three places."

"I didn't hear anyone mention the word 'arm' or 'leg,' " Violette said.

Dahlia took no notice of what her sister said. "He broke his arm first . . . then he broke his leg."

"He did not." Violette gave her sister the sternest of looks. "Dally Bradford, you are making that up as sure as the sun comes up in the morning. I don't mind telling you that is something that has caused me quite a bit of concern of late."

"Why would my telling you that Mr. Smithers broke his arm or his leg cause you concern?"

"What concerns me is . . ." Violette stopped, then started up again. "As much as I hate to say it, Dally, it appears to me that more and more lately you are exercising your unpleasant habit of telling fibs."

"Fibs!" Aunt Dahlia said, doing her utmost to sound insulted, sounding insulted being something she excelled at.

"Yes, fibs, and don't bother to sound so persecuted. Well, it's worse than fibs, Sister. I have personally caught you in several falsehoods this past week. Untruths. On occasion, you're telling downright lies."

Susannah, who had also noticed Aunt Dahlia's newly acquired habit of telling falsehoods, listened with acute interest, looking to Aunt Violette and back to Aunt Dahlia. She noticed that being called a liar was something that did not seem to offend Aunt Dahlia in the least.

In fact, she seemed to be taking it all in stride. Susannah was just wondering if Aunt Dahlia was going to defend herself when she said, "Maybe you won't have to put up with it much longer. I've been feeling as close to my end as a body could feel."

Susannah knew it was time for Aunt Vi to say something to mollify her sister, as she usually did whenever Aunt Dahlia ended her sentences with a dash of self-pity. So she was very surprised when Violette came right out and asked, "Well, are you going to tell the truth, or are you going to be evasive and pretend you don't know what we are talking about? You have been telling falsehoods of late, have you not?"

Dahlia went right on with her sewing, her words coming slowly and matter-of-factly. "There is no point in telling the truth when one's life is so terribly dull. I hate getting old. I've lost my hair, my teeth, my bloom. What's next?"

Violette looked at Susannah. "That is why I tell you not to let your regrets take the place of dreams."

Dahlia rallied long enough to ask, "Now which one of us is fibbing? You aren't sitting there trying to say you enjoy getting old, are you?"

"I don't mind getting old. You get to sit on the front pew at church."

Susannah ducked her head and hid her smile behind the gown she was embroidering. How dear her aunts were, and how much she enjoyed these quiet evenings together, with the three of them sewing, her with her pot of hot tea, her aunts taking an occasional sip of the one luxury in their life, a glass of port, which now seemed to be making her aunts feel drowsy. Dahlia started to doze off, her glasses slipping far down her nose before she gave a start and pushed them back up.

Aunt Vi suddenly went limp and dropped her embroidery. Her head fell back against the chair.

Susannah's heart fluttered. In a panic, she sprang to her feet and rushed to her aunt's side. "Aunt Violette . . . Aunt Violette," she repeated, slapping the older woman's hands. Violette did not move. For a moment, Susannah was numb; she held her dear aunt's wrinkled hand. Aunt Vi couldn't be gone. Not now. Not like this.

A tear rolled down her cheek, followed by another and another. Soon she was crying. "You can't leave me. Aunt Vi! You can't leave!"

Susannah put her ear against her aunt's chest and listened, praying desperately to hear a sound, however faint. She heard nothing. She held her breath. She was about to pull back when she heard the faintest sound. She wanted to shout with joy, but since Aunt Vi was still motionless, Susannah knew that time was precious. If Aunt Vi wasn't dead, she might not be far from it. God, she couldn't be dying.

"She's dead, isn't she?" Dahlia asked. Susannah paused only long enough to take her hands. She kissed each of them.

"She is still breathing. I could hear her heart beat." Susannah dropped her hands and rushed forward.

For the first time in her life, Susannah saw them not as the women who had raised her but as two white-haired old ladies without too many years left to live. She had never confronted the reality that her aunts would not always be with her. The thought of losing them wrenched her heart. She turned quickly away.

Susannah reached the door and opened it.

"Are you going after the doctor?" Dahlia's voice sounded high-pitched and frightened.

She paused just long enough to say, "No, Aunt, I'm going to find Reed. I'll send him to town for the doctor. He can make better time on horseback than I can in the buggy."

Susannah hurried outside and went running down the path that led to Reed's house. She was screaming out his name even before she started pounding on the door.

The moment he opened the door she burst into tears. "Aunt Vi . . ."

He stepped outside and put his hands on Susannah's shoulders, trying to calm her. "What is it? What's happened?"

"It's Aunt Vi! She's dying! Go after Dr. Bailey. Quickly! She's unconscious. I don't know how long she can hold on."

"Where is she?"

"She's in the parlor!" Susannah screamed. "You're wasting valuable time. If you let my aunt die, I'll–"

Reed was halfway up the path. Susannah turned and ran after him.

By the time she followed him into the parlor, Reed was dropping down beside Aunt Vi's chair. He checked her pulse. Next, he put his head against her chest and listened to her heart. He removed the wilted zinnia that was pinned to her dress and unbuttoned the tight collar at her throat. That done, he lifted each of her eyelids before leaning closer to her face.

Susannah was mesmerized. All her attention was focused on the manner in which he examined her aunt. His hands. His beautiful, beautiful hands. She was captivated by them as they moved over her aunt. Truly they were gentle, knowing hands. Reed Garrett's hands.

But they were not the hands of a rough-and-tumble drifter.

He rose to his feet, turned to Susannah, and the first thing she noticed was the smile stretching across his face. When he chuckled, she could not believe what she heard. Then he said, "There's nothing to worry about." Susannah was stunned.

For a confusing moment, all she could do was stand there feeling bewildered. Nothing to worry about? Who did he think he was? A man of medicine?

Susannah had never felt more like slapping anyone in her life. Her aunt was unconscious, probably dying, and he laughs? "Nothing to worry about!"

she shouted, waving her arms. "I don't know how you can say that! Look at her! For God's sake, she's unconscious! She might–"

"Calm yourself." He held his hands up. "She isn't dying. She's drunk."

"What?"

"She's not unconscious. Your aunt is drunk. Dead drunk."

"Drunk?" Susannah couldn't believe what she was hearing. "Drunk?" she repeated stupidly.

"As a skunk. Let her sleep it off and she'll be fine in the morning . . . a headache perhaps, but otherwise fine."

"Drunk? My aunt is drunk?" She shook her head. "I can't believe it." Suddenly, she narrowed her eyes and gave the bottle of port sitting on the silver tray next to Aunt Vi's chair a suspicious look. "You don't know what you're talking about. She can't be drunk. Look at that bottle. It's practically full. She couldn't have had enough to make her drunk. Why don't you stop trying to play doctor and go to town for Dr. Bailey like I asked you?"

"I can go for the doctor, but he'll tell you the same thing. Your aunt doesn't have a thing wrong with her that a good night's sleep won't cure. She's drunk. I don't know how to make it any plainer than that."

"I told you she couldn't have had enough to drink. Look at that bottle of port if you don't believe me. Hardly any of it is gone, certainly not enough to make anyone drunk."

"That was our second bottle," Dahlia said in her softest tones.

All the anxiety drained out of Susannah's body.

She had never felt so many different emotions in one day. This must be what made a person grow old, for truly she felt as if she had aged ten years since breakfast. She could not believe it, so she asked her aunt, "That was your second bottle?"

Dahlia nodded. "I opened it not long before Vi passed out."

"Why?"

"Because she drank what was left in the other bottle. If I was going to get any, I had to open a new one."

Reed leaned over and gathered Violette into his arms. "If you'll show me to her room, I'll carry her to bed."

"This way." Susannah picked up a candle and led the way. She stood to one side of the door as Reed walked into the room and gingerly placed Violette on her bed.

"Get her out of this dress and into something loose and comfortable so she can breathe. Let her sleep as long as she wants. If she feels bad in the morning, let me know. I can mix up a little seltzer water for her to drink."

Dahlia, who had trailed them, now opened the wardrobe and crossed to her sister. She held one of Violette's gowns. "I'll get her ready for bed," she said.

Reed, Susannah noticed, was beginning to look a bit uncomfortable, and for good reason. He did appear to be out of place in her aunt's bedroom.

"I guess I'll be getting on back," he said. "Call me if you need me."

"We will," Dahlia replied. "Thank you."

Reed nodded.

Susannah watched him cross the room, but she

said nothing. She couldn't. She was too lost, too deep in thought, too confused to be able to push aside what she had just seen—or what exactly it could mean.

How calm he had been. How professional. How correct. Him. Reed Garrett. The same Reed Garrett who had ridden into their lives a short while ago, a homeless drifter.

Without realizing she was doing it, Susannah followed him, a jumble of questions in her mind. How had he known to take her aunt's pulse? What was he doing when he'd gently thumped her chest and felt along her neck? How did he know to lift her eyelids and, more important, what to look for when he did?

Reed reached the front door and turned to Susannah. "Go on to bed and get some sleep. Don't worry about your aunt. She'll be fine tomorrow. You've got my word on it."

"Who are you?" she asked boldly.

If her words caught him off guard, he did not show it. He was good at hiding his emotions, but for the slightest fraction of a second there was a glimmer of a response in his eyes. It had been there just long enough for Susannah to see it.

"Who are you?" she whispered again. "What are you? What are you hiding?"

"I'm no one you should be afraid of, so rest easy on that score."

"You're hiding something. I know you are. You are not what you say you are . . . what you want us to believe."

"I am what I said I am."

"But, Aunt Vi . . ."

"I am a drifter, a man down on his luck, as I said. I needed work and your aunt was kind enough to give it to me. You are trying to blow things out of proportion. Naturally you're worried about your aunt. Tomorrow you will feel foolish for asking these questions. Good night."

Before she could say anything more, he walked out the door.

She watched him tramp down the porch and into the night. Her pump was primed, and Susannah had never been a woman to let a primed pump go to waste. Once she focused on something, she stayed focused. She never left anything undone. Tomorrow she would get her answers. No! She would get them this very night.

Chapter 11

Susannah had gotten only as far as the orchard when she saw the orange circle of a cigarillo glowing brightly in the dark. Suddenly it flew through the air in an arc, a scattering of sparks lingering for only a moment.

Reed stepped into her path. "My, my, you must be very curious indeed. Unless I miss my guess, I'd say this is the first time you've ever sought out a man's company in the dark. That sort of thing is a little out of character for you, isn't it?"

Her heart skidded to a stop, thumped erratically and began beating as if she were running up a hill. The lateness of the night, coupled with the potential intimacy of their being alone together, made her feel terribly nervous. It occurred to her, too, that charging into the night after him was an impulsive act that he would probably see as more panic than poise.

She took a step back. "I . . ."

He moved closer, out of the darkness into the pale wash of moonlight, the angles of his face etched with shadow and giving him a frightening look. She inhaled deeply and was assaulted by the sweet, familiar smell of peach blossoms mingled with the scent of his body. A man's warm body. A man breathing heavily.

The scent and sound brought back memories of her childhood, memories of the time before she came to live with her aunts. Sudden panic overtook her. She began to run.

She darted through the trees, feeling the shower of pale, velvet-skinned peach blossoms; they brushed her skin with the texture and softness of a fawn's nappy nose.

Reed was following her, calling out her name again and again.

When he caught up with her, he grabbed her by the arm. As he spun her to face him, the world about her shattered. She was too surprised to move. Before she knew what was happening, she felt the touch of his lips on hers. The suddenness caused an inadvertent response within her, and she shivered. His hands moved over her back, lifting her to him, fitting her body against his as he began to kiss her neck.

Reality slapped her in the face. It was a cold awakening and she felt an instant surge of anger. She shoved him and when he would not release her, she fought him, swinging her arms, feeling her hands come in contact with his flesh. She pulled one arm free and hit him hard.

She heard him grunt, then exclaim, "What's the matter with you?"

She threw her head back and closed her eyes, feeling her back pressed against the rough bark of a tree, the feather weight of peach blossoms dropping onto her, their fragrance suddenly sickeningly sweet.

"Look at me."

She shook her head. She couldn't. Not now.

He was a man, and long ago she had branded men as the enemy. Yet deep, deep down within her she knew that it wasn't really this man who was the enemy. The enemy lay within her, a legacy, an inheritance from her mother, her beautiful, honey-voiced mother who had died at the age of twenty-nine in a bordello in New Orleans and left behind a daughter who knew far, far more than any child should.

"Tell me," he said. "Tell me what it is that you are afraid of." His voice was whisper soft, his presence, his very nearness frightening, and yet somehow welcome. "Tell me what it is. Tell me what you fear." His voice was lyrical, as if he treasured each syllable he spoke. "You don't have to be afraid of me. I won't hurt you."

How could she tell him? How could she make him understand that it wasn't him she was afraid of? How could she explain that the greatest fear in her life was that she would turn out to be exactly like her mother–her lovely mother, who threw her life away in a whorehouse on Basin Street and gave birth to an illegitimate daughter, a "trick baby," delivered upstairs in the attic by a backstreet midwife?

Would he understand that she spent the first years of her life growing up with the knowledge that she would one day join the ranks of many scarlet sisters, mother-and-daughter combinations, of which there were a number in all New Orleans brothels, a duo that would bring as high as fifty dollars a night for both of them together?

Susannah turned her head away. Shame seeped into her very soul. No, he would not understand. How could he, when she did not understand herself? How could she expect it to matter to him that her mother was born a lady, refined and educated, or that she had once worn real silk stockings? Presented engraved calling cards at the homes of friends and acquaintances? She hadn't words to explain that her sweet, sophisticated mother, who always smelled like honeysuckle and roses, had been a whore.

She felt the warmth of his hand as his palm shaped itself over her cheekbone. At the touch of his flesh against hers, she stiffened, and the rest of his words seemed barely audible, their meaning unintelligible to her. He drew his hand back and she stared at it, at that same hand that had mesmerized her when he had tended to Aunt Vi.

Those beautiful hands. She fought the urge to turn her face against them, to kiss the palms, to absorb their strength. She remembered a drawing she had seen of Michelangelo's sketches. In it the hand of God was stretched out, his forefinger extended to his newly created Adam. She'd known exactly what it meant. By touching only the tip of His finger to His lowly creation He could bring it to fulfillment.

Reed had such hands. If they touched her, could she resist him?

Her mind went blank. She could process no thoughts. There was no apparent avenue of escape. She could only stand there and stare at him, stupidly feeling herself at the mercy of those hands. Only her body told her just how very frightened of him she was. She saw her own hands come up, as if they would cover her face. She closed her eyes and prayed he would disappear.

She heard him chuckle. Then he said, "I am a man of infinite patience."

His nearness made her throat feel strangely tight. She opened her eyes and saw the white of his smile.

"There," he said, "that's better."

"Better for you, perhaps."

"You are painfully shy around men, aren't you?"

Painfully shy around men? Her? She wanted to throw back her head and howl. Should she tell him how every part of the male body looked–*every* single part? How foolish he was. How gullible. She almost laughed out loud

Still, she thought, *Miss* Eleanore Savannah had protected her daughter enough that she was still a virgin when her great-aunts had come swooping into Madame Broussard's Parisian Club, like two avenging angels swathed in gray bombazine. And Reed might actually be impressed to learn that even now, sixteen years after Vi and Dahlia had brought her back to live with them in Texas, she was still a virgin: pure of body . . . if not of mind.

"Tell me something," she asked

"What?"

"Why did you follow me?"

She did not answer.

He reached out a long, well-shaped hand to cup her chin, drawing her face farther into the soft moonlight. "Infinite patience, remember?"

She remembered. "I wanted to know who you are . . . who you really are."

"What do you mean?"

"I know you aren't just a drifter. There is more to you than meets the eye. You have an air of refinement about you, and it's obvious that you are educated. I cannot help wondering why such a man would choose the life of a drifter, a ranch hand, when he has obviously been accustomed to so much more.

"I watched you with my aunt tonight. You have done that sort of thing before. You were too comfortable, too knowledgeable, too confident. No mere drifter would have been so practiced, so skillful. Tell me. Are you a doctor?"

He did not answer.

"You are not the only one with infinite patience."

He stroked her cheek with the back of his fingers. "There was a time in my life when I wanted to be a doctor. I even went so far as to study medicine for a year in Edinburgh."

It was a good attempt and a valid explanation, but she did not buy every slice of that pie. She would bet her best Sunday bonnet *and* her paisley shawl that this man was hiding something. But he had so disturbed her emotions that she knew she'd best let it ride for now. She was about to head back to the house when he changed the tone of things.

"I must say that I've never encountered anyone as charming as your Aunt Violette and her fondness for port."

Susannah could not help smiling at that. "She does love her port."

"She has earned the right."

"Yes, she has."

"I think that might apply to you as well."

"I don't know what you mean."

"I think you do. I think you know exactly what I mean, but you are afraid to admit it."

Something twisted in her heart, a subtle wrenching. It hit her that she was experiencing a feeling she had never felt before, a feeling she warily identified as desire, the one thing she had been terrified of all her life—terrified that it ultimately would cause her pain. How strange that when desire did come, it was not terrifying, nor did it fill her with shame or pain.

Instead, it filled her with longing, and the knowledge of just how truly empty her life had been.

Odd. How could something be so new and yet so familiar? It was as if her senses had suddenly come to life, for she was acutely aware of the nearness of him, of the scent of his flesh, even of the texture of the softly troweled earth beneath her feet, the fragrance of warm air that floated over her, the rhythm of her beating heart. She wanted to turn away from him, to run as fast as her legs would carry her back to the house, to the safety of her room, but something stopped her.

"What would you do, I wonder, if I touched you?" he asked. "If I drew my finger down the side of your face, or traced the line of your neck where it forms the curve of your shoulder? How would you react if I put my arms around you, as I have thought about doing so often these many weeks? Would you slap my face? Or would you turn and run away?"

"And if I did neither–what would you do?"

"I would keep on touching you," he said, "touching you and touching you, until I had to know more."

"More?"

"Much more. I have thought of little else since coming here."

"Tell me," she dared to whisper.

"The way your body would fit itself against mine if I took you in my arms like this. The way your breath would feel against my skin when I kissed your face as I am doing now. The feel of your mouth opening under mine. The sound I knew you would make when you kissed me back."

His lips touched the curve of her cheek, petal

light. Her breath caught in her throat, overpowered by the strength of the heartbeat that constricted her chest and made her temples ache. The mouth that had been searching her face and whispering such mesmerizing words closed over hers. Knowledgeable as she was, she was completely unprepared for the flush of feeling that seemed to be everywhere at once, rushing even to the extremities of her body.

She suddenly understood that all her knowledge, taken from observation, was a world away from real knowledge based on action and feeling. How clean he smelled, how soft was his hair skimming along the side of her face, how warm those lips that moved over hers with such a gentle, searching pressure that left her mouth tingling, her heart pounding with excitement, her mind screaming more, more, more!

Afraid she would fall, she gripped his shoulders, wondering if he could feel the way her body trembled.

"I think we have found a far better way of communicating, and as difficult as it is to stop, I think this could be continued in a more comfortable place."

A shudder passed over her, and she stared at him through a thick haze of longing, but the words he had spoken began to penetrate the fuzziness in her brain. *Continued in a more comfortable place . . .*

Visions of naked bodies entwined upon a bed came rushing back. That was reality, not this heady feeling. Well she knew that no matter how ardent, how heated, or how passionately it was expressed, desire did not last.

But shame did.

She shoved him, and he stumbled back far enough for her to dart beneath his outstretched arm. A split second later she was again rushing between the peach trees. She dashed up the path toward the house, leaving nothing behind save the man with a look of regret etched on his face and the peach blossoms that fell like snowflakes onto the ground.

With a curse, Reed brought his forehead to rest on the tree trunk. Later, when he had regained his composure, he took out his knife. Moved by thwarted desire, he carved a heart and then her initials into that tree.

At that moment he would never have guessed that the next afternoon she would come seeking the very spot where they had caressed, would stand beneath the tree's knotted boughs and kiss the heart and the initials she found there.

Chapter 12

Reed was up well before daylight. He finished the morning chores early, then went to see how Violette was feeling. At least that's the story he wanted everyone to believe. Of course, he knew that Violette would be feeling fine–a little headache, perhaps, but otherwise fine. What he really wanted was to see Susannah.

He spotted her before he reached the house. She was hard to miss, bathed in the yellow light of dawn, talking to Peony as she led the milk cow up from the pasture, picking her way across the wet grass like a dancer. Behind her the sun spread out like a halo on the horizon. The early morning air was crisp and fragrant with the smell of damp grass and the heavy sweetness of honeysuckle in bloom. A mockingbird in the mulberry bush, filling the air with the celebration of his song, seemed as carried away with the moment as Reed was.

She stepped like a ballerina, her movements lissome, smooth, and elegant, yet artless. Her motions flowed in perfect rhythm, each movement with a purpose, creating a dance he had never seen before. How unaffected she was now, how childlike and natural. He had never seen her like this, because, he realized, she allowed the beauty of her soul to shine forth only when she was alone.

He wanted to see more of this real, expressive, and emotional Susannah, so he stayed where he was, partly obscured by the wagon, content to observe her until she sensed his presence.

Just outside the gate, Peony stopped and stretched out her neck, letting loose with a long, mellow *moooooo,* which must have delighted Susannah, for she threw her arms around the cow's neck and began to laugh. Never had he heard such laughter from her. Gay. Spontaneous. Heartfelt. Beautiful. He wanted to capture it, to hold it in reserve for the time when he knew there would be no Susannah in his life. But he could dream. . . . *If I had someone like you.*

Susannah removed her arms from around Peony's neck. She took up the lead rope and began to dance ahead of the cow, singing, leaping, twirling, then bouncing back to give Peony a few words of endearing encouragement. It occurred to him that her body was speaking for her, that there was power there and the ability to say and be all the things that Susannah could not, would not allow herself to show. Her soul was wild and free, just as her body had the ability and desire to be. It was her mind that was frozen.

Question was, why?

A rooster on the fence behind him crowed. He heard the flapping of Daffy's wings and then a crash followed by a dazed honk. Normally he would have looked and more than likely laughed. But not today. Today all his attention was for Susannah, only Susannah.

He saw her glance in the direction of the commotion and freeze when she caught sight of him. Right before his eyes her naturalness and childlike manner vanished. In their place was the rigidly controlled woman he knew. He walked up to her.

"What are you doing here?" she asked. "Your chores–"

"Are all done. I was up early."

"You look like a man with a mission. Where are you off to now?"

"I'm on my way up to your house to see how your aunt is faring."

"Aunt Violette is fine. I don't think it's a good idea to disturb her."

He started to say something, then realized he could not. To say more would cause her to ask questions, and when that happened, he might reveal things about himself better left where they belonged–in the past.

He realized all of a sudden just how alike they really were. There was something in her past that she kept hidden away, too, something that made her strive against her true nature, no matter what the cost. By not allowing her past to speak out, she became silent and this silence had quieted her very soul. Quieted the joy, the gaiety, the laughter. She was a peacock who thought herself a sparrow. How long, he wondered, could she keep up the pretense?

Not that he was casting stones at her–far from it, for he carried too similar a burden. But whereas she closed her eyes to her burden, he had opted to run from his. How strange that he had to see her blindness before he could see his own. Now that he saw it, he did not know what to do about it. Running was all he knew. It helped him forget, at least for a while.

"Why are you staring at me like that? Is something wrong?"

Shaken out of his daze, he realized she had spoken. All he could manage was a weak "What?"

Peony tossed her head and Susannah calmed her. It was obvious that Susannah was a bit put out with him, and she let it show. "I asked what you were staring at. You were looking a hole through me."

"I'm sorry. I was lost in thought."

"You were lost all right. It didn't look like there was anyone there for a moment."

Reed wanted to laugh outright. If only she knew there hadn't been anyone there for a long, long time . . . He had been dead inside for years, and yet, observing her a moment ago and standing here with her now he perceived a slight thread of remembrance, a fragrance he had smelled before, a road he had traveled down once, long ago.

He forced out his words, trying to make them sound light. "It's a bad habit of mine–this tendency to lose myself to the point I'm not aware of anyone or anything around me."

"What were you thinking?"

"I was remembering something."

"From the painful past?"

"Is that how you see the past? As painful?"

She rolled Peony's lead rope around her hand, obviously agitated. "Don't put words into my mouth."

"I was curious, that's all."

"Curious people have bad memories."

"Are you speaking from experience?"

"I am merely repeating what I've heard."

"I've heard it said that curiosity is a keyhole to which many an eye is pasted. Much as I hate to admit it, curiosity is another fault of mine. Alas! In less than five minutes you've discovered two of my faults."

She wasn't amused. "I'm not interested in your faults. I've got Peony to milk."

"Ah yes, Peony. The cow with the unusual name. Did you name her?"

"Aunt Violette did."

He smiled.

"You find that funny?"

"In a way, I suppose I do. It is when she is most amusing that I am reminded of what a remarkable woman your aunt is. An original. A bundle of delightful eccentricities."

She stroked Peony's neck and fixed him with a bewildered look. "Sometimes you speak strangely. You use words ordinary people don't use. It could be because of where you come from, but I don't think so. There is something else that makes you different. I don't know what it is yet, but I intend to find out."

"I was trying to say that your aunt is different. She's herself. She never does anything in exactly the way one expects, or the way everyone else does it. Not even when naming her farm animals."

Her eyes were suddenly bright and full of warmth. "Her soul is afire with a wild sort of joy."

"You are very close to her, aren't you?"

"I adore her. I owe her so much. She has been like a mother to me. I cannot imagine what my life would have been like without her. Of course, I love Aunt Dally and I don't mean to slight her in the least. It's just that Aunt Vi . . . I will miss her terribly when she is gone."

Her tone touched him. She touched him. He wanted to touch her in return, and not only in the physical sense. She looked so fresh now, so pure standing there in her plain blue dress. "You will always have a part of her that will live in your memories, in the things she taught you."

"Yes, she has left deep footprints. They will be easy to follow."

He absorbed her words and thought about what she had said. "You have a knack for expressing yourself and a wisdom far beyond your age."

"Humph! It isn't age that gives one wisdom, but experience."

"And you've had a lot, I imagine?"

She paused for so long that, not wanting to keep his gaze on her face, he had time to fix in his mind the exact slope of her neck, the narrow shoulders, the dusting of blond hairs on her arm, the taper of her waist, the flare of her hips, and every detail of the things in between.

"I've had enough."

A reply came swiftly to his lips, but he was never able to utter it, for at that moment Peony shook her head violently, her bell clanging to signal the end of her patience and their conversation, or at least Susannah must have thought so, for she said, "I must get the milking done. Excuse me."

She tugged at Peony's lead and started around Reed, close enough now that he could have reached out and touched the enchanting curve of her cheek. He knew better, of course, so he had to be content to watch her, which he did for some time, until she disappeared behind the darkness that lurked behind the barn door. It was only after she was gone that he whispered the poetic words he had learned long ago–words that had held no meaning for him until now: *Many a flower is born to blush unseen, and waste its sweetness on the desert air.*

He stood where he was for some time, staring at the last place he had seen her, as if doing so would prolong his time with her. The yellow light of dawn grew brighter. The rooster crowed as he had earlier, only this time his cries were not punctuated by the flapping of Daffy's wings. In the mulberry bush, the mockingbird went on with his song.

Everything was as it had been before. And yet it was different.

Reed waited around a bit; then, in spite of what she had said about not disturbing her aunt, he walked on to the house. When he stepped onto the back porch, he saw Dahlia sitting in a rocker. She was sorting through a basket of greenery at her side.

"Good morning," he said, eyeing a red mark on her arm. "Did you burn yourself?"

Dahlia didn't look up. "Burned it last night when the kerosene lamp fell off the table, not that anyone cares."

"The kerosene lamp? Are you sure? I was told we were all out of kerosene. Susannah said you'd been burning candles since last Monday."

Dahlia finished tying a bundle of wild buckwheat, but he didn't miss her quick glance in his direction, or the subdued voice when she spoke. "Maybe I burned it on the stove, then."

He forced himself not to smile. "It's a pretty nasty

burn. Have you put anything on it?" He asked this even though he knew she had doctored it thoroughly with one of her remedies.

"What do you take me for? A fool? Course I did."

"With what?"

She tilted her head to one side and gave him a look that didn't come within a hundred miles of trust. "Why do you want to know?"

"I just wanted to make sure you put something on there that will keep it from getting infected. You . . ."

"Boiled onions and salt," she said, not really listening to him. "Then I used elderberry bark mixed with fat. This morning I made creosote tea and mixed it with badger oil."

"Good God! You drank it?"

"Now why would I do a stupid thing like that? What do you take me for, an idiot? The burn is on my arm."

Reed shrugged. "Good." He looked toward the kitchen door. "Is Violette up?"

"Of course she's up. You think she's a lady of leisure?" She paused. "What do you want with Vi?"

"Just checking to see how she's feeling."

"Like she had too much port, how else?"

He knocked on the door anyway. "I want her to know I'm concerned."

"If that's all you're about, I can tell her."

"I want to tell her myself."

"Oh, go on in, since that's what you want to do anyway. Don't know why you wasted all this time dawdling with me. I'm not the one you came to see. Nobody ever comes to see me."

"Are you certain it's okay to go in?"

"Of course. You afraid you'll catch her in her drawers?" She laughed at that. "Well, don't stand there looking like a sack of potatoes. Go on in. She's in the parlor pretending she's doing the mending, but she's catnapping."

He removed his hat, opened the door, and went into the kitchen. A pot of chicken stew bubbled on the stove, filling the room with a delicious smell and reminding him that he had missed breakfast. He snatched a cookie from the plate sitting on the table, then went down the hallway to the parlor.

He found Violette sitting in a rocking chair next to an open window. Today she was wearing her red petticoat under her dress, but he could see part of the ruffle peeking out beneath her skirt. A pink knit shawl was draped around her shoulders. Her hair was slicked back into a bun with three buzzard feathers poked into it.

He tapped lightly on the wall. "Are you awake?"

"Of course I am. I saw you talking to Susannah," she said, turning away from the window and looking at him. "Come on in."

He stepped into the room.

"You finished your chores mighty early this morning."

"I wanted time to check on you. How are you feeling?"

"Fit as a fiddle, save for this cannon going off in my head. Dally said I was as stewed as a boiled owl. Course, I can't remember if I was or not." She laughed and waved her hand toward a chair across from her. "Take a load off your feet and have a seat."

He smiled. "You aren't trying to tell me that's the first time you've ever overindulged, are you?"

Her eyes sparkled with humor. "Lord, no. Probably won't be the last time I overindulge either. You know, there comes a point in everyone's life when the only thing that will help is a drink. When you get older, those times seem to come closer together. Take me, for instance. I used to wonder why I liked to have a drink in the evening."

"I take it you don't wonder anymore?"

"Nope. No point in wondering when you know the answer."

"What's the answer?"

"A drink makes anybody seem more interesting. Can you imagine what it would be like to spend every single evening for the rest of your life with Dally?"

"I noticed she's in one of her good humors this morning. Our conversation was tart enough to have been soaked in brine."

"Dally should be gagged."

Reed laughed.

"Sure is nice to hear a man's laughter. Makes me remember my husband. He's been dead twenty years. I hear you start remembering all those who have gone before you when you start getting old."

"I wouldn't say you were getting old."

"Listen, when I was young the Dead Sea was alive."

"My mother always said age was a matter of mind. If you don't mind, it doesn't matter."

Buckwheat came into the room and curled himself on Violette's lap. Violette stroked him a time or two as she considered Reed. "You a drinking man?"

"I have been known to imbibe on occasion."

"But not on a regular basis?"

"No."

"Good. I need you sober in case I fall asleep again. Dally said Susannah was frightened."

"Yes, she was quite frightened. She thought you were dying. She is very devoted to you, you know."

She stopped petting Buckwheat and looked off. "Yes, I know. That bothers me. I'm not going to live forever. I worry sometimes . . . about what will happen to her when I'm gone."

"I have a feeling you will live a long time. You appear to be in excellent health."

"My health is fine. It's my age that's bad."

He smiled. "By the time you're ready to cash in your chips, Susannah will probably have a husband and a dozen children."

"I'm not so certain. You see, Susannah has never had a beau–has not even come close to having a beau."

He couldn't have hidden his surprise if he'd wanted to. "Not ever?"

"No, not even once."

"But I thought Tate . . ."

"Tate has wanted Susannah for years, but Susannah never cared for him. She made that plain enough. She refused to allow him to court her. He came by once, a long time ago. Susannah had warned him not to come out here, but Tate does pretty much as he pleases, you know."

"What happened when he came here?"

"He knocked on the door. Susannah poked her head out of her bedroom window and told him to leave. He refused and she dumped a washbasin full of water on him."

"I can understand her disinterest in Tate, but what about other men?"

"It was the same. She was simply not interested. Never."

Reed was puzzled. "I know she doesn't care for men, but I figured that was because she'd had an unhappy experience with one sometime in her past—but never? She is too lovely a woman to end up a spinster."

"My sentiments exactly. I don't want you to think it was because there were no other men interested in her. There have been plenty, but Susannah never gave them the time of day. And it isn't because she had a tragic love affair either."

"I knew there was something strange . . ."

"Not strange at all, considering that . . . well, perhaps we should let that dog lie for a spell."

His curiosity was stirred. "What were you going to say? Considering what?"

"Nothing."

Judging from the firmly clenched jaw, he didn't think she would be volunteering any more tidbits during this conversation. His only leverage was to tell her about the things Susannah had said the other day, but something held him back. He would let it ride for now. Before long, he was going to ask the questions he had been wanting to ask. And when he did, he wanted some answers.

Right now he had his own ghosts to deal with. He stood up and patted Buckwheat on the head. "I guess I'd better be getting back to work. I didn't intend to stay so long. I just wanted to see how you were feeling."

"I hear you took pretty good care of me last night."

"All I did was carry you to your room. Susannah did the rest."

"That's not the story I heard. I'm told you have quite a way with doctoring."

"A man does what he has to do," he said. "I've always been a great improviser." He headed toward the door. "I'll see you at suppertime."

"Count on it," she said. "I never miss a meal."

Reed went to the henhouse and began nailing up the new chicken wire and mashed his thumb three times. He didn't curse, even though he knew the reason he smashed his thumb in the first place was because Susannah and not chicken wire was on his mind. Yes, she was puzzling. Yes, he was frustrated. And the thing that frustrated him the most was that he was allowing his thoughts to linger on her longer than they should, that he was involving himself in something he knew he ought to stay out of.

You cannot save the world, Reed, no matter how badly you want to. His mother's voice came to him as sharp and clear as if she were standing beside him. He remembered the way she looked when he saw her last, wearing dark blue velvet with Venetian point lace, her Etruscan gold bracelet on her arm. He imagined his lovely mother walking next to him here, through the clucking hens and chicken droppings. And he laughed.

Good Lord, how far away Boston was . . . how very, very far.

That night, when he lay in bed, he relived the pain he had tried to put behind him. Yet the more he tried, the more the past came back to haunt him. When he finally fell asleep, he dreamed of Boston.

Reed was leading Rosebud outside the barn when Susannah suddenly appeared in the doorway wearing a bright, saffron-colored dress of simple cotton that seemed to capture all the sunlight on this dewy morning. He was blinded by the sight.

"Good morning."

"Good morning. You're looking as fresh as a buttercup," he said.

"It's because of my yellow dress."

"No. It's not the dress. It's you."

She smiled hesitantly, as if uncertain of herself, but her confidence returned as she walked toward him with steps as careful and measured as a bride's.

"You look troubled? Is something amiss?"

"It's Daffy. I can't find her anywhere. I was hoping you had seen her."

"Not this morning. But don't worry. I'm sure she will turn up."

"I'm not so sure. There were a lot of goose feathers near the pigsty. I hope she didn't fall prey to a coyote during the night."

"Perhaps she's down at the creek."

"I don't think so. She never goes down there."

"There's always a first time. Don't forget that geese are waterfowl. I think it would be quite natural for her to migrate toward water on such a fine spring morning."

She looked thoughtful, then her expression turned to one of relief. "She has been spending a lot of time in the watering trough of late. Perhaps you're right. I'll walk down that way. If you should see her . . ."

"I'll let you know."

She did not say anything, nor did she make any move to leave. When Rosebud began rubbing her head impatiently against Reed's arm, it broke the spell of silence between them.

"I'll head on down to the creek and let you get on with your plowing."

He watched her leave, and once she was out of sight, he led Rosebud toward the door.

They had almost stepped through the doorway when much to Reed's surprise, he saw Tate Trahern entering the yard. Tate rode up to Susannah and dismounted.

Reed waited just inside the barn.

She must have heard him coming up behind her, for she turned toward him and held her hand up to shield her eyes from the sun. "Tate Trahern," she said slowly, as if allowing the surprise of seeing him to settle. "What are you doing out here?"

"I came to talk to you."

"I'm busy."

"This will only take a minute."

"I really don't have time. Our goose is missing. I've got to find her."

"I'll buy you a dozen damn geese. I want a few words with you."

Even from where he stood, Reed could hear her weary sigh. "What about?"

"About this drifter your aunt hired."

"Reed?"

"What is he to you?"

"The same that he is to my aunts–a farmhand. Not that it's any of your business."

"Are you seeing him?"

"I see him every day. He works here."

"You know what I mean. Is he courting you?"

"Don't be silly."

Tate stepped closer.

Susannah took a couple of steps back, until she was against the wall of the equipment shed.

"If it's a man you're looking for–"

"If I wanted a man, Tate Trahern, I wouldn't look in your direction. Now, go away and leave me be." She made a move to leave, but Tate leaned forward and placed his palm against the wood planking, blocking her way.

Reed tied Rosebud and started outside when Susannah suddenly ducked under Tate's arm and rushed to the door of the shed. She picked up a rake that was leaning against it. Tate had almost reached her when she whirled around and thrust the rake toward him.

Tate jumped back just as she said, "If you want that pretty face of yours all scratched up, keep on coming."

"You wouldn't hit me with that," he said, and took another step. "Not that it matters. I like a woman with a little fight in her."

He lunged and Susannah brought the rake down. It caught the brim of his hat. When she drew the rake back, his hat came with it, held by three tines.

"Good God almighty! You could have killed me."

"Get on your horse and leave." She thrust the rake toward him. Tate leaped backward, tripped, and fell. Susannah shoved the rake at him one more time. "And take your hat with you."

Tate scrambled to his feet and grabbed his hat. "You're crazy."

"I've also got a good aim. Next time I won't miss."

Tate didn't say a word as he went to his horse and mounted.

Once he had ridden out of the yard, Reed walked quickly over to Susannah. "Are you all right?"

"Of course. I can take care of myself."

He laughed. "Yes, I saw. You're pretty good with the working end of a rake. I thought for a moment you were going to plant that thing in his head."

"Don't worry, Yank. I never intended to hit him. I just wanted to let him think I would. Tate is really a coward, like all bullies. And he can only bully people who are afraid of him."

"Which you aren't, apparently."

She shook her head. "I'll go down to the creek to see if I can find Daffy." She leaned the rake against the shed and walked away.

Reed stared at Susannah's retreating back. She was brave in so many ways, timid in so many others. She baffled him frequently and intrigued him always these days. She was all closed up. A tightly wrapped box . . . that he wanted desperately to open . . . like a Christmas present.

His stomach knotted. Who was he to even think about disrupting the fragile peace Susannah had wrenched out for herself? She'd stayed put and gone on. He'd run away from the troubles in his past as soon as he'd been able. She'd called Tate Trahern a coward. If she knew how he'd dealt with the problems in his life, she'd have every right to call him a coward . . . and worse.

Chapter 13

Susannah opened the door. Reed was there with Daffy in his arms.

"Daffy!" she exclaimed. "Oh, Reed, where did you find her?"

"Honking hoarsely in the feed bin. She must have wandered in when I wasn't looking."

Susannah took her from him. "Oh, poor Daffy. Were you in there all this time–all yesterday and this morning while we were in church?"

Daffy honked her delight and nibbled at Susannah's face.

Violette joined them on the porch. "I locked her in the privy once."

Susannah laughed. "I remember that," she said, then put Daffy down. "I imagine she's hungry."

Dahlia walked up in time to say, "She shouldn't be hungry. She was in the feed bin."

"Yes, but Daffy is a grazer. I doubt she ate much grain."

"No matter," Dahlia said. "A missed meal or two won't hurt her. She's fat as a brood sow."

Daffy didn't seem to mind the name-calling, for she waddled off with her bill to the ground in search of food.

"Come on in the house," Violette said, taking Reed by the arm. "We've got Sunday dinner ready."

"I thought I'd eat a couple of those biscuits and the ham I took home with me last night."

"Save those for later. We'd be mighty honored to have you join us for a nice, hot Sunday meal." She leaned toward him and whispered, "We've got pork chops, collard greens, a mountain of potatoes . . . and rice pudding."

"The biscuits can wait," Reed said, and followed them into the house where he ate too much and enjoyed every bite.

Once everyone had finished, Reed was invited to join them in the parlor.

"Aunt Vi thinks Sunday afternoon is the best time to read," Susannah said, leading the way.

Reed nodded. "I agree, but I don't have anything to read."

"Don't worry about that. We've got plenty of books for you to choose from," Dahlia said.

Susannah began pulling out books, trying to find a title that interested him. Before long, her aunts joined her. By the time he decided on *The Farmer's Almanac*, there must have been at least a dozen books scattered about.

Susannah settled herself into a chair across from Reed. Occasionally she would look up from her book, only to find him reading intently, his eyes moving over the page at a very rapid rate. She was thinking he must have had a lot of schooling to read that fast, when she began to notice how long his legs looked, thrust out over the carpet as they were, crossed at the ankles.

Much to her surprise, she found it a nice, pleasant feeling to have a man in the house, stretched out comfortably with his attention on a book. Having spent almost all of her life in a household of women, she found his presence both welcome and perplexing. She was thinking about that when Aunt Vi stood up and went to the window.

"It's hot as a baker's oven in here," she said. "I think I'll open a few–Oh, my Lord! It's Reverend Pettigrew coming up the road."

Susannah leaped to her feet. "Hurry! We've got to hide these books!"

The three women sprang into action.

"Here, Aunt Vi! Stuff *The Wayward Wanton* under the sofa cushion; toss *The Sultan's Captive* in the piano bench. Aunt Dally, get that copy of *The Dastardly Deed* and shove it behind the clock on the mantle. Oh, dear, where can I put this copy of Ovid?"

"Here, give it to me," Violette said. "I'll cram it into this copper urn."

"Hurry!" Dahlia said. "He's almost through the gate."

Susannah grabbed the Bible and put it on the skirted table next to Reed, who seemed mightily amused. "There," she said, "I think we're ready."

Susannah was just about to sit down again with a copy of *Twelve Steps to Piety* when Violette suddenly said, "Susannah! Get that copy of *The Ravishing Prince* lying on the table and put it somewhere! Quickly! I hear him on the porch."

Susannah grabbed the book and looked frantically around the room. Not a moment too soon, she dashed toward the family Bible and thrust the thin and tiny copy of *The Ravishing Prince* inside.

A second later Dahlia led the Reverend Pettigrew into the parlor. "Good afternoon, ladies . . . Mr.

Garrett," he said. "I was on my way back from the Donnally place and thought I'd stop by. I was hoping Susannah might have some of that cold buttermilk she gave me last time I was here."

Reed stood and shook hands with the Reverend Pettigrew as Susannah hurried into the kitchen.

She came out a few minutes later with a tray of glasses filled with buttermilk, which she passed around.

"I must say I didn't expect to find all of you inside on such a fine day."

"We were reading," Dahlia said.

"Oh?" Reverend Pettigrew looked around the room and Susannah groaned. She knew he was looking for the books.

"We were reading the Bible. . . . That is, Mr. Garrett was reading to us."

Reed, she noticed, raised his brows at her, but thankfully said nothing.

"Why, that's a mighty nice way to spend a Sunday afternoon. I think I'll suggest that to the rest of the congregation next Sunday." He looked in Reed's direction and said, "What book were you reading from?"

"The Song of Solomon," Reed said smoothly.

Susannah wanted to choke him. Of course he was aware that the Song of Solomon contained some very descriptive passages on the female anatomy.

"The Song of Solomon, you say," Reverend Pettigrew repeated thoughtfully. About that time his wandering gaze landed on the family Bible sitting on the table next to Reed. "That's a mighty fine-looking Bible you've got there," he said, rising to his feet.

He had no more than started toward it when

Susannah leaped up and dashed toward the Bible. "Here! Let me get it for you!" she said.

Susannah picked up the large Bible. Her fingers slipped between the pages to retrieve the slim volume of *The Ravishing Prince.* As she turned toward the reverend, she dropped the small book into Reed's lap, vowing to put tacks in his biscuits if he didn't hide it.

Reverend Pettigrew looked through the Bible as he sipped his buttermilk. When he finished, he stood and thanked Susannah. "Your buttermilk was as good as I remembered."

"You needn't hurry off, Reverend," Susannah said.

"I've got two more stops to make, so I'd best be on my way."

When Reed got to his feet and stepped forward, Susannah's horrified gaze fell on the copy of *The Ravishing Prince* lying in his chair. He'd been sitting on it. Violette must have seen it about the same time, for she moved quickly to the chair and sat down.

"I do hope you will forgive me if I don't walk you to the door, Reverend," Violette said. "I suddenly feel a bit light-headed."

"It must be the heat," Susannah said.

"You stay right there," the reverend said as he and Reed walked toward the door. After farewells, the two men went outside.

Susannah watched them from the window, wondering what Reed would say to them when he returned. When the men finished talking, Reed waited until the reverend drove off, then walked toward the barn. Susannah watched him go, unable to understand the sudden stab of disappointment that gripped her.

Later that night she could not sleep for thinking about him. Were these the kinds of thoughts her mother had? Did she think about men until her curiosity got the best of her? What was it like to dress provocatively, to feel the hot glances, the roving hands? She had often wondered about how it would feel.

Susannah rolled over and punched her pillow, but sleep would not come. With an exasperated sigh, she threw the covers back and climbed out of bed. Across the room, she saw the old humpback trunk that had belonged to her mother. She went to it and threw back the lid. After rummaging through the contents, she found what she was looking for—the low-cut, scarlet satin dress with the black feather trim. She dug a little further until she found the black silk stockings and the black satin shoes. She turned toward the mirror and looked at herself in her green cotton nightgown.

A moment later the nightgown lay on the floor at Susannah's feet. In its place was the scarlet satin dress. Susannah glanced down at an ocean of bosom. She had more cleavage than the tufted cushions in the judge's fancy carriage. She turned to one side and allowed the long slit in the skirt to part, revealing a length of leg covered in the black silk. She looked at her reflection, then lifted her hair to the top of her head. She imagined herself in a smoke-filled room swimming in the scent of cheap perfume. She saw herself as she had seen her mother when she watched from behind the stair rails, slowly descending the steps in a graceful and fluid manner until every man in the room turned to watch. But she imagined Reed Garrett watching instead. Susannah felt beautiful, desirable, aching to know what it would feel like to let Reed see her like this.

"No!" she said, and whirled away from the image of herself in the mirror. She began jerking the black feathers from around her neck, then ripping at the satin. When she stood over the pile of tattered satin, feathers, and silk, she began to cry. Susannah had destroyed the only bit of her mother's clothing she had left. She stared down at the pile, not trying to stop the tears.

Now she knew how it felt to wear those clothes. She knew, and she was terrified she might want to know more.

A few days later Susannah glanced out the kitchen window and saw Reed leading Rosebud out for the smithy to shoe. Ordinarily she would have gone to talk to Jess Oliver. She had known him since she was a child, for he was one of the first people she met when she came to live with her aunts in Bluebonnet. She could still remember clearly the day he stopped by to shoe her new pony. He would be wondering why she stayed in the house, why she did not come out with a cup of coffee and the offer of a slice of fresh-baked pie.

Until now it had not been so difficult to keep men in their proper perspective, to allow them to be in her life but to play only a minor role. That had all changed with the appearance of Reed Garrett. For all her life she had lived with the knowledge that her aversion to men came from the fear that she might turn out like her mother, from the abhorrence of the sordid things she had seen and heard the first nine years of her life.

She had a new fear. What if the contrary was true? What if her fear came not from despising the things her mother and the other whores did with men, but from knowing that she wanted to do the same things? If she were honest, she would have to admit she had thought about such things with Reed, more than once.

Now she understood why the shadowy images of naked bodies, the sounds and smells of lovemaking haunted her dreams at night. The only difference she could find between her mother and herself was that while her mother made love indiscriminately with any man, Susannah could see herself doing those things with only one. And that made Reed someone she had to avoid at all costs. If she ever gave in to her desire, to her will, she would be lost.

She chastised herself for thinking about things like this when she had a bushel basket full of tomatoes that needed to be cooked and ladled into jars, and forced herself to turn away from the window.

"Oh," she said, when she saw Violette standing in the doorway looking at her. "You startled me. How long have you been there?"

"Long enough to wonder if you were going to be content to watch, or if you were going to do what you wanted to and go on out there."

"Out where?"

"Out where Jess is working. Jess and Reed."

"That isn't what I want."

"Hogwash! This is your Aunt Vi you are talking to. My body may be old and wrinkled, but my mind is as sharp as it ever was. I'm not so old that I don't know what it feels like to want a man."

"I don't want him." She went to the sink and took some tomatoes out of the basket and began washing them, as if she could wash this conversation away with the dirt.

"He's a nice man."

"You don't know anything about him."

"I'm a good judge of character."

"Yes, you are, and if I remember right, it was your good judgment that persuaded you to buy that worthless divining rod from the peddler last year."

"It wasn't worthless. It's made a right nice support to prop the window open."

Susannah put down the tomato she was holding and faced Violette, drying her hands as she did. "All right. What is going on here? Are you trying to whet my interest in this hired hand?"

"Since when did you start referring to him as a hired hand? He's not just an ordinary drifter, and you know that as well as I do. He's educated. He has an air of refinement about him that makes me think he comes from the kind of family we've only read about in books."

"If that's true, then he is running from something . . . more than likely the law."

"If there's anything in his past, it's pain, not something criminal."

"What makes you say that?"

"Look in his eyes."

"I have."

"I mean really look. Those are the eyes of someone who has suffered, and suffered deeply."

"Well, what do you want me to do about it? Console him?"

"No, but you might try being just a little bit nicer."

"I'm nice."

"You are about as cold as that norther what blew through here last February."

"You know why I can't be nice, Aunt Vi. You of all people know."

Violette's face softened. "I do, child, but it's time to lay those ghosts to rest, time to accept your mother for what she was, to allow her to be a human who made mistakes."

"And if I can't? Oh, Aunt Vi, what's going to happen to me?"

"You've only to look at your Aunt Dally to see what happens to an unforgiving woman. I don't think you want that."

Susannah felt the burn of tears at the back of her throat. "No, I don't want that, but I seem to be helpless to prevent it. If he knew . . . if he really knew the truth about me, do you think he would be interested?"

"I don't think it would matter to him, if he cared for you."

"If he cared . . . if I cared . . . if I could stand the thought of him touching me."

"He cares, but that isn't the issue here."

"Oh? What is the issue?"

"I don't think for a minute that you abhor the thought of him putting his hands on you. I think you're afraid–no, terrified–of what you might feel, what you might do if he did. You are so afraid of becoming like your mother that you won't give yourself the opportunity to live, to feel, to care."

"I thought you understood."

"I do. How many times have we talked about this, Susannah? I have tried so many times to reassure you that you have control of your life, that you don't have to end up like your mother."

Tears clouded Susannah's eyes. "I know you have, Aunt Vi. You have treated me like your own, but you could never undo those nine years and what they did to me. No one could. It wasn't that you did not try. It was simply that those nine years made me different."

"I feel it's my fault, that I failed you somehow. At the time I was reluctant to talk about the kinds of things that went on between men and women because I figured you'd had enough of that. Maybe I was wrong. Maybe we should have talked about those things. It would have helped, I think, if John had been alive, if you'd had a man around, an example of what a normal, loving marriage is all about. It always grieved me that John was not here so you could learn to love a man in a healthy way, just as it grieved me that I could never have any children of my own."

Susannah was crying harder now. "It isn't your fault. It's the things I remember, the things I saw that I can't forget. You couldn't possibly understand what it was like to stand in the shadows and watch your mother disrobe in front of a man, or the horror of watching a man mount her like an animal, taking her roughly, while she stared at the ceiling."

"Dear, dear child. I had hoped you could forget."

"Forget? I can never forget the glassy look in my

mother's eyes, the smell of lovemaking that sickens me still, or the way my mother would barely wash one man's residue from her body before another one took her. The horrible, vulgar things those men said ring in my ears to this very day. There were times that they would even reach for me, times when a man would offer my mother money if she would let him undress me."

"Oh my God. You never told me *that*, Susannah!"

"Once, when my mother was ill, just before you came for me, one of the other whores took me to her room. A man was there. He had given her money. She held me while he pulled my dress up. He unfastened his pants and rubbed himself on my leg. My mother came into the room screaming. She picked up a bootjack and hit him over the head with it. He fell against me. I had his blood all over me."

Violette, too, was crying now, and she put her arms around Susannah. "We should have had this talk a long time ago," she said.

"I don't know if that would have helped. Aunt Vi, don't blame yourself. You've been wonderful to me–you and Aunt Dally both have–but, well, not a day goes by that I don't wonder what my life would have been like if I'd had a mother and father to live with like other people. I am like a tree that was cut down. I have no roots. I cannot grow."

Violette wiped the tears from Susannah's cheeks. "You can, child. You can grow new roots, but you've got to let yourself try. You can't keep lopping off every little root that starts. Let it go. See what happens."

She cried harder. "I can't."

"You can."

"Oh, Aunt Vi, don't you understand? It's too late for me. I can't change what I am."

"It isn't too late."

"It is, but it doesn't matter. Not really. I don't want to change. I like the way I am."

"You can't mean that."

"I do mean it."

Violette paused. "I have never been able to understand a mind hardened by stubbornness any more than I could understand a life frozen in dignity. Strange bedfellows both."

Violette left and Susannah simply stood, staring at the vacant doorway. She wanted to call her back, but she was unable to do so.

She was vexed beyond anything she could ever remember. Never had she felt so inadequate, so agitated. There was no denying the truth of what Aunt Vi said. It hurt to know she had been such a disappointment to the ones she loved most. A ghastly vision of herself reduced to the status of a bitter old maid rose up before her; the awful consequences of the loneliness she would experience, the guilt she would constantly feel, the regret she would live with for the rest of her days.

Question was, what could she do about it? She was a grown woman, and life already pointed in a certain direction that, set in motion, would be nigh impossible to turn around. She might as well wish for the moon.

And if she did transform her life, what then? What would she have to show for it? The answer came swiftly to her.

Reed Garrett.

* * *

After lunch the next day Susannah was in the parlor knitting. She almost dropped a stitch when Daisy Hitchcock came into the room. "Why Daisy, how nice to see you. It's been quite a spell since you were here last."

"I know," Daisy said, taking a seat across from Susannah. "I haven't had time to do much of anything since I started working at the post office. I've missed our visits."

"As I have." Susannah jabbed her needles into the ball of yarn in her lap and put the knitting into the basket on the floor. "There. Now we can visit."

"What are you making?"

"A shawl for Aunt Vi."

Daisy smiled. "Purple. I should have known. It's still her favorite color?"

"Oh, yes. Just the other day she was going on about what a dreadful shame it was that one couldn't find purple drawers."

"That would look divine with her red petticoat."

"Wouldn't it?" Susannah said, and they both laughed.

"Is it true that you're sweet on Mr. Garrett?"

Susannah could only stare at her for a moment, completely astounded. "Sweet on Reed Garrett? I should say not. Whatever gave you that idea?"

"Tate said–"

"Tate! Well, that explains it. Listen to me, Daisy. You shouldn't believe a word Tate Trahern says. And don't you go letting him sweet-talk you into doing something you'll regret. Do you hear me?" She shook her head. "Sweet on Reed Garrett . . . Why that's the most preposterous . . . Why, Reed Garrett and I go together like stripes and plaid."

"I'm sorry I brought it up. I was curious, that's all, seeing as how we used to be such good friends."

Susannah leaned forward and put her hand on Daisy's. "We're still good friends. We just don't get to see each other as much as we did when we were younger."

"Sometimes I wish we were still in school. We were happy then, weren't we?"

"Very happy."

"Sometimes I wonder if I'll ever be that happy again."

"You will be."

Daisy started crying.

Susannah stood and went to sit on the sofa beside Daisy. She put her arm around her and asked, "Daisy, what is the matter?"

"Oh, Susannah, I've done something awful." Daisy sobbed.

"You couldn't do something that bad. You're too nice a person."

"I'm going to have a baby."

"Oh, Daisy. Don't carry on so. You can always get married."

"No, I can't."

"Why not?"

"He won't marry me."

"You've told him about the baby?"

"No. I'm afraid to tell him."

"Afraid? Why would you be afraid to tell the father of your child? He has a right to know. It's his child, too."

"I know he won't marry me. Oh, Susannah, what am I going to do?"

"Daisy, who is the father?"

"I can't tell."

"You've got to tell him, Daisy. You can't let it go too much longer. How far along are you?"

"A month or so. I just missed my woman's time."

"Daisy, if you don't tell him so the two of you can get married, you will be forced to have this baby and raise it by yourself."

"I know. My pa will kill me if he finds out."

"Isn't there someplace you could go until you have the baby? Any relatives?"

"No."

"Well, perhaps you could come out here. We're far enough from town that we don't get many visitors. It shouldn't be too difficult to keep you hidden away."

"What would I do with the baby?"

"I don't know, but we would think of something by the time it came."

Daisy wiped her eyes and said, "I've got to be going. I've got to get back to the post office. I told them I was coming out here to deliver an important letter to Mr. Garrett."

"You have a letter for Reed?"

"Yes. Is he here?"

"He's down by the barn helping Jess Oliver shoe our horses. Do you want me to take the letter to him?"

"No, I want to do it. That way I won't be telling a lie."

Susannah smiled and gave her childhood friend a

hug. "You are a nice person, Daisy. Don't you ever let anyone convince you otherwise."

The two of them walked to the kitchen. Susannah stood at the door while Daisy went on down to the barn.

As Susannah watched Daisy walk up to Reed, she noticed the friendly manner in which he greeted her. Susannah's heart stilled and her blood ran cold. Was Daisy's tale all a pretext? Was her real motive in coming out here to tell Reed about her baby? Was Reed the father?

Reed looked up and saw Daisy walking toward him. He was wondering what she was doing there when she said, "You got some mail. It's from Boston. I thought it might be important."

"Why, thank you, Daisy. That is very nice of you to go to so much trouble. I appreciate it." Reed took the envelope from her and glanced down. He recognized his father's writing. A warm current of affection flowed through him. "It's been a while since I've been anywhere long enough for my folks to write. I really am looking forward to reading this. It was nice of you to bring it out here. I owe you a favor."

Daisy looked down at her feet. "It wasn't any trouble. I'm happy to do it. I hope it's good news." She glanced at Jess. "Hi, Mr. Oliver."

"Didn't expect to see you out here, Daisy. Are you looking for work?" He winked at Reed. "I suppose I could use another hand. Do you know anything about shoeing?"

Daisy giggled. "I think I'll keep my job at the post office." She carefully looked over the horse he was shoeing. "Me and horses, well, we don't get along too well. I'm kinda scared of them."

"That's probably a good thing. Wish I'd learned that before I got hurt the first time by one of them. If you change your mind, you let me know."

"I sure will, Mr. Oliver." She looked back at Reed. "I guess I'd better be getting back to town."

"Thanks for bringing this out. That's just about the nicest thing anybody ever did for me. You let me know if there's ever anything I can do for you. I mean that."

Daisy nodded. "I will." She turned away. "Good-bye," she said, then added, "Good-bye, Mr. Oliver."

Jess waved a hand at her.

"Good-bye, Daisy," Reed said. "Thanks again."

He watched Daisy as she made her way back to the house. He saw Susannah open the back door and let her in. Reed looked down at the letter in his hand, then ripped the envelope open.

Dearest Reed,

Your mother and I were elated to hear from you and to know all is well. I know how difficult it must be for you to write when you're on the move, but I'm thankful you understand what it must be like for us to wonder where you are and how you are doing. Your mother gets especially fretful when we don't hear regularly.

Things haven't changed much since we wrote to you last. Your sisters are doing fine and send their love. I'm getting a little more bald than I was when you saw me last, but your mother still looks as beautiful as she did the day I married her. I've purchased a smart new buggy to drive her around town. Next week I'm going out in the country to look at a pair of carriage horses. Hannah and Dandy are getting a bit old. I guess it's time to turn them out to pasture. It's hard to believe that you were just a young boy when Hannah was a foal, and I remember the day I bought Dandy at the fair and you insisted on riding him all the way home. Where have the years gone?

I saw Harriet Van Meter at the opera last week. She asked about you and said to please tell you hello next time I wrote. I don't know if you remember but she's Alana's mother. She said Alana's rich husband had hired some New York lawyer and was getting a divorce. Harriet was reminiscing about the days when you and Alana were sweet on each other. She wanted your address so Alana could write. Forgive me for taking the liberty of lying, but I told her we didn't have an address where we could write you. She truly seemed disappointed.

Mrs. Harrison Brewer returned from a trip to South America, sick with malaria. She died three weeks after she arrived home. A pity. Your college friend, Jackson Haggerty, just had his fifth daughter. Our former neighbors, the Morisettes, now have seven sons. I wonder if they'd be interested in a trade?

I hear that Adam Copley is in poor health (it couldn't be poor enough to suit me). I pray that once he's gone things will settle down a bit. It would be wonderful to have you back home where we could see you frequently. I miss our Sunday afternoon visits more than I can say. I rarely go into the library without expecting to see your long legs resting on the ottoman and you in the chair with a book in your hands. This old house retains your memory, just as that dilapidated leather chair by the fireplace in my study still holds the imprint of the last time you sat there. Next time you're in a town large enough to have a photographer, have your picture taken for your mother and myself.

Speaking of your mother, she is standing beside me now, wringing her hands and telling me to hurry. Seems she has a few things she wants to say to you, so I'll end with just a reminder of all the love and affection I hold for you.

God bless you,
Your father

Reed swallowed back the emotion that lodged, thick and painful, in his throat. A thousand memories of special times spent with his father came rushing back. Of all the things he regretted in life, being separated from his parents was the most difficult to accept. He took a deep breath and looked down at the familiar hand of his mother.

My dearest son,

I cannot tell you how thankful I was to see your physician's scrawl across the envelope that came the other day. It seems as time passes that I grow more and more anxious for your letters. Separation does indeed make the heart grow fonder–if it were possible to love you any more than I already did.

I just read over what your father wrote. He is always such a dear to write you the news so that I might spend my precious few lines telling you how terribly we continue to miss you. The gardener unearthed an old top of yours in my rose garden. When I saw it, I cried. I was worthless for two days. The metal tip is rusted and the paint is gone from the wood, which is cracked and split, but that precious top now occupies a place on the bookshelf, along with your great-grandfather's pipe, my mother's spectacles, and the old family Bible.

I know you have always trusted my woman's intuition, and pray you will not scoff when I tell you that I have been having the most blessed assurance whenever I pray for you of late. I truly feel that God is tempering my pain by this assurance that your present circumstances are not permanent. I hope this is true and that we may all be together soon. Even more, I pray that you will find someone to love, that you will no longer be denied that richest of blessings.

My darling son, your father tells me he must leave now if he is to post this letter today, so I must end, as I do with all my letters to you, with the feeling that there were so many more things I wanted to say. Since time does not permit, I ask you to simply remember that you are always in my thoughts and that there is hardly a day that goes by that I don't remember the warmth, the joy of how your little-boy's hand felt in mine. May the Lord bless you while we are apart, one from the other.

As always,
Your loving mother

* * *

An hour after Daisy left, Jess Oliver drove the last nail into Milkweed's shoe. When he finished, he released the horse's foot and straightened up, grimacing as he stretched out his back. "Lord-a-mercy! I sure am glad that's the last of them. Don't think I could shoe another horse today. I'm getting too old for this."

"I don't think age has anything to do with it," Reed replied. "Even a young man would have trouble working for hours all hunched over like you do."

Jess stretched his back once more, then began putting his tools back into his wagon. "I guess you're right. Maybe my back doesn't hurt any more than it used to. I just like to complain more."

"You could always let your son take over some of the more strenuous jobs for you."

Jess tossed the used horseshoes into the back of the wagon. They landed with a clang. "I've thought about that, but then I'd miss all the nice things the ladies give me to eat, like Miss Susannah's pie."

"Her pie?"

"You ain't never eaten any of Miss Susannah's pie?"

Reed thought back. He'd had pie on several occasions, but it was always Aunt Vi's pie or Dally's. To his knowledge he'd never eaten one of Susannah's. He shook his head. "Not that I remember."

"Then you really missed something. Her pies have won prizes at the fair for the past five or six years. Come to think on it, I believe my wife said she also won a prize last year for her sour pickles."

Reed could believe that.

Jess glanced toward the house. "You don't suppose she's upset with me for not coming to shoe the horses last week, like I intended, do you?"

"No, I don't think she's upset with you at all. Why would you think that?"

Jess scratched his head. "Well, I don't rightly know, but she's always brought me a cup of coffee and a nice slice of pie before I finished, and today I haven't seen hide nor hair of her."

"She's putting up tomatoes."

"Heck! That ain't no excuse," Jess said as he removed his shoeing apron and tossed it into the wagon. "She's been busy before–tomatoes, squash, okra, corn, you name it. She would leave it for a spell and come to say hello." He shook his head and glanced fondly back at the house once more. "I must have done something to make her mad at me, although"–he scratched his head a bit–"I don't rightly know what it could have been."

"You know women. They don't always need a reason, at least not one any man can understand. I'm sure it isn't anything you've done."

"I can't think of any other reason for her to act so standoffish."

Reed had a feeling he knew the reason, but he wasn't going to tell Jess Oliver. He simply figured that if Susannah was ignoring Jess, it was because Reed was helping him.

"I bet she's so busy she doesn't realize you're almost finished. Why don't you go wash up, and I'll see about that pie?"

"I don't want to put you to any trouble."

"No trouble. I'll drop Milkweed off in the barn as we go."

The kitchen door was partly open, and the warm, pungent smell of cooked tomatoes drifted out to greet him. Reed rapped on the wood and pushed the door open.

"Come in," Susannah called out.

She kept on working, saying nothing until she'd finished. "Is Jess gone?" she asked at last.

"No, he's washing up."

She straightened and looked at him. She seemed different. Her whole face looked different . . . rather solemn, or perhaps severe, as if something were weighing on her mind. The look in her eyes had changed, too, more private, as if she resented his coming here.

She turned back to what she was doing, leaving him standing there like an extra shoe. He stared at a knothole under the table leg. The floors were scrubbed and oiled. Three rows of jars full of tomatoes lined one end of the table. The sunlight coming through the window glinted off the shiny tops. She dabbed at her damp forehead with her sleeve. "Did you need something?"

"Pie."

She gave him a curious look. "Pie? You came in here in the middle of the afternoon looking for pie?"

"For Jess. Seems you've always given him a cup of coffee and a slice of pie whenever he came out here to shoe the horses. Now, after sixteen years of coffee and pie, poor ole Jess can't understand what he did to make you stop."

Her face seemed to melt and rearrange itself into a softer, kinder version. She glanced at the half-eaten pie sitting on the top shelf of the stove. "I–"

"Didn't want to go out there when I was there,"

he said, knowing that was the reason, and wondering if she would admit it.

"It would take more than you to make me a prisoner in my own house. I go where I want to."

"But not if I'm there."

"I wouldn't want you if you came rolled in gold dust." She clapped her hands on her hips. "Now, what makes you think I would give a fig about being around you?"

He grabbed the dipper and dipped it into the water bucket. "I don't know, but I'll think about it," he said, and took a long drink.

"You do that," she said, going to the stove and taking the pie down from the shelf. "And while you're thinking, you might be thinking about marrying Daisy Hitchcock."

He choked on the water. "Marry Daisy Hitchcock? What on earth would make you think I'd want to marry Daisy Hitchcock?" He stomped across the kitchen. "What possessed you to say a thing like that?"

"Have you been seeing Daisy?"

"Hell! I see her every time I go into the post office, but that doesn't mean I want to marry her. I just go in there to mail letters."

"You haven't been . . . you know . . . intimate with her?"

"Good God! Is that why she came out here? Is that what she told you?"

"She's going to have a baby."

"Well, it sure as hell isn't mine."

Relief washed over her, wave after wave, until she was saturated with it, to the point of going weak in the knees.

"Did she tell you I was the father?"

"No, she wouldn't say who the father is. I just naturally assumed–"

"I'm getting fed up with everyone around here accusing me of things. I suggest that if you want to know who the father is, you start with Tate Trahern."

"Tate? What makes you suspect him?"

"Because he's low enough to do something like that. Because I see him sweet-talking her every time I go in to mail a letter."

Susannah was certain he was telling the truth. She felt terrible. And joyous that he wasn't the father of Daisy's child. "I'm sorry I jumped to conclusions. I hope you will forgive me."

"Forget it. Just give me the damn pie, and I'll get out of your way."

"No need to trouble yourself with the pie. Tell Jess to come on up."

"I'll deliver the message," he said, walking to the door. "Don't bother to cut any of that pie for me."

"I wasn't."

Reed went straight to Jess and delivered Susannah's message, which seemed to cheer him. It didn't do much for Reed, and the more he thought about the encounter in the kitchen the more frustrated and angry he felt. He had to get off the farm . . . for a little while at least.

Susannah was in her bedroom when she heard the sound of a horse and looked out the window to see Reed riding toward his place. He brought a bottle to his lips and tipped back his head. Then he tapped the cork back into the bottle as if he intended to save it. But he didn't. He tossed it into the air and drew his pistol. He fired at it twice and missed.

Under other circumstances Susannah might have laughed. But not now. Reed was drunk as a skunk. And she was at least partly to blame because she'd jumped to conclusions.

Reed's bottle rolled a few feet before coming to a stop. He shot at it a few more times until he finally shattered it.

She shook her head and turned away. She unbuttoned her dress and was about to change into her nightgown when she remembered the food she had put away for him. More than likely, he had not had anything to eat, and if he needed anything right now, it was something in his stomach besides liquor.

She buttoned her dress again and wondered if she was doing the right thing, but guilt over the hostile way she had treated him was disturbing her. The plate of food she had saved him from supper might not do him any good, but taking it to him would ease her mind a bit.

Carrying the plate of fried catfish, hush puppies, and turnip greens covered with a kitchen towel, she picked her way over the uneven ground. All her courage vanished the moment she reached his door. She started to turn around and go back, but she looked down at the plate of food and decided she could knock and leave it outside.

She knocked twice. She bent over and was about to place the plate on the step when the door opened. She raised her head. "I . . ." The sight of him sucked the words right out her throat. He was obviously undressing, for he was wearing only a shirt. It was a long-tailed shirt, so everything major was covered.

She glanced down. His feet were bare. His legs were well shaped, the muscles hard. She looked away.

"It's a little late in the evening to be making social calls, isn't it?"

He slurred the words, and the alcohol fumes were strong enough to loosen paint. "I saved your dinner. I thought you might like something to eat."

He stepped back, motioning for her to come in. "You can put it on the table."

If she had possessed an ounce of wit, she would have handed the plate to him, but she was caught off guard by his appearance. It had been a long, long time since she had seen a man's naked legs. The sight brought back a flood of memories. All unpleasant.

She stepped inside and carried the plate to the table, where she deposited it in a businesslike manner. "I'm afraid it's cold, but it should stick to your ribs."

When she turned around, he was blocking her way. His gray eyes seemed hidden and dark. His hair was mussed, and he looked at her in a sleepy way. He wobbled on his feet a bit, and she was reminded of just how drunk he really was. She started around him.

His hand shot out and grabbed her wrist. "What's your hurry?"

"I need to get on back."

"What for? It's a little early to be going to bed. If you thought enough to bring me something to eat, the least you can do is keep me company."

She took a step back. He released her wrist. She looked around. "Where's your silverware?"

"What do you need silverware for?"

"Do you intend to eat with your hands?"

"It's in the drawer over there," he said, "but I

don't intend to eat. As for my hands, I can think of something better for them to hold than silverware."

"I should have let you go to bed hungry."

"Yes, you should have, but you are here now, and I'm a bit too drunk to act in a civilized manner."

"Go to bed and I'll forget this ever happened."

"There is nothing to forget–yet."

"You know what I mean."

"I'm not so certain I do. You are a woman of contradictions. You are not what you seem. You bedevil me. You're seductive as hell one minute, as innocent as a babe the next."

"That's not true."

"Yes it is. You knew exactly what you were doing when you came out here."

"I only came out here to bring you something to eat. I saw you ride in. A fool could see you'd been drinking. I felt it was partly my fault."

"Correction. It was all your fault."

"I was trying to make amends."

"Why?"

"I don't believe in letting the sun go down on anger."

"Don't start getting biblical on me."

"I'm surprised you noticed."

"Why? Because you thought I was too drunk to pick up on the biblical reference, or because I have some knowledge of the Bible?"

"Both."

"Why are you here?"

"I told you."

"You better leave now, because–"

"Why?"

"Because you came out here all soft and sweet

smelling and playing on a man's desire. I'm drunk and I'm a man. Don't you understand what that means? What are you trying to do to me? Do you want me to make love to you? Is that it?"

"Nothing could be further from the truth."

"Good. I'm glad to hear it, because it wouldn't have done you any good. I'm not interested."

"That makes two of us, then, and if you'll get out of my way, I'll get out of here and leave you to brood and wallow in whatever sins of the past you are running from."

She knew the moment the words left her mouth that she had said too much, that for once she had goaded him beyond even what his gentlemanly manner would take. Before she could think about escape, she found herself hauled up against him, her words muffled against the hard, unforgiving mouth that covered hers.

He kissed her deeply and with rough abandon, as if by doing so he could leave her feeling used and cheap.

When he broke the kiss, he held her at arm's length. "I have loved only one woman in my life and I lost her. I have no desire to love anyone ever again. But I am a man, and I have a man's wants and needs. If you are interested, then by all means let's explore the possibilities. If not, then stay the hell away from me." He released her. "Well? What's it to be? Your bed or mine?"

She slapped him harder than she intended. She looked away, afraid to see the expression in his eyes. But when she did look at him, she was surprised by what she saw.

"I deserved that, I suppose. Perhaps it was good

that it happened this way. Now you know. In the future you would do well to remember what could have happened here tonight. You think about that the next time you feel the urge to come out here to relieve your guilt."

She hurried around him, pausing at the door, and said, "It was a good thing you lost the woman you loved. You would have made her life miserable."

"Oh, I did worse than that," he said bitterly. "Believe me. I did much, much worse."

Chapter 14

The following Sunday morning Susannah was up early. After breakfast she went to the barn to fetch a halter and lead rope. Then she walked out into the pasture where the horses grazed. As soon as she saw Rosebud was not there, she remembered letting her out into the bigger pasture the day before.

Well, she thought, there was nothing to be done about it now. She would simply have to go after Rosebud. It wasn't so much the going after her that Susannah minded, but the unfortunate circumstance of having to pass by the little house where Reed stayed.

She walked toward his house, forcing herself to focus on what a lovely morning it was, which wasn't too difficult–until she neared his open window and heard him talking.

She paused and listened, wondering who he could be talking to. Her aunts were at home, she knew, for they hadn't finished dressing for church when she'd left. Who else could it possibly be?

She was about to move on down the path, when she realized that it was only *his* voice she heard. She listened a bit longer and understood then that he must be talking in his sleep.

She heard the bedsprings creak beneath his weight, the hollow sound of the brass headboard when it clanged against the wall. The bed creaked again. Her heartbeat escalated. She imagined him tossing restlessly in his sleep and saw vividly the sheet tangled around the long, muscled legs she remembered so well. Suddenly he cried out.

"Philippa . . . you don't know what you're saying. Don't ask me to do this. Please. Trust me. I know he's your father, but he is wrong. Trust me . . ."

Suddenly she heard an agonizing sound, as if someone were being tortured. Over and over he moaned pitifully, and Susannah had to fight the urge to go to him, to offer him comfort.

But she remembered what had happened the last time she went to him. Without a backward glance, she hurried toward the pasture to find Rosebud so they would make it to church on time.

If there was anything she needed today, it most definitely was to go to church.

A warm patch of sunlight on his face woke Reed. He looked at the clock next to his bed, unable to believe he had slept so late, even if it was Sunday.

After he dressed and finished his coffee, he stepped outside and saw Susannah leading Rosebud from the pasture.

"Need any help?" he called.

"No, thank you. I can manage."

He stepped off the porch and walked up the narrow path that joined the one she used. She slowed down a bit, then stopped. Something he was happy to see, for she did look fetching in that yellow dress. The color did something wonderful to her hair, and it brought out the gold flecks in her eyes.

"I'm driving my aunts to church, and I've got to hurry."

"Why are you running so late?"

"Ask her," Susannah replied, indicating Rosebud. "I had to chase this blasted horse all over the pasture. She wouldn't come even when I offered her oats."

He reached out and took the lead rope. "I'll hitch her to the buggy; then I'll drive you to town."

"I wasn't hinting for your help. After all, it's your day off."

He shrugged. "One day is pretty much like another. I've nothing better to do." He started walking and Rosebud trotted behind.

Susannah fell in step with him. "Thank you."

"Anytime," he said, and pulled ahead.

"Reed?"

"Hmmm?"

"Could I talk to you?"

He slowed the mare. "About what?"

"I . . . I want to apologize for what I did the other night . . . for coming to your place and invading your privacy."

"No apology needed. The fault was mine. I had too much to drink."

"Regardless of whose fault it was, I am sorry it happened. My aunts are sensitive women. They've grown accustomed to . . . to having you around. They don't understand why you don't drop in anymore, and they miss your visits in the evenings."

He stopped and looked at her. "And you?"

She gave him a puzzled look. "Me?"

"Are your aunts the only ones who miss my visits?"

"No . . . no, of course not. Your presence is a nice diversion."

Well, he had wondered where he stood with

her, hadn't he? He shook his head. "That's a first. I've been called a lot of things, but never a nice diversion."

"Who is Philippa?" she blurted.

He felt as if someone had punched him in the stomach. For a moment he was sure his body was turning to stone, and he was helpless to do anything about it. Every muscle seemed to grow rock hard. Not even the sudden gust of breeze disturbed his hair. It was as if he and the world around him shut down the moment she said that name. Philippa . . . Oh God, Philippa. Would he ever be free of the pain?

He saw the soft look in her eyes. What touched her? Was it his grief, his sorrow, or his anger that reached out and touched her? "I'm sorry. It's none of my business. I shouldn't have asked."

"Where did you hear that name?"

"You said it."

"When?"

"Not too long ago this morning . . . when I passed by your house on my way to get Rosebud. I couldn't help hearing you talk. At first I thought you had a visitor, but then I realized it was your voice only that I heard. I figured you must have been dreaming. You cried out. The window was open. It's a still morning. The sound carried. I didn't mean to pry."

They were standing stock-still, staring at each other. Suddenly, Reed said, "Philippa was my wife."

She looked as if someone had sucked the breath out of her, and because of that, her next words were weakly spoken. "I'm sorry. I didn't know . . ."

"Of course you didn't know. How could you?"

"I am very sorry."

"Don't worry overmuch. The wound is not as fresh as it once was." He felt strange saying that, but he realized it was true. Actually, he was glad that Susannah knew he'd been married.

Susannah did not ask any more questions, and Reed did not volunteer any more information. They started walking to the house again and soon reached where her aunts waited.

Reed drove them to church, finding he enjoyed the outing on such a fine, sunny morning as much as they did. The buggy moved slowly through the flat terrain, passing old, abandoned farmhouses and a few thickets of mesquite, where they jumped a covey of quail that took flight with a whirring of wings.

During the trip, he cast a glance or two at Susannah. She was perched on the edge of the seat as if she were ready to flap her wings and take flight, just like the quail. Normally when he drove them to church, she would have an expectant look on her face and her eyes would be alert, taking everything in. Today her expression was different, one of deep speculation. He knew she was mulling over what he told her, trying to put two and two together. He figured her biggest question was about what had happened to Philippa.

He wasn't ready to answer that question just yet.

They arrived at church a little ahead of schedule. Violette told Reed to pick them up at half past twelve. "If you have anything you want to do, go on and do it; then come back here."

"I don't have anything pressing. I guess I'll just hang around."

"Then why don't you join us inside?" Aunt Vi asked.

He gave her a teasing smile. "Worried about my ornery hide?"

"No, it's the rest of you that I'm worried about. Sure you won't change your mind and join us?"

"I've never been much of a religious man."

"Interesting," Violette said, "that a man with no religion would know the Song of Solomon."

"I was religious . . . once."

"Then join us and try being so again."

"I can't do that."

"Why?"

"I've turned my back on the church."

"And God?"

He shrugged. "You can't have one without the other."

"Why did you turn away?"

He looked off into the distance. "Because God turned away from me."

"God never turns his back on his sheep, although it may seem that way for a time. Have you never read the book of Job?"

"A long time ago."

She thrust her Bible at him. "Then I suggest you try reading it again. You might be surprised at what you find."

Reed took the Bible. "For instance?"

"Has it ever occurred to you that God might be testing you, that he has allowed your faith to be tried, just as Job's was? Don't you remember that in the end, because Job had persevered, God restored everything he had taken from him, but in greater abundance? 'Oh ye of little faith.' "

He looked from Violette to Susannah, but he saw

no encouragement in her eyes. "Thanks for the invitation, but I think it's a little late for me."

"Don't be so certain. Even the blackest sheep can become as white as snow."

"In my case, that would take a miracle," Reed said. "A real honest-to-God miracle."

"Miracles always happen against overwhelming odds. Otherwise they wouldn't be miracles."

"You're a shrewd old woman and I like you."

"You're a lost lamb and I like you, too."

"Well, when you two get through liking each other, do you think you could help me down?" Dahlia asked.

Everyone laughed and Reed said, "Always happy to oblige a woman who knows her own mind."

Just as he extended a hand to help Dahlia down from the buggy, Reed caught a glimpse of Tate Trahern who was sitting with Daisy in a buggy. He must have seen Susannah, because he stopped talking. Reed paused a moment to observe how Tate followed Susannah's every move. The man was a real bastard, Reed thought. Tate might be sitting by the woman who carried his child, but it was Susannah who captured his attention, Susannah he wanted.

Susannah must have sensed that Tate was gazing at her, for she glanced at him once, then turned her head away as if hiding behind the protective curve of her bonnet.

"I'll take Aunt Dally on inside," she said, grasping her aunt's arm.

"I'll be along in a minute," Violette said. "I want to say something to Maude Whittaker."

Reed moved to Violette's side.

"Tell me about Tate and Susannah," Reed said. "Besides her dousing him with a basin of water, was there ever any real romance there?"

Violette glanced at Tate. "No. He came out to our place a dozen times or so, but Susannah wouldn't have anything to do with him. He got real angry once when he asked her to a dance and she wouldn't go. He's a possessive sort, and he doesn't know how to take no for an answer. I thought he'd never get over her spurning him. He was sweet on her for a long, long time."

"It doesn't look like he's gotten over anything. I'd say he's pretty sweet on her right now."

Violette gave Tate another quick glance. "Yes, it does look that way, doesn't it? I feel sorry for poor Daisy. I don't think Tate gives a flip for her. In fact, I don't think he is capable of giving a flip for anyone except himself. I blame his pa for that. He ruined Tate by giving him everything."

"My father gave me everything, but I don't think it ruined me."

She smiled. "No, it sure didn't." She paused a moment, then put her hand on Reed's arm. "Be careful around Tate. I've seen the way he looks at you. It's obvious he's jealous of your working for us, of your being so close to Susannah. He's a troublemaker, Reed. For that reason, I was always glad Susannah never paid him any mind."

"I can handle Trahern," Reed said.

"It isn't just Tate you have to worry about, though. He's got all those hands who work for his pa."

"Thanks for the warning."

Violette nodded. She walked over to where

Maude Whittaker and Miss Abby Hungerford were standing.

Reed stayed put, watching Susannah as she and her aunt walked up the church steps. They paused just outside the door when Sam Smith said something to her and Susannah stopped a moment to talk to him.

Susannah and Sam talked for a minute before Jess Oliver joined them. They stood there talking for quite a spell, occasionally punctuating their conversation with a burst of laughter. Much to his surprise, Reed found Susannah to be lively and animated. It wasn't that she hated men, Reed realized, but that she seemed threatened by men who might see her as a woman. He didn't speculate further, for at that moment he saw Tate approaching Susannah. With her back to him, Susannah didn't see him coming. When Tate reached Susannah, he took her by the arm and led her to one side. Even from where he stood, Reed could see Tate was standing closer to Susannah than propriety allowed. He could see, too, that it angered her.

Reed started in their direction when he felt a hand on his arm. "She can take care of herself," Violette said. "She's been rebuffing him for years. I don't think he would ever harm her, but if you interfere, it could create quite a stir. I don't want her humiliated like that."

Reed stood still, clenching his fists. He could not believe his eyes when he saw Tate lean toward Susannah as if he intended to kiss her.

Suddenly Susannah shoved him.

Tate took another step toward her, but the Reverend Pettigrew put a detaining hand on his shoulder. He and Tate talked for a minute. Then Tate turned angrily away.

Reed smiled.

Violette took a deep breath–one Reed identified as a sigh of relief. "Well, I think I'll be moseying on into church now. This is your last chance. Are you sure you don't want to join us?"

"No, I think I'll do a little meditating out here."

Violette looked around and tilted her head back to gaze at the sky. "You picked a mighty fine day for it. This is cloud-gazing weather."

He glanced heavenward. "Maybe I'll do a little cloud gazing, then."

"Couldn't hurt you none."

He laughed. "No, not as long as I remember a man gazing at clouds is at the mercy of puddles in the road."

Violette patted him on the back. "Don't worry yourself none. Puddles are few and far between in these parts."

He gave her his arm and walked her inside.

He was returning to the buggy when he heard a horse nicker. He looked up and glanced in the direction the sound had come from. To his complete surprise, he saw his dapple-gray mare tied to a tree next to the graveyard. The same mare that had been stolen from him that day when he was robbed.

Gray Girl whinnied again and began pawing the ground as she tossed her head up and down. Reed couldn't help smiling, but he wasn't surprised that his mare had recognized him. Besides being a very beautiful animal with a refined head and long, sleek body, Gray Girl was probably the smartest horse he had ever owned, or at least the best trained. She could count, do tricks, and give him kisses. She was fond of grabbing the hat off his head, and never missed an opportunity to pull the saddle blanket off before he could get the saddle on.

He walked up to the mare and scratched her between the eyes, pulling his head back when she tried to reach for his hat. "Oh, no you don't! You haven't been gone so long that I've forgotten all your bad habits," he said as he gave her the once-over.

He had bought her a little over two years ago from a man who raised and trained horses for the circus. At the time Reed hadn't been looking for a show pony, but he was in the middle of nowhere and needed a horse, and she was the only one around. Even then, it took a lot of persuasion to convince the owner to part with her, and he made Reed pay dearly. But she was more than worth the money, and it wasn't long until Reed was so attached to her that he wouldn't have parted with her for any sum of money.

Reed started to untie her, but when he reached for the reins something made him stop.

He would bide his time until church was over, when the thieving bastard came back to claim her.

Gray Girl nickered at him again when Reed left. He walked back to the buggy and climbed in. He looked down at the Bible in his hands. Without knowing why, he opened it to the book of Job and began to read.

The sound of singing reached his ears, and he closed his eyes as he listened to the words of "Amazing Grace."

Amazing grace, how sweet the sound that saved a wretch like me. I once was lost but now am found, was blind but now I see. 'Twas grace that taught my heart to fear, and grace my fears relieved. . . .

When the song ended, tears slipped down Reed's face. He knew now that there was more at stake here than just Susannah. He prayed for the first time in five years. When he finished, he knew that next Sunday he would be in church.

Half an hour later, the service was over. Tate Trahern was one of the first to leave. Reed watched him come down the steps and walk across the grass to where Gray Girl was tied. He unfastened the mare and managed to get one foot in the saddle before Reed rushed over to him and grabbed the bridle. Gray Girl stopped and wheeled. That sudden move left Tate unbalanced enough that Reed easily pulled him from the saddle. The mare bucked a few times, then stood with her front legs far apart, switching her tail.

"I think you've gotten on the wrong horse," Reed said.

Tate had his fists doubled when he turned to look at Reed. "I think you'd better mind your own business." He started to mount again, but Reed stopped him. This time Tate took a swing at him, but Reed ducked.

About that same time, Sheriff Jonah Carter was leaving church. He saw the confrontation and came over at a trot. "Now, hold on here just a gol-darned minute. Looks to me like you two fellas left church a mite early. Maybe you didn't stay long enough to let any of the preacher's sermon soak in. What seems to be the problem?"

"This good-for-nothing doesn't want me to get on my horse," Tate said.

The sheriff looked at Reed as if he expected an answer.

Reed gave him one. "I don't have a problem with him getting on his horse. It's getting on *my* horse that I mind."

"You trying to tell me that this is your horse?" The sheriff pushed his hat back and scratched his head as he looked from Reed to Tate and then to the gray mare. "Tie the horse until we get this solved," he said and one of the men nearby obeyed.

"This horse belongs to the Double T," Tate said.

"So, both of you are laying claim to this horse–is that right?"

Tate nodded. "The horse is mine."

"The horse was stolen from me," Reed said.

"You got any papers that prove the horse is yours?" Jonah asked Reed.

"No."

"How about you, Tate? You got any papers?"

"The horse was born on Double T land. We don't have papers on horses we raise."

"Seems to me there ought to be a way to prove who this horse belongs to without having to fight over it," the sheriff said, "but I don't rightly know what that would be."

The congregation, including the reverend, had gathered around. "Ask him if the mare has any marks or scars that he can identify," Reed said to the sheriff.

Tate scoffed at the idea of being asked anything. "It's pretty obvious there are no marks on the mare. Her hide is as smooth as a baby's cheek."

Jonah bore down on him. "So what you're saying is there are no marks you can identify on the mare?"

"That's what I'm saying."

Jonah looked at Reed. "How about you? Can you identify anything special?"

Reed began to describe a long scar on the underside of the mare's belly. "Why don't you take a look?" he asked the sherrif.

Sheriff Carter had no more than bent to examine the mare's belly over when he righted himself. "There's a scar there, all right. Just the way he described it."

A gasp went up from the crowd, which was followed by a sudden buzz. Reed paid that no mind but went on to validate his ownership even further. This time he directed his question to Tate. "I don't suppose you know of any special training this mare has received?"

Tate looked at Reed as if he was speaking Greek. "Special training? She's broke to ride, if that's what you mean."

"It's not."

Tate seemed uncomfortable, and Reed knew he had struck gold. He turned around and whistled. Gray Girl's head jerked up, and her ears pricked forward. "Untie her," he said to a young sandy-haired boy standing nearby, "and let her go."

"You mean turn her loose?" the boy asked.

"Yes."

The boy threw the reins over the mare's neck and released his hold on the cheek piece.

Reed whistled again.

Gray Girl snorted and tossed her head, then trotted toward him. When she reached him, Reed stroked her and scratched her beneath the chin, talking to her as he did. Gray Girl tossed her head a couple of times, and began nibbling at his face.

When five-year-old Jessica Suiter said, "Mommy, that horse is kissing him," everyone began to laugh.

Everyone, that is, save Dahlia, who did not look amused when she said to Violette, "I knew it! I knew he was a deadbeat the moment I saw him. He worked for a circus."

"Oh, for crying out loud! Dally, have you taken complete loss of your senses?"

"He's a circus worker and you can't trust them. They'll steal you blind."

Distracted by the laughter and shouts, Reed was down on his guard. It was just the opening Gray Girl needed, and she yanked his hat from his head and began shaking it. Whenever he reached for it, she would yank her head back or turn it one way or the other. Everyone was rolling with laughter. It took Reed a solid five minutes to get his hat back.

He asked the mare how old she was. Gray Girl pawed the ground five times. Children began laughing and clapping their hands. "I want a horse like that one!" someone shouted.

It was Sam Smith who called out, "That's the first female I've ever seen that would tell her age."

Everyone laughed and the sheriff stepped forward. "Well, I think I've seen enough." He turned to Reed. "Take your horse."

"The saddle is mine," Tate protested.

"The saddle goes with the mare," the sheriff said.

"According to my way of thinking, you can either go to jail for horse stealing, or you can forfeit your saddle." He looked at Reed as he said, "You may have to do both, if Mr. Garrett wants to press charges."

"I only want what belongs to me," Reed said. "I'll forget about the rest." He removed the saddle and placed it on the ground. "I don't want Trahern's saddle."

"Keep the saddle," Tate said. "I don't accept charity." He turned and walked away. It was obvious that Tate was angry. Very angry.

Chapter 15

Susannah was sitting near an old swing down by the creek, thinking about Reed, when suddenly he appeared. She could tell by the surprised look on his face and his abrupt stop that it had been accidental.

"Sorry for the intrusion. I didn't see you here. I hope I didn't interrupt anything."

He was such a nice, decent person, Susannah observed. Why couldn't she be herself around him? Why did she think of her mother and a scarlet satin dress when she saw him these days? She cleared her throat. "It's all right," she said. "I wasn't doing anything. I just come here out of habit mostly. I used to love this place when I was a little girl. In the summertime Daisy and I would swing far out over the creek, then bail out, landing in the water. It frightened my aunts to death. They forbade me to do it." She leaned back a bit and gave the swing a push. "It seems like it was a million years ago."

He sat on a tree stump nearby. "I didn't realize you and Daisy were close friends."

"I don't suppose you would call us close friends anymore, but we were very close at one time. She was my first friend in school."

"What happened? Did you have a falling out?"

She thought about that and shook her head. "No. It wasn't any particular thing that caused it. It was a gradual thing, like erosion. As we grew older, our differences became more noticeable."

"What differences?"

"The things we wanted out of life. Daisy was interested in boys and always had a beau."

"And that didn't interest you?"

"No, and before you ask, it still does not interest me. Daisy is a natural mother. She comes from a large family, and she is very good with children. She would like nothing more than to be married with a house full of children. . . ." Susannah's voice dwindled off to nothing. She took a deep breath and said, "Poor Daisy. Since her father's illness she has worked hard to support her family. It just doesn't seem fair. Wealthy people seem to have all the advantages."

"Not always," he said softly.

She wondered what cross he had to bear, what dark secrets he kept locked away, the same as she. "What happened to cause you to lose your faith?" She could not help asking, "Or did it go away gradually . . . eroding like my friendship with Daisy?"

He leaned forward and gave the swing another push and did not answer her question.

The two of them sat in silence, each of them watching the swing move back and forth. At last he said, "I can almost picture you as a little girl down here swinging and giving your aunts an attack of apoplexy."

"I am certain there were times when they came close. Now that I'm older, I see how my coming down here probably frightened them to death. Neither of them had ever spent much time around children. They must have worried greatly."

"But you didn't let that stop you."

She couldn't resist smiling. "No, of course I didn't. Not because I was willfully disobedient. It was more out of ignorance. I knew my aunts were terribly soft when it came to me. They let me get away with far more than a mother would have."

She did not tell him, however, the reason why her aunts were so easy on her–that they were trying, in their own way, to make up for the life she'd had before she came to live with them, a life that was anything but easy.

"I take it your mother died when you were young. Was that why you came to live with your aunts?"

She could feel a tightening in her muscles. He was encroaching upon forbidden territory, causing her past to rise up before her like a monster surfacing from the deep. Anticipation reached her extremities and left the tips of her fingers tingling. She had known for some time that this moment was coming. She had prepared herself for it. Yet when he asked the question, she was totally unsure how to answer it.

After a lengthy pause, she said softly, "Yes, she died."

"How old were you?"

"Nine . . . almost ten." No more questions, please.

"And your father? What about him?"

She stared coldly at him, then said, quite frankly, "I don't know who my father was. That makes me illegitimate, doesn't it? Are you shocked?"

"No. Should I be?"

She shrugged, trying to show him it did not matter what he thought. But it did matter. It mattered a lot.

"When your mother died, you were nine or ten. You came to live with your aunts immediately after that?"

"My mother wrote them when she realized how sick she really was. They came after me as soon as they received word of her illness. Unfortunately, she was dead by the time they arrived."

"They are your great-aunts?"

"Yes, they are my mother's aunts, so that makes them my great-aunts."

She stopped the swing. "You know something? You ask too many questions, and I'm tired of answering them." She left the swing and started to walk away. He stepped forward as if to block her, though she was not at all hemmed in. Something made her pause to see what he would say, what he would do. Part of her wanted to run, to retreat as she had always done, and yet there was a part of her that wanted him to know, to understand, to offer comfort. She had been denied the love of a mother and father, the affection, the tenderness, the loving pats. Her aunts loved her and nurtured her in the only way they knew, but there were times when she yearned to have someone put his arms around her, to hold her and tell her everything would be all right.

"Don't go."

She looked around, calculating, trying to decide the best way to handle this. Should she simply tell him their talk was finished, or walk off and leave him standing there with no explanation whatsoever?

He must have anticipated that, for he stepped closer. Instinctively, she countered with a step back. He took a step forward. She stepped back and felt herself against a tree. She recalled another time when he'd had her in such a position, and she remembered what happened. She could not let him kiss her again. She could not.

While her heart beat with fright, his arms went around her to rest against the tree, leaving her trapped between them. He did not touch her but simply leaned forward, bringing his mouth to hers.

"Trust me," he whispered. "Trust me like you did your aunts."

"My aunts were family. They loved me."

"Are you certain that I don't?"

"Yes . . ." His kiss stopped what she was going to say.

The touch of his lips against hers was soft, gentle, inquisitive, as if he wanted to show her there was another way to do this sort of thing, a way that was neither sordid nor rough. She felt consumed by a force that sapped the strength, the readiness from her muscles to escape. She tried to fight the lethargy that swept over her, the feeling that she wanted to see what else he could show her.

His gentleness undid her, as it had from the beginning, and now the attraction that had been growing took control. She could not fight him any longer. She remembered the things she saw as a child, the couplings, the sounds of lovemaking, and she knew she wanted those things, that she wanted him to do all of those things to her, over and over, until she cried out. She wanted him to make love to her. God help her, but she did.

"You don't have to be afraid of me. I would never do anything to hurt you, anything you did not want me to do."

How could she tell him that was precisely what she was afraid of? He was speaking softly to her, the words no more than whispers against her skin, and she knew she had needed, wanted this for so very long. All her adult life she had yearned to know what it felt like to be loved, to be desired, but she was afraid to allow it to happen. How very well she knew the price. Now she was weak against what she knew, against the warning in her mind. She melted against him.

He slipped the shoulders of her dress down to her waist. "You are so beautiful." Still kissing her, he touched her breasts, kissed her there. Her head fell back against the tree, and a moan escaped her lips, a moan that took her back to another time, another place . . . until she remembered. She saw herself as she had been that day so long ago–the first time she watched and learned just what it was that her mother did–a little girl observing her mother with a john from a curtained-off alcove.

It was raining outside and dreary for such a warm, sultry afternoon. Because of the rain, Susannah could not play in the courtyard, so she came inside to play with her doll. Before long a customer called on her mother, and Susannah was sent from the room. Unable to find a place to play, she carried her doll into the alcove behind a portiere, but soon it was not the doll who commanded her attention but her mother.

Susannah could never rid herself of the memory imprinted upon her mind that day, of the stranger and the way he looked with his pants off, or the look on her mother's beautiful face as she removed her clothes in front of him.

It wasn't the movement or the moaning that Susannah remembered most, or even the way the john's face was twisted with passion, but the way her mother's face was turned toward her with an impassive expression. Not once since that day had Susannah seen anyone with a face so devoid of emotion. It was not the face of her mother, but that of a stranger—detached beyond recognition, bereft of tenderness or love.

And all that was left behind was a child who possessed a peculiar mixture of innocence and knowledge. A child robbed of her freshness, her purity. Susannah squeezed her eyes closed, wanting to shut out the vision of what happened next, of the john slumped over her mother and the way he rolled off and walked to the curtain. He paused only a moment before he jerked back the curtain, and Susannah's life was changed forever.

"Well, lookey what we got here. You're mighty curious for such a little tyke. How old are you, kid? Six? Seven?"

Susannah could not speak.

"It doesn't matter, I suppose. If you are old enough to be curious, you are old enough to participate. Come here." He picked up a wash cloth. "Come here and wash me."

Susannah squeezed her eyes tighter against the pain that throbbed in her head. She could not breathe.

"Leave my daughter out of this," her mother had said.

The man had laughed. "A daughter should help her mother." He held out the cloth. "Come here."

Come here . . . come here . . . come here . . .

Again and again it reverberated in her head. At night she could not sleep for hearing the words over and over. It will never leave me, she thought. Too long ago something had crept inside her and poisoned her, and, like poison, it was something that was killing her slowly. With the image of her lovely mother before her, Susannah wondered what would happen when Reed left. What if, after Reed, there was another? And another? And another?

"No!" she screamed, and shoved him. "Stay away from me!"

With he dropped his arms, she took a side step, struggling to get her dress up and refastened. She wiped the back of her hand across her mouth.

"Don't . . ." He reached for her hand with his, but she slapped it away.

She saw the pain in his eyes and knew she must look wild, even desperate. Her breathing was shallow, rapid. The voice that spoke was not hers, for it sounded foreign even to her, and the words that came felt strange upon her lips. "You can't seduce me. No matter how hard you try, you can't, because I know men. I know what you want in the end. First you try to divert me with a few soft words and a kiss. Then you will touch me here and there until I cannot resist. The next thing I know you'll be trying to put your prick inside me."

She wanted to cry at the expression she saw upon his face. If she lived to be an old, old woman, she would never forget the look of utter disbelief, the breathtaking gasp of surprise, the disappointment that seemed to gush up from somewhere deep within him.

Well, let him be shocked. Let him gasp at her vulgarity. Let him know, once and for all, just what she was and who she was. Maybe now he would leave her alone. His look of utter devastation only hardened her and gave her the strength to say the words that drove the stake home. "Don't look so shocked. You know that's what you want. That's what you all want."

She turned and ran, knowing that this time the righteous Reed Garrett would not lift a finger to stop her.

Reed was so stunned he couldn't move. He couldn't have heard correctly. It was a mistake. A terrible mistake.

But he knew in his heart that there had been no mistake, that the words she said were the words he heard. He remembered another time when she had shocked him with the phrase "turn a trick"–something no lady would know or say. And yet she *was* a lady in every sense of the word. Still he could not fathom where she learned to talk like she did.

Suddenly and without warning, the shock, the utter disbelief, vanished and in its place was a surge of anger. No, he didn't know where she learned to talk like that, but he damn sure was going to find out. He had a lot of questions that needed answers and he wanted them now.

"Susannah!" he called out, going after her. He looked for quite some time and was on the verge of giving up his search when he found her a mile or so farther down the creek. She was standing waist deep in water beside a thin stretch of sand.

Rarely traveled, this stretch of the creek had bushes and vines that grew taller and were more thickly entwined. An ancient, uncommonly large cottonwood curved out over the water; its fluttering leaves filtered the sunlight to dapple the earth and spangle the water.

He paused only long enough to catch his breath, unable to do more than hoarsely whisper her name–"Susannah"–unable to believe the abundance of emotion eight simple letters could carry.

She had stripped out of the bodice of her dress and had waded out into the water, her breasts bare. He watched, transfixed, as she scooped handfuls of river sand and brought them to her chest. With tears running down her face and great heaving sobs escaping her, she scrubbed the places where he had touched her, over and over, until her flesh burned red. "Oh, Mamma . . . Mamma . . . I did love you," she said in a low, hoarse voice he could scarcely hear. "I did."

He started to go to her, but something held him back. Perhaps it was better this way. Perhaps this was something she needed to settle and lay to rest in order to heal the wound that still festered.

Still she scrubbed, more frantically now, and the beautiful pale skin he had kissed a moment ago was ugly red. He heard her moan, then cry out: "I can't be like you! I can't! I can't!"

Her words made little sense, but her anguish tore into him. Still he did not go to her–not until he saw the tender skin of her breasts rubbed to blistering red with no sign of her stopping.

"No!" he shouted. "Don't!" He waded out into the water. "Susannah–don't! There are other ways to deal with pain besides inflicting more upon yourself."

When his words had no effect on her, he took her

by the arms. Energy spent, she did not resist him. He chastely washed the sand from her skin and tugged at the bodice of her dress. As he did, he talked to her in a soft, soothing voice devoid of sexual intent.

Once her dress was in place, he stood with her in the water, holding her up when she could no longer stand, allowing her to cry, neither asking her to stop nor encouraging her to go on. He wanted her to trust him above all.

Too many thoughts and a jumble of emotions overpowered him, and he felt as useless, as helpless as a fresh-hatched gosling, trying to soothe a pain he did not understand, to offer sympathy and comfort when he was not certain what she needed. And yet when he looked down at the small, wet head pressed so tightly against his chest, he felt a nurturing tenderness that seemed to flow out of him naturally, without thinking. He could feel the rise and fall of her soft breasts against him, and marveled that he had been able, after all this time, to hold someone close like this, to give solace.

When she'd cried herself out, he was still holding her against him. He whispered into her hair. "I'm sorry. I never meant for this to happen. I know you don't believe me, but you don't have to worry. I won't touch you again."

She pulled back. Tears still rolling down her face. "You don't understand, do you? You don't understand that the problem isn't you."

"Susannah, help me to understand."

"You can't understand. Don't you see that? You can't comprehend any of this because I don't understand." She cried harder. "It's me, Reed," she said, poking herself hard in the chest. "It's all me. Me! The blood in me is bad."

"I told you, it doesn't matter who your father was. I don't care."

"It's not because I'm illegitimate. It goes much deeper than that."

"It doesn't matter. None of it matters."

Her look turned cold. "It matters to me," she said, and pulled away from him. "It matters to me."

Chapter 16

It was twilight and Reed had come to the house to see Violette. "You don't seem surprised that I want to speak privately with you," he said.

"I was expecting you." She held the door open. "Come on in. Dally and Susannah are upstairs hemming Dally's dress. We can sit in the parlor, if you like. Or would you prefer to sit on the porch?"

"Susannah's window . . ."

"Is open," Violette said. "The parlor, then."

He followed her into the parlor, sitting in the chair she indicated. Violette took a chair nearby and looked at him sternly, leaving little doubt that she knew precisely why he had come.

In a way he was relieved. "I suppose you have as many questions about me as I do about Susannah. Primarily, what I want to discuss–"

"I know what you want to talk about. Susannah told me what happened."

"She did?"

"Yes, and you must understand that although I like you, my first loyalty is to Susannah. I won't do or say anything to cause her the least discomfort."

"Nor would I want you to."

"Tell me why you want to involve yourself in this? What do you hope to gain from it?"

"Nothing."

"Why become involved, then?"

"I want to help her. If I can."

"Don't you have enough troubles of your own?"

He did not respond right away. He realized he had to tread carefully here. He'd come to get some answers about Susannah's past, not to give answers about his own, but Violette was a woman who would expect fairness. "Let's just say it's part of my nature to be caring."

"Translate that into plain English for me."

"I have never seen anyone with so much potential hold themselves back because of something in their past. If I could help her face her demons, she might be able to drive away whatever it is that has forced her to settle for half a life."

"You know nothing about her past, I take it?"

"Nothing more than snatches, bits of information she's dropped here and there, observations I've made. Nothing that explains her behavior, yet just enough to make me want to help."

"You have to understand one thing, Reed. Susannah is a cold, passionless woman, and it's a well-known fact that a woman of that ilk is better off without a man in her life. Sad as it may be, some women are born to be spinsters."

Why did Violette say those things? If it was her purpose to anger him, she got the response she wanted. He, who prided himself on being an easy-going man, got not merely angry but quite angry. "I don't think you know your niece as well as you believe you do. In fact, I don't think you know her at all. It isn't her natural bent to be cold and passionless. I kissed her and she kissed me back–and with a great deal of feeling. For someone who was born to be a cold, passionless woman, she sure changed.

Something or someone made her the way she is. She was trained, like my horse was trained. It isn't her nature and she is fighting against it. My concern is, if she doesn't conquer her fear, it might destroy her."

"Calm down, boy. We aren't enemies. I'm on your side. Susannah is as dear to me as any human could be. I had to be certain about you, you understand. I had to know what your motives were before I could trust you."

Reed settled back in the chair, feeling himself relax. "And do you trust me now?"

"I do. I suppose I've trusted you since the day I first saw you. That day in town, when they were fixing to string you up for a pie-stealing cow thief, I had a feeling you were the one."

She stood up and he started to rise. "Keep your seat. I'll get us a glass of port–just one glass," she said with a wink.

"You are quite a woman. Why did you never have children of your own?"

"I lost two children in infancy to the croup. I was never able to have another."

"I'm sorry. I shouldn't have pried."

"It was a long time ago. The pain has healed, and I'm not sensitive to it. I'm glad you did ask. It gives me the right to ask you a few things," she said, laughing when he groaned.

She went into the kitchen and returned a few minutes later with two glasses of port. She set one down by her chair and handed him the other, then took a sip and settled back. "Susannah said you were asking questions."

"Yes."

"What did she tell you?"

"That her mother sent word to you when she was ill, but died before you arrived. That she came to live with you when she was almost ten."

"She didn't tell you anything else about Rachel?"

"Rachel? Was that her mother's name?"

"Yes. She was the daughter of our brother Matthew. When she was a young woman, she was the toast of the county, so beautiful that she could have married anyone."

"So why didn't she marry?"

"She did marry. Her husband was killed in the war."

"He wasn't Susannah's father?"

"No, he wasn't."

He thought about Susannah's illegitimacy. "There's no way to find out who her father was?"

"None that we know of. Dally and I asked that same question a million times over. We tried to find out when we went to New Orleans, but ended up on dead-end streets. To be honest, I doubt that Rachel knew."

"Why would you think that?"

Violette took a deep breath and released it slowly. "I don't know rightly how to put this, other than to be blunt. Susannah's mother was a whore–a prostitute on Basin Street in New Orleans."

Reed felt a stab of pain for Susannah. It was all coming together now. "What a horrible thing for a child to know."

"It gets worse."

"I can't imagine how."

"Susannah was born in a bordello. She lived there until she was almost ten, when Dally and I went to

New Orleans to see about Rachel, only she was dead and buried by the time we arrived, so we whisked that poor baby out of there as fast as we could."

"Good God! Raised in a bordello? What kind of a mother would subject her child to such–why didn't she contact you sooner? If not for herself, at least for her child."

"I have asked myself the same question a hundred times. I never came up with an answer. What makes it so difficult to understand is that we knew Rachel quite well. She was like a daughter to us. This whole thing seemed so contrary to her nature. She was such a loving, caring person. Dally and I couldn't figure out how someone could change so drastically in a few short years. We were convinced that something must have happened, something quite dreadful, to change her, but we could never find out what it was."

A dozen emotions churned in Reed. He wished Rachel weren't dead. He would personally like to choke her. He was angry, overwhelmed. He couldn't fathom what Susannah must have endured. He thought of his own two sisters and the childhood they had, the love, the nurturing, the privilege of being children. He no longer wondered where Susannah had learned to talk the way she did. God only knew it was a miracle that she didn't grow up to be a prostitute herself. Now he understood why she was so reserved around men, why she had no interest in them, why she was afraid to let herself feel. She was obviously terrified of turning out like her mother.

"What was Rachel's husband's name?"

"J. D. Carpenter."

"Carpenter?" He pondered that. "If his name was Carpenter, then why did she give Susannah the name Dowell?"

"Rachel went by the name Rachel Dowell in New Orleans. Of course, she had one of those fancy names for her gentlemen friends. I don't remember what it was. I think it had Savannah in it . . . Lady Savannah or something of that ilk."

"Why would she change her name?"

"Why would she become a prostitute? At first we were determined to learn the reason but we had no luck. After several years we admitted defeat and gave up. The answer died with her."

"Her husband was dead, so it couldn't be because she was hiding from him."

"It's my guess that she did it to protect her husband's name. I never met Mr. Carpenter, you see, so I didn't know much about him. Rachel married him when she was in the South visiting relatives with her mother. After they married, they lived on a beautiful plantation in Mississippi. The only other information I have about him is in a letter Rachel received, notifying her of her husband's death."

"What did the initials J.D. stand for?"

"I don't know. In her letters, Rachel always called him J.D."

"Do you have the letter?"

"Of course I have it. I kept everything of Rachel's–what there was left. It was all Susannah would ever have of her mother."

"Could I see that letter?"

"I'll get it."

When Violette returned, she handed the letter to Reed.

According to the accounting he read, Captain J. D. Carpenter was a Confederate soldier who died in a Union encampment near Manassas. In the last paragraph, there was mention of some personal effects of Captain Carpenter's that could be forwarded to her if Mrs. Carpenter would write back authorizing it and telling where she wished them sent. There wasn't anything in the letter that Reed found particularly useful, but there was something that he found strange. When he reached the bottom of the page and read the signature, he felt as if someone had slammed him in the stomach.

Dr. John Joseph Ledbetter.

Difficult though it was to believe, it seemed that his family's friend and next-door neighbor in Boston had treated Rachel's husband.

"Is something wrong?"

Reed shook his head. "This is amazing, but I knew a Dr. John Joseph Ledbetter, a surgeon in the Union army. There couldn't be two Dr. John Joseph Ledbetters. The name isn't common. It has to be the same man."

"Stranger things have happened," she said.

Reed looked thoughtfully at Violette. "Why do you think Rachel went to New Orleans after her husband's death if she was living on their plantation in Mississippi?"

"I have no idea, unless the plantation was destroyed during the war. Maybe Rachel was desperate because she lost everything–her husband, her home. Who knows?"

"What I don't understand is why she didn't come here. Surely she knew you would give her a home."

"Of course she knew that. She had to."

"Becoming a prostitute in New Orleans was a desperate act. No one ever wondered what happened to her? No one tried to find her? What about her father?"

"Matthew was killed in the war."

"What about her husband? Did he have any family?"

"More than likely, but I don't remember." Violette paused for a moment, looking reflective. "You know, I do recollect he had a brother. Lordy, Lordy, I completely forgot about him. I don't remember his name, but it must have been at least a year after the war was over when he just dropped by one day, right out of the blue, and asked if we had heard anything from Rachel or had any idea of her whereabouts."

"What did you tell him?"

"The truth, of course. We didn't know anything."

"What did he say?"

"He thanked us for our time, then left. We never heard from him again."

"You had no inkling why he was looking for her?"

"He never said. Dally and I figured he was concerned for her welfare. Maybe he promised his brother he would look out for her if anything happened to him. What do you make of it?"

Reed stared at the floor. "I don't know. I need time to digest all this. It's a bit overwhelming." He stood up impatiently, thanked Violette, and left.

That night, after going to bed, he found he could not sleep. He lay awake trying to imagine the things Susannah must have seen and heard. He tried to imagine what she would have looked like as a little girl of four or five, with her chestnut hair in ringlets, pushing her baby carriage down a dark hallway as she listened to impassioned moans and vulgar language instead of nursery rhymes. He shuddered.

Suddenly he remembered the letter from Dr. Ledbetter and had an idea. It was probably more on impulse than anything else, but he climbed out of bed and began writing to his father in Boston.

Reed had intended to ride into town to mail the letter to his father the next morning, right after his chores, but as luck would have it, the hand he'd hired to run the harrow came in from the fields early. The harrow was down, so Reed had to help him get it back in working order.

It was later that afternoon when Reed went into Bluebonnet with his father's letter and one he was mailing for Violette in his pocket. As he rode down the main street, he passed several horses from the Double T that were tied in front of the Roadrunner Saloon, but he didn't give them much notice.

He went straight to the Buck and Smith General Store. He didn't realize his face was stern and determined until Daisy commented on it.

"Afternoon, Mr. Garrett. You having a bad day?"

"No. Why? Do I look like I'm having a bad day?"

"Well, you appear a mite unhappy," she said.

He laughed. "I'm just a little preoccupied." He took the letter out of his pocket, placed it on the counter, and pushed it toward her.

"Oh, another letter to Boston," she said, looking at the envelope. "That reminds me! You got something . . ." She turned around and sorted through a bundle of letters. "Here we are." She handed him the envelope.

"It's from your family." His look must have made her think he thought she had been prying, for she added, "I know it's from your family because I read the name on the envelope."

He took the letter and tucked it in his pocket. "Thanks."

"It's always a pleasure, Mr. Garrett."

Reed tipped his hat and bid her good day, then walked out of Buck and Smith.

Across the street, he saw Tate Trahern step out of the Roadrunner Saloon, two cowhands with him. Tate's mouth tightened into a grimace, then he leaned over and spat in Reed's direction.

Reed ignored Tate and his gesture. Nonchalantly, he untied his horse and climbed up, then rode out of town as if he hadn't a care in the world.

"Hello, Daisy."

Daisy jumped and spun around in midair. "Tate Trahern! You scared the daylights out of me! What on earth are you doing in here?"

"Why, I came to see you."

"Humph! Tell that to someone who believes it. I haven't seen you in a month of Sundays. What brings you around now?"

"Aw, Daisy, don't be so hard on me. I've been real busy, but even then, I sure did think about you a lot."

Daisy's face brightened. "You did?"

"Sure I did, honey."

"What are you doing in town so early in the afternoon?"

"I wanted to see you. I thought you might want to go to the prayer meeting on Thursday."

She scowled at him. "You don't ever go to prayer meeting, Tate Trahern, and you know I know it."

"A sinner can always repent."

"I'd sooner believe that pot-bellied stove over yonder would get up and walk."

"I sure have missed seeing you."

"Shhhh, don't talk so loud. Do you want Mr. Smith to hear you?"

"I don't care who hears me."

"Well, I do!"

"Then don't be so standoffish. I told you I rode all the way into town just to see you. Can I help it if I wanted to see my girl?"

Daisy wanted to believe him, but doubted she could. "What do you want, Tate?"

"I want to see that letter Reed Garrett mailed."

"How do you know he mailed a letter?"

"I saw him come in here, and he didn't carry anything out."

Daisy glanced around the store nervously, then whispered, "I can't let anyone look at the mail. I've told you that before. It's government property."

"Honey, I don't want you to give me the letter, just let me see it."

"Shhhhh! Don't talk so loud. Do you want me to lose my job?"

"Okay, I'll be quiet," he whispered. "Now, give me the letter. I'll give it right back."

"You promise?"

"I said I would, didn't I?"

Daisy didn't look convinced. Tate sighed, trying not to let his exasperation show. "I promise. Now, let me have a look at that letter."

She went to the bag that contained the outgoing mail and rummaged through it. "Here it is." She handed Tate the letter.

He glanced down. The letter was addressed to Mr. and Mrs. R. Alexander Garrett II, in Boston.

"Give me something to write on, will you?"

Daisy handed him a piece of paper. Tate copied the name and address from the letter. He folded the paper, put it in his pocket, and handed the envelope back to Daisy. "You see? No harm done."

She glanced around the store. "I sure do pray you're right, Tate."

He gave Daisy the kind of seductive look that usually brought her around. "I'm always right, Daisy. Calm down. Nothing is going to happen. Nobody noticed a thing. I'll see you tonight."

"Tate, you aren't going to do anything to get me into trouble, are you?"

"Don't worry your pretty head about nothing."

"Tate . . ."

Tate blew Daisy a kiss and left. He went directly to the office of the *Bluebonnet Weekly*. The editor, Jefferson Holt, looked up.

"You wouldn't, by any chance, know the name of a newspaper in Boston, would you?" Tate asked.

"Well, there's the *Boston Herald* . . ."

"That'll do," Tate said. "Much obliged."

Tate left Jefferson staring curiously at him and headed on down the street. He was whistling when he walked into the office of Western Union.

Chapter 17

Susannah watched her aunts on an evening stroll and sighed fondly. No one knew how to be old as well as her aunts.

Her reverie was broken when Reed suddenly appeared on the porch steps. She picked up the bowl of black-eyed peas she was snapping, intending to leave.

He quickly came to her and put his hand on her arm. "Don't go. I want to talk to you."

"I've got work to do."

"You are going to have to face this sooner or later. You can't ignore me indefinitely. I know you're concerned about my talk with your aunt and that you're angry."

She clutched the bowl against her. "I never get angry at Aunt Vi."

"All right, then you're angry at me."

"You had no business prying."

"I can't undo what has happened any more than I can change the fact that I know about your past, but I can make things even."

She cast him a skeptical look. "And how can you do that?"

"Fair is fair. I can tell you about mine."

"I doubt you have anything as colorful."

"You might be surprised."

Susannah stared at him for a minute, trying to decide if he was sincere. There was something about the way he spoke, something about the way he looked that made her think he was. She was not a trusting person. "You have a talent for choosing the right thing to say."

"Trust not the argument but the word."

And he had such a way with words. With people, too, she feared. "It all sounds good."

"The power of sound–greater than the power of sense."

"In spite of your eloquence and obvious education, what it all boils down to is this: I don't trust you any more than I trust myself," Susannah said.

"Trust and be deceived, is that it?"

"Something like that."

" 'To long for that which comes not. To lie abed and sleep not. To serve well and please not. To have a horse that goes not. To have a man who obeys not. To lie in jail and hope not. To be sick and recover not. To lose one's way and know not. To wait at the door and enter not, and to have a friend we trust not: are ten such spites as hell hath not.' "

He must have been amused at the expression on her face, for he laughed and said, "Alas, those are not my words, but the words of the English author and translator John Florio."

Alas? What kind of man talked like that? she wondered. She found herself envious of Reed, of the knowledge he possessed. *The English author and translator* . . . She couldn't name an English author if someone held a gun to her head. She tried to sound nonchalant when she said, "I never heard of him."

He laughed again. "No reason why you should. He died in the early sixteen hundreds."

"Apparently you heard of him."

"Only because my father was a scholar. My mother swore my first words were 'To be or not to be.' "

She gave him a blank look. The words had no meaning to her, and she found herself growing resentful of the education, the opportunity he obviously had. He was unlike anyone she had ever met. He knew so much. She was suddenly overwhelmed by the prospect of discovering more about him, of understanding who he was and where he came from. She could learn from him if she would just let herself. Part of her wanted to trust him. Another part warned her away.

" 'Life is short,' " Reed suddenly said, " 'the art long, opportunity fleeting, experiment treacherous, judgment difficult.' "

"Another quote from a man who died two hundred years ago?"

"No. It's from Hippocrates. He died about four hundred years before Christ was born. He was a Greek physician. What I quoted was the first of his *Aphorisms* on the art of healing."

"Who are you? How do you know those things?"

"Do I have your word that what I say does not go any further–not to your aunts, not in your journal, not anywhere?"

She nodded.

He sighed and sat back. "I come from an old and prominent Boston family. My father is wealthy and educated, an architect by trade, a scholar by choice. My mother's maiden name was Adams. She is descended from President John Quincy Adams. I am their only living son. My younger brother died when he was six. I think that is when I became interested in medicine. My parents both supported my choice, and I was sent to the best schools. I studied medicine in Edinburgh and Vienna."

Susannah was astounded.

"You're a doctor?"

"I received my M.D. from Georgetown University in Washington, D.C. In Vienna I received a diploma for proficiency in obstetrics operations and gynecology."

Susannah listened raptly. His life sounded like something out of a fairy tale–Prince Charming, perhaps, for he must have led a charmed life.

"Shortly after I returned home and set up my medical practice, I married the catch of the season, Philippa Copley, the daughter of Adam Copley. He was president of the Boston Society for Medical Improvement and founder of Copley Hospital."

He paused and looked at Susannah. His hand came up to stroke her cheek, and she found herself leaning into his palm. "You are looking at me with such wide-eyed wonder. I know all of this talk about Boston society and Copley Hospital doesn't mean much to you."

"No, it doesn't, but it helps me understand the importance of the man whose daughter you married." She paused, then plunged ahead. "What happened to your wife?"

"About a year after our marriage, when Philippa was about to give birth to our child, she asked me to deliver it. Her father thought the privilege belonged to him. For a while she was torn. Philippa was her father's favorite child, his only daughter, and she adored him."

"But you were the child's father. It is scriptural that when a man and woman marry, they shall leave their families and cleave one to the other."

" 'Devout' is not a word I would use to describe Adam Copley."

"Did you deliver the baby?"

"Yes, at least in the beginning. I told you that I had gone to school in Vienna. I studied in the childbirth wards of the Allgemeines Krankenhaus. It was there that I first heard of a Hungarian doctor who believed that childbed fever was contagious. His name was Ignaz Semmelweis, and he believed a great many of the deaths from childbed fever were caused by the doctors who assisted the births."

Susannah was certain she misunderstood. "You said they were *caused* by the doctors?"

"Yes."

"I don't understand."

"The medical profession is young, Susannah. Primitive. There is so much we don't know. There are too many men practicing medicine who left their apprenticeship or graduated from medical school without ever observing or delivering a baby. Many of them have never used a microscope. There are still places where doctors apply hot poultices of cow manure to cuts. Many doctors were trained only to lance abscesses, administer age-old remedies, set fractures, or sew up cuts. Semmelweis was different. He was well trained. He observed. One of the things he noticed was there was a much higher rate of deaths from childbed fever in the wards where medical students trained than there was in the wards where midwives assisted. When he began investigating, he discovered the doctors and medical students often came into the childbearing wards straight from autopsy rooms, something the midwives did not do. He also noticed the women who had childbed fever were often in a row of beds where they were examined one after the other."

"And that's how he knew it was the doctors?"

"His proof came when his colleague, a doctor, died from an infection from a scalpel wound."

"I don't understand."

"His colleague received the scalpel wound while doing an autopsy on a woman who died of childbed fever."

"What did that prove?"

"It proved there was a link. You see, when Semmelweis viewed the autopsy of his colleague, his friend's organs showed the same changes as seen in the women who died from the fever."

"So what did he do?"

"Everyone under him had to scrub his hands with soap, then soak them in chlorinated lime solution before and after going into the wards. Over the next few months the deaths, which had been as high as twenty percent, dropped to one and two-tenths percent."

"That's wonderful."

Reed frowned. "You would expect the hospital staff to hail his discovery and follow his lead. Instead, Semmelweis was condemned and found his rank lowered, his practice limited. When he reported his results to the Medical Society of Vienna, he was ridiculed and jeered, the victim of virulent attacks."

"Oh, how awful. The poor man. What happened?"

"Although some supported him, he was too deeply hurt to continue his practice in Vienna. He returned to Hungary and practiced in Pest, in the wards of Saint Rochus Hospital, where he reduced the death rate of women in childbirth. Ten years later, in 1861, he wrote a book about his beliefs."

"Did they believe him then?"

"No. Hardly anyone took notice. And the ones who did, like the renowned scientist Virchow, opposed and ridiculed his ideas."

"What happened?"

"They broke him. A brilliant, intense, and sensitive doctor was broken by the callous indifference of his superiors and colleagues. He was committed to an asylum and died in 1865 of a blood infection–virtually the same illness that had killed the mothers he tried to save."

"Poor man. To die in such disgrace." She suddenly thought of something. "You know, it's strange, but I don't remember hearing anything about this. I've helped with a few birthings. I was never told to wash my hands or to rinse them in–what was the name of the . . . of the . . ."

He smiled at her. "Chlorinated lime."

"Yes, that was it. I've never heard of it."

"That doesn't surprise me. Even today few have heard of it, or they have heard and refused to believe. Even when prominent, educated men have joined in support–men like Oliver Wendell Holmes, who read his essay 'The Contagiousness of Puerperal Fever' before the Society for Medical Improvement, and that was in 1843."

"Society for Medical Improvement? Isn't that the–"

"–one Philippa's father was president of?"

She nodded.

"Yes, it's the same."

She frowned. "How does all of this fit together?"

"You have to understand that although I was convinced of what Semmelweis discovered, I didn't jump to conclusions. An English surgeon by the name of Joseph Lister and a Frenchman by the name of Louis Pasteur made further discoveries to support Semmelweis's theories. Pasteur sterilized with heat; Lister with carbolic acid. In 1867, Lister published the results of his findings. Like Semmelweis, he was greeted with indifference or open hostility. When he came to America, it was the same thing. Even the most prominent physicians, like the leader of American surgery, Samuel Gross, criticized Lister and failed to see the connection between sterilization and infection. Even now, it isn't accepted very widely here."

"But you believed."

His voice turned cynical. "Oh yes, I believed . . . for all the good it did me."

"You wanted to follow these ideas when your wife gave birth, but your father-in-law did not. Is that right?"

"Yes. I think Adam's complete disregard went back to a long-standing feud he had with Oliver Wendell Holmes. Since Holmes supported the idea, it was Adam's natural bent to oppose it. Of course, I don't think he accepted the idea, even on its own merit."

"So your wife did not benefit from what you had learned. She died, didn't she? She died with the fever?"

"Philippa died, and our son with her."

Her heart went out to him. "Oh, Reed . . . I'm so sorry. So very sorry. What a terrible loss." She was quiet for a few moments. She understood his pain, of course. She could even grasp why he might not want to live in Boston. But there was one thing she could not comprehend. "Why would that make you turn away from medicine? I would think you would have been even more determined to prove Semmelweis was right."

"That isn't the end of the story."

"There's more?"

"Yes. In the beginning hours of Philippa's travail, I followed the procedure I learned in Vienna. I scrubbed my hands and soaked them in chlorinated lime solution. I used carbolic acid to scrub down anything that would touch her or our baby when it came. Philippa's father saw me and was furious. He said it was an extremely controversial procedure, that he would not subject his daughter to such speculative medical procedure."

"That must have been difficult for you."

"Extremely so. Adam said it was because I was educated in Europe and studied medicine with heretics."

"What did you do?"

"I am sorry to say that I did not use my head. I played into his hands and endangered the very person I wanted to save. I accused Adam of being narrow-minded and too stupid to see what was clearly before his eyes."

"Your poor wife. Was she listening to all of this?"

"She was in labor. It was her first child. She was hurting and terrified. We did nothing to alleviate her fears by our arguing. In the end it came down to her having to choose between her father and her husband."

"Oh, no. Oh, Reed. She chose her father."

She saw the tears in his eyes. How difficult that would be for anyone to understand, to accept. That a wife would turn against her husband, against the man she married, the man who fathered her child.

"She . . ." His voice broke. He paused and breathed deeply, gaining control. "What it all boiled down to was the simple fact that she trusted her father more than she trusted me. She begged me to let her father deliver the baby."

"And you stepped aside?"

"Not at first, but after Philippa became hysterical, I relented. I was hurt by her rejection, so I complied with her wishes. I foolishly gave my place over to her father."

"You had no choice. Did her father deliver the baby then?"

"Adam tried, but after hours of hard labor, the baby still had not come. It was apparent to me after the first few hours that we needed to do a cesarean procedure . . ." He glanced at Susannah. "That is where you have to cut the mother's stomach to get to the baby."

Susannah nodded.

"When I mentioned this to Adam, he refused to consider what he called 'another of your far-fetched ideas.' "

"You had to stand there and watch your wife and baby die?"

"No, I couldn't. I had to do what I could to save them. At last, fearing for Philippa's safety and believing in the cesarean procedure, I shoved Adam out of the way and took over. And it enraged him. He accused me of using savagery."

"I'm so sorry."

"So am I. I should have realized it was too late when I took over, that Philippa had been in labor too long. Our son was stillborn, and Adam's rage went one step further. He accused me of killing my own child."

Susannah put her hand over Reed's, unable to find any words of comfort.

"I was devastated over the death of our child, but I hid my grief in order to console Philippa. But a few days later Philippa developed childbed fever and died."

"Her father blamed you for her death as well."

"He more than blamed me. He said I caused her death by using witches' brew, which was what killed her. He called me a murderer at Philippa's funeral."

The tears were running down his cheeks faster now. He could not go on.

Susannah rubbed his hand, as if that one gesture could impart all the empathy she had for him.

"And," she murmured, "you became a loner, drifting around the country, working at this job and that, never staying in one place too long, never giving the painful memories of the past a chance to catch up with you."

He wiped his eyes and pulled himself together.

"Now I understand," she said, "what you meant that day, when you told me you could never love anyone again."

He turned and kissed her softly on the mouth. "No, you don't understand. It isn't as you think. It isn't because I'm still in love with Philippa. I got over her death a long time ago. But I'm empty inside. I have nothing to offer a woman."

Suddenly Reed added, "I see your aunts returning

from their walk. I'd best be running along." He stood, still holding her hand.

She looked up, and their gazes locked. Pretense seemed to fall away, and she felt she could see clearly now. She allowed him to draw her to her feet.

"You will remember your promise? Say nothing to your aunts, to anyone."

"Your secret is as safe with me as mine is with you."

"We are partners in grief, then."

"Partners in grief." She squeezed his hand.

"What's this?" Violette called out. "A handshake on the front porch?"

"Reed was showing me how they shake hands in Boston."

"Better make sure that's all he shows you," Dahlia said in a sour tone.

Susannah held her breath, trying not to laugh. She made the mistake of glancing at Reed, whose face was full of soundless mirth. And they lost their composure and they did laugh.

"A loud laugh, a vacant mind," Dahlia said.

Violette laughed, but Reed was thinking he and Susannah were beginning their friendship with laughter. A fine start.

Tate Trahern was still brooding over what had happened at church when Reed Garrett had made a laughingstock out of him. It didn't help matters that he hadn't received a reply to his telegram to the *Boston Herald*. Tate was angry, seething. He was not accustomed to being ignored or not getting his way.

Then, when he least expected it, some three

weeks after he'd sent the telegram, Tate received a reply. Reading the message, he smiled. He folded the piece of paper neatly and tucked it away in his pocket. He had just been given the ammunition he needed to rid himself of a varmint. All he had to do was wait for the right time to use it.

He mounted his horse and rode out of Bluebonnet. He would have been a happy, happy man, save for the fierce pounding in his head and the humiliation he felt whenever anyone in town looked at him. Both of which he blamed on Reed Garrett.

September came, ushering in the first day of fall, but nobody remembered to tell the heavens, so the weather remained as it had all summer, hot, dry, dusty, and near to unbearable. Not even an occasional breeze that stirred the dry leaves in the cornfields could offer much relief. As Violette said, "It's too hot to talk."

Reed stood at the gate of the pigsty. Miss Lavender had given birth to fourteen piglets during the night. Susannah had four of them in her arms–pink, wiggling, squealing, and, to his surprise, rather cute. He shook his head. Life took strange turns. He would have never believed ten years ago, when he was the toast of Boston society, that he would be standing in a dried-up town in west Texas contemplating a farrow of piglets.

Susannah looked at him, joy reflected in her face, and he felt as if the sun had come out from behind a cloud. For a moment they both stood still, like two hastily caught forms captured on a canvas, frozen in time. The atmosphere was charged with luminosity.

One of the piglets began to kick its hind legs furiously. Susannah laughed and gave it a kiss. "I shall call you Rowdy," she said, and Reed had the sound of a soft, Texas drawl to add to his jumbled senses. She kissed the piglet again, and Reed was overwhelmed with desire. He wanted to give her a child.

For a moment Reed was taken aback. The idea of giving her a child surprised him. He had not thought about that before. But it was true–and he hadn't felt that way since Philippa died.

"This one I shall call Runt," she said, holding up the smallest of the farrow. "This one is Chubby. And this one"–she held up the most docile of the quartet–"I shall call Pansy, because she is so shy."

"That leaves only ten more to name, and then you must worry about remembering which name goes to which piglet."

"Oh, I never forget," she said, her eyes growing round, amazed that he would even suggest such a thing.

"Doesn't it make it difficult for you to give them names and to treat them as pets . . . later on, I mean, when it comes time to butcher them?"

"We only butcher one hog a year. The rest we keep to breed or to sell. But no, it doesn't bother me overmuch. It's a natural part of life, to live, to die. We all have our roles to play. We must be content to grow where we're planted."

She returned the piglets to their mother, then began the process of picking up the other ten and bestowing names on them: Clementine, Rosemary, Flora, Sweet Pea, Sassafras. She paused a moment, then came up with names for the others. Willow, Lily, Petunia, Willie–a nickname for Sweet William. She turned toward Reed, her brow creased by a frown as she looked down at the last piglet in her arms.

"Don't tell me you forgot a name."

"No . . . I can't seem to think of the right name for this one. He's a plain little fellow, don't you think?" She turned the piglet so it was facing her, the flat little nose working back and forth, the small beady black eyes looking at her with an unfathomable expression. She sighed and released him with the others. "I'll have to wait for him to distinguish himself in some way."

"And if he doesn't?"

"Then I will have to think of something. He cannot go through life without a name."

"Why not?"

"It wouldn't be right."

Like her aunts, she had a preference for using flower names for animals, but unlike them she would occasionally, as now, throw in a few nonfloral names spontaneously. He wondered what name she would give to herself. He thought of the lovely ice flowers he saw on the windowpanes during the cold Boston winters and wondered if the cold, frozen side of her would vanish if touched by the sun of love . . . his love.

Miss Lavender grunted and stood, then walked away, the piglets falling off the teats one by one–all except the piglet with no name, who clung to his mother for all he was worth. He was dragged halfway across the pigsty before he fell off. By the time he did, Susannah was laughing so hard, she could scarcely speak. It was only after she picked up the persistent piglet and turned to him that she found the breath to say, "Tenacity. I shall call him Tenacity." The last piglet named, she put him down, dusted her hands on her apron, and walked toward Reed. He opened the gate as she approached, then closed it after her. She turned and stood beside him, looking back at Miss Lavender, who rubbed an apparent itch against one of the slats in the fence, then ambled over to the trough.

"You don't know much about pigs, do you?"

"Until now, our only association was at the breakfast table."

She smiled. "I don't suppose there were many opportunities to come face-to-face with a pig in Boston."

He thought about some of the fat-faced matrons in his mother's study group, with their beefy jowls and small eyes. "Not the four-legged kind."

She didn't say anything, but when he looked at her, humor danced in her lovely eyes. After a few seconds of silence, she asked, "Did you like Boston?"

"When I was there, I liked it very much. Even now, there are many things I miss about it, and an equal number of things I don't."

"I would not like living that kind of a life, I think."

"You prefer the country?"

"I know I do."

"Why?"

"Because I have learned far more from observing life in its wildest forms than I ever could from living a civilized life."

"Its wildest forms?"

"When I first came here this was all so unfamiliar. I was accustomed to a city and being surrounded by people. All of a sudden I found myself in the middle of nowhere, living with two old women I did not know. I felt lost and so terribly lonely. I became a wanderer, a nomadic child who preferred a grassy prairie, hollowed-out trees, and rain-washed ravines to hard, polished floors and creaking beds surrounded by four confining walls. I took long walks and spent hours lying on my back in the tall, wind-swept grass, watching the clouds move overhead, listening to the wind as it whispered in my ear. Rummaging along the creek, I unearthed arrowheads and bits of pottery, and I learned I was not alone, that there had been others wandering here before me. In the summer I would stand outside and watch violent thunderstorms move across the prairie, nurtured by thunder and lightning, that taught me death can come unexpectedly and that life can pass all too quickly."

"Nature was your schoolroom."

"Yes, it was, and it was there that I learned from the animals I came in contact with. Not the housebroken pets, or the gentle and tamed farmstock, but the wild, misunderstood creatures that I identified with–deer, pronghorn, coyotes, prairie dogs, the gray wolf. Over and over I observed their traits, their character–the playful nature, the steadfast devotion, and the keen instinct. I saw how they could be themselves, independent and aloof, yet dependent upon one another for survival and protection, how they were inquisitive and cautious, curious yet wary. Rubbing a porcupine in the wrong direction and getting quills in my hand taught me there is a right way and a wrong way. Red ants taught me the virtue of hard work; honeybees, its reward. From prairie dogs I learned indulgence and the joy of lying in the sun. Birth taught me faith; death, that life should have a purpose. The wobbly-legged newborn who kept on trying to stand, in spite of repeated failure, taught me determination. I saw from their example how to rely on intuition, to be fiercely protective of the young, to be devoted to one's mate and one's community."

"The kind of things you cannot get from the civilized world."

She paused and stared beyond the pigsty. He saw that she was gazing at the fields where stacks of hay rose up like so many grassy pyramids, but he said nothing, not wanting to break her reverie.

"You can't reproach a hayfield for partiality, or a pig for being conniving. You cannot challenge the beliefs of a sunflower, or the convictions of a summer storm. I am surrounded by Nature's infinite patience, her impassioned fury, and I have learned to speak many of her languages, to find pleasure in pathless fields, to delight in isolation. The peace of nature and the innocence of creatures reaches out to me. There is a security here, a sense of belonging, a soothing salve for the troubled mind, a sanctity in knowing we dwell in God's finest work of art." She turned to look at him. "Does any of this make sense to you?"

"All of it makes sense. You have a rare gift of understanding, an even rarer gift of expression. You don't just say words. You convey feelings. There is rhythm and motion in everything you say. It's as if I can hear the voices of another level of being calling out. You don't just love the country. You are part of it."

"Yes. I love it."

"It goes beyond that, I think. I see your face, your spirit in the things around you, in the contrariness of the wind, the mystery of seeds, the frolic of animals, the beauty of flowers, the sense that nothing is ever complete, that it goes on and on.

" 'And this our life, exempt from public haunt, finds tongues in trees, books in the running brooks, sermons in stones, and good in everything.' "

When she looked up at him, her expression was awestruck. "I am not the only one who has a way with words, it seems. That was beautiful."

"Beautiful, but not mine. The words are Shakespeare's."

He saw the color steal up her cheeks. He did not mean to embarrass her by being such an ass as to stand there spouting Shakespeare. Not to her, with her understanding that went so far. "Susannah . . . I'm sorry."

"It doesn't matter."

"It does matter. There are two kinds of asses. The four-legged kind and the pompous. Forgive me."

She turned to look at the piglets again. "Pigs are really clean animals, you know, and very intelligent."

He looked at Miss Lavender wallowing in a puddle, her white hide gleaming with mud, and he knew that, in her way, Susannah had forgiven him. "Miss Lavender is the exception, I take it?"

"They roll in mud to keep cool and to bring comfort when they itch."

"And they told you this?"

She laughed. "In a roundabout way. It works, you know. Mud is very soothing."

He raised his brows and gave her a questioning look. "You've tried it?"

Her grin was impish. "Once."

He burst out laughing.

She put a damper on his humor with her next comment. "Aunt Vi said she spoke to you about castrating some of the young hogs."

"She mentioned it, yes."

"You sound reluctant."

"I'm not a pig farmer. I know nothing about pigs . . . precious little about animals at all. As far as castrating a pig . . ."

"Well, you were a doctor."

"Castration was not my specialty."

She laughed. "Is it anyone's?"

"Did you tell your aunt?"

"About you?"

He nodded.

"No, I said I wouldn't, didn't I?"

"Then why did she ask me?"

"You are the hired hand, and it's a man's job."

He scowled, feeling as if he'd been manipulated into doing something he did not want to do. "If I'm going to practice medicine, I'd rather work with humans."

"Maybe you'll get the chance."

"I doubt it, not that it matters. That life is behind me now. I can't go back."

"Of course you can't, but if the opportunity arises, you could start over."

"Never."

"Don't be so certain. Opportunity is a strong seducer."

"Opportunity," he said, knowing he sounded cynical, yet unable to keep himself from it. "Opportunity in the form of pig castration?"

"Expect the unexpected. Sometimes the brightest fires are kindled by unexpected sparks."

"Ever the optimist."

"No. A believer in miracles."

Chapter 18

On Sunday the Reverend Pettigrew preached on the consequences of good and evil, and how life is a chain of events, each link an incident that hangs upon a former one.

"There is never a present moment that is not connected with some future one. Good," he said, "may at some future time bring forth evil, just as evil can bring forth good, and they are equally unexpected."

A week later, the evil came in the form of an epidemic, a devastating outbreak of chills and high fever. And no one saw anything good about it.

The Thursday following the Reverend Pettigrew's sermon, Sheriff Carter stopped by. He was on his way back from the Carmichael place. It was late in the afternoon, and Susannah was with her aunts in the garden. She was pulling up the last of the onions to store in the root cellar.

The three of them watched him ride up as they walked to the fence where it was shaded by a Dutch elm. "Afternoon, Sheriff," Violette said. "What brings you to this neck of the woods?"

"There's a sickness going about. I just fetched Doc Bailey."

"Did you say sickness?" Dahlia asked.

Jonah nodded. "Three of the older children are sick, and Will Carmichael has been running a high fever for three days. This morning his wife woke up with a headache and fever."

"Does Doc Bailey have any idea what it could be that ails them?" Violette asked.

"Nope. Says it's too early to tell. Lots of things start out with headaches and fevers according to him. Says he's got to wait for more symptoms."

"Is there anything they need?" Susannah asked. "I could send food. Should I go over and help?"

"Don't think that would be a good idea, at least not according to Doc. He advises folks to stay put. He said for me to ride around and alert everyone that this could be the start of an epidemic. It's the third case of fevers he's been called on in two days. If it's an epidemic, the best thing to do is to stay home, away from other folks."

Susannah raised her hand to shield her eyes from the sun. "If the Carmichaels are sick, they will need food, someone to care for them."

"I know you want to help, Susannah, but you don't want to go sashaying about and carrying something home. You've got your aunts to think about."

Susannah glanced at the concerned faces of Violette and Dahlia and felt a bit foolish. "Yes, of course."

Jonah must have sensed her discomfort, for he said, "Tell you what. If you want to throw some things together, I'm going out there tomorrow afternoon. I can stop on my way and carry it to them for you. Lord knows they could use it, with all those mouths to feed and their ma and pa sick."

"Thank you, Sheriff. I'll have a basket of food ready."

Jonah tipped his hat and turned his horse around.

Susannah and her aunts watched in silence as he rode away.

Later that evening, when the supper dishes were cleaned up, Susannah was sitting on the porch with her aunts when Dahlia said, "Well, shoot me for a sidewinder, but it looks to me like Reed Garrett is coming a-courting. I do believe he's carrying a bouquet of flowers, Susannah."

"They might be for you, Aunt Dahlia," Susannah said.

She was suddenly like a little bird with her bright eyes and quick, bustling movements as she began picking at bits of imaginary fluff on her skirts and patting the fat sausage curls on her head into place. "Won't do him no good. I'm holding out for something better."

"Better?" Violette snorted. "At our age men are like wanted posters: dead or alive. There isn't anything in-between. If you find one and he's still kicking, you better latch on to him."

Reed stepped onto the porch and began distributing a bundle of flowers to each lady. "Found these growing along the creek with no one to enjoy them. Thought you might find a better use to put them to."

"Why, thank you, Reed," Violette said. "I'll put them in a vase right next to my bed, that way I can extend the summer just a bit longer."

"Why would you want to do that?" Dahlia asked. "You've done nothing but complain about the heat, and now you want to extend it?" She looked down at her own bunch of flowers. "They look wilted."

"They were fine until you looked at them," Violette said. "Honestly, Dally, your sour disposition is enough to wilt a cast-iron skillet."

Susannah stood. "Here, let me have them, and I'll take them inside and put them into water for you."

Violette handed her hers. Susannah turned to her Aunt Dally and said, "I'm sure a little water will perk them right up, Aunt. Would you like me to put them by your bed, like Aunt Vi's?"

"No, flowers make me sneeze. Put them anywhere you like. If I had them near me, they might die, seeing as how I've got such a sour disposition and all." Dahlia came to her feet and started into the house. "I've got a headache and a fever. I think I'm coming down with the plague." She stopped and looked at Reed. "Did you hear the Carmichaels are all dying from the plague? Sheriff Carter was by this afternoon. He said Doc Bailey said we've got a plague epidemic and it's spreading to everyone." With that, she opened the door and went inside.

"The plague?" Reed glanced quickly in Susannah's direction.

"She's telling fibs again," Violette said before Susannah could respond.

"The Carmichaels are sick, though," Susannah said. "And Sheriff Carter did stop by this afternoon. He said Doc Bailey thinks it could be the start of an epidemic."

"An epidemic of what?" Reed asked.

"He said it's too early to tell," Susannah said.

"Here, let me have those flowers," Violette said, and took the blossoms from Susannah. "I'll put them in water. Why don't you two take a little stroll and enjoy this nice evening. I love this time of year when we begin to get some relief from the heat. The best time of day is right now, late in the evening."

After Violette went inside, Reed turned to Susannah and said, "Walk with me?"

"How could I resist? As Aunt Vi said, it's so lovely outside this time of evening."

He extended his hand, palm up, and she knew he meant for her to put her hand in his. It was an innocent gesture; he was being his gentlemanly self.

What he did not know was how difficult that was for her. His hand looked warm, inviting, secure–all the things she knew it would be, but she could not forget the scarlet satin dress. Her heartbeat escalated; she tried to swallow some moisture into a throat that had gone bone dry. No one could imagine the effort it took, nor the clamoring reaction it caused to perform such a simple act, nothing more than placing her hand in his. It was something she had dreamed about and wondered about and now the opportunity presented itself. Would she do it? Could she do it?

She glanced at his face and saw infinite patience in his eyes. Did he know that she had never held a man's hand before? Did it matter?

His words were reassuring. "It's only my hand. It doesn't come with a long list of implications or obligations. I think you know by now that you can trust me."

"I . . ."

"Come on." He made the decision for her and took her hand in his. The simple contact of skin to skin, warm flesh to warm flesh, was beautiful, sheltering, and very disquieting.

She did not pull her hand away.

He helped her down the steps, then released her hand, but the feel of his skin, the warmth of his touch remained, long after they walked along the stone-lined path that ran between the flower beds. They were well beyond the gate before Reed said, "Tell me about this epidemic."

Susannah told him what she knew, mentioning how Doc had been treating a lot of people with fevers and headaches.

"Did he mention any other symptoms?"

"No, nothing. Do you have any idea what it could be?"

He shook his head. "There are endless possibilities at this point. The sheriff was right when he said it was too early to tell, that they needed to wait for more symptoms."

"But waiting . . . it's like sitting on a powder keg with the fuse lit."

"Unfortunately, all we can do is pray the fuse goes out."

"And if it doesn't?"

"God help us," he said, "if it turns out to be something serious."

"If it does turn out to be something serious, will you help?"

His expression was pained. "If anyone needs help . . ."

"I mean as a doctor."

He screwed up his mouth and exhaled, then lifted his eyes to stare over the top of her head at something far, far away. He said nothing for what seemed to her a very long time. She was on the verge of asking the question again when he said, "I told you before; I can't go back to that."

"You can't let people die."

"And you are worrying unnecessarily. We don't know that lives are in danger."

"But if they are?"

"We will cross that bridge when we come to it."

"You're a doctor. You can't go through life pretending to be something you're not."

"That's a strange thing to hear someone like you say, since you have done precisely that."

"What do you mean?"

"You have been living your life in the darkness. You are existing as a shadow of yourself. You have pressed your life, who you really are inside, down into a little box, put on the lid, tied it with a colorful ribbon, and made it into a neat little package."

"As long as I'm happy . . ."

"But you aren't. Not really. You're only holding your head underwater. It's just a matter of time until you are forced to come up for air–or drown."

"I don't want to talk about me."

"Of course you don't. You don't want to wake up, to take responsibility for yourself. You couldn't help the circumstances you were born into, Susannah, any more than you could help what your mother became. But it doesn't have to end there. You were released from that prison a long time ago when your aunts brought you here. The door to your cage was thrown open, only you chose to remain inside." He stopped and turned toward her and took her in his arms. "It's time," he said, "time to come out, time to let yourself be who you really are."

She wanted to pull away, to run back to the house, but something within her could not obey. Tears slid silently down her cheeks. He was unmoved. Determination seeped out of his pores. She was afraid, confused. She didn't know what to do.

"You told me once that you had learned much

from animals in the wild. Tell me what you would have done if you found a young wolf with its leg caught in a trap. Would you walk on by and leave it there to starve slowly to death?"

"You know I would not."

He wiped the tears from her face with the fleshy pad of his thumb. "If those are cleansing tears, let them flow. If they are for pity, they are pointless. Tears won't save you because what I feel for you is far from pity."

"So you are going to hold me here, caught in your arms, like the wolf caught in the trap?"

"You said you wouldn't leave it caught in the trap. What would you do? Release it with a broken leg?"

"No."

"Bring it home with you to raise for a pet?"

"No, of course not. I would never try to make a pet out of a wild creature, especially not a wolf."

"Why not?"

"A wolf was never meant to be a domestic animal."

"Interesting, but we'll get back to that later. Right now, I want you to answer my question. What would you do?"

She almost snapped at him with the answer. "I would bring it home and nurse it back to health. Are you satisfied?"

"Almost. And then? What would you do when it was well?"

"I'd release it."

"Why?"

"Because there would be no reason to keep it in captivity. If it was completely healed, it would be able to take care of itself."

"Wouldn't it be hard to let it go after having it around for a while, after becoming attached to it?"

"I suppose so."

"Then you could keep it for a while longer. There would be no reason to hurry."

She thought for a moment, considering what he said. "No," she said at last. "It would not be wise to keep it any longer. To do so would only serve to make it more like a dog. It would become domesticated and lose its wild spirit."

He released his hold on her. "And that is precisely what you are doing to yourself. You are a wolf who has been domesticated and taught to behave like a dog."

She slapped him.

"Do it again if it makes you feel better, but remember this. Slapping me won't change anything for you. You can put a dog in a silk dress, but its tail will still stick out."

She slapped him again and then burst into tears. She covered her face with her hands and turned her back to him, sobbing in earnest now. She had never hit a person–until Reed. She was sorry, but she wished with her whole heart he would leave her alone. Her life had been nothing but turmoil since he arrived.

She wasn't certain how long she cried, but it did seem awhile before she felt his hands on her arms as he turned her toward him. She did not look at him, and he did not say anything. He drew her closer to him and allowed his hand to slip around to the back of her head. He held her there, with her head pressed against his chest, and she felt her tears come with renewed vigor.

She cried for some time, but he never said a word, nothing to encourage or discourage her. It was as if he was simply offering to be her support, and she guessed that, in a way, he was.

When she was all cried out, he took his handkerchief and dried her face. "My mother always said there was nothing as medicinal as a good cry. Blow," he said, holding the kerchief to her nose.

She did as he asked, feeling too drained and exhausted to do anything else.

"You call that blowing?" He pushed the handkerchief back to her nose. "Try again."

She blew harder this time. Apparently it satisfied him, for he wiped her nose and put his kerchief away.

She had never felt so washed out, or so close to another human being, in her life.

"Better?"

She nodded and looked around, seeing for the first time where they were, surprised at just how far they had walked. She could not see any sign of the house or barns, but she recognized the old feed trough as one in a pasture they no longer ran any cows on. She walked over to the trough and sat down, the backs of her legs resting on the lip of the trough. She began swinging her feet.

Reed joined her, parking his big frame on the edge next to her. He gave her a quick look and held out his hand as he asked, "Friends?"

She leaned up and kissed his cheek. "Friends," she said before feeling overcome with shyness and turning her head away.

He scooped up a handful of small rocks and began chucking them at a clump of grass, missing mostly.

She scooped up a handful of her own and showed him how it was done.

"You're better than me."

"I've had more practice."

He laughed and chucked another rock. He hit the clump of grass this time.

"I'm sorry I slapped you."

"I knew you were going to before you did."

"I've thought about what you said . . . about the wolf. I understand what you were trying to say. When I came here to live with my aunts, I was like the injured wolf."

"Who allowed the memory of painful traps to keep you living as a house pet instead of returning to the wild and being what you were destined to be."

"It is much easier to solve the wolf's dilemma than my own."

"Regaining lost or injured instinct is difficult, but not impossible. You need to learn to lead a normal life. A good way to do that is through observation, by watching those who lead normal lives and allowing your own instinct to run free." He sighed. "Your aunt Dally is still caught in the trap, so she snarls and snaps at those around her, living in a world of her own imagination that is peppered with falsehoods and lies. Vi has learned to hold on to the joy of life, to give her spirit the freedom to roam at will, to wear red petticoats on top of her skirts if she is moved to do so."

"I don't want to be like Aunt Dally."

He chuckled. "I don't blame you. She could be quite a woman. It's such a waste."

"What can I do?"

"If you want to return to the wild, if you want to find your pack, you better learn to howl."

"Howl?"

"Loud and often."

"And you? When are you going to set yourself free?"

She felt his arms come around her, his mouth closing gently over hers. Her first thought was to pull away, to run, but she remembered his words and pushed thought aside and allowed instinct to take over. It was instinct that caused her head to fall back, instinct that prompted her to return his kiss. She opened her mouth to his kiss and realized that it could not go on long enough, nor could she get close enough to him to ever want it to end. Her breath caught, trapped against the quickening that beat in her throat. As ready as she thought she was for his kiss, she was unprepared for her reaction to it, for the rush of feeling, the absence of breath, the languid pleasure she found in being touched by him.

"You have so much living to do, so much to learn. There are things I could teach you, Susannah, beautiful things, exquisite things that happen between a man and a woman, things I *will* teach you."

"When?" Her voice came out a mere whisper.

"When you are free," he said. "When you learn to howl."

How could she tell him she felt like howling now?

Jonah stopped by a few days later, on Monday. Susannah was in the yard, hanging out clothes. When she saw him coming, she took the clothespins out of her mouth and tossed them into the basket. She walked up to the fence and waited until he rode up to her.

As he drew closer, she could see he looked tired and worried. "Good morning, Sheriff Carter. Not more bad news, I hope."

"Doc Bailey thinks it's typhoid."

"Oh, my God! No! Not typhoid!"

"Two of the Carmichael kids are dead. Doc doesn't think Mrs. Carmichael will make it through the night."

Visions of the Carmichaels' darling children rose before her. A sharp, piercing pain gripped her heart. "Oh, no. The children. Which two?"

"The twins."

"Oh, dear God. Matt and John." Susannah felt like her heart had been ripped out. She kept seeing the Carmichael twins sitting a few pews ahead of them on Sunday mornings, the sun coming through the window and turning their silky blond heads a brilliant white. "They were such sweet boys. They deserved to grow up. It's such a shame. Such a wasteful shame. My heart grieves for the family. Is there anything that we can do?"

"Stay home."

She sighed. "Yes, I suppose that is best. You look tired, Sheriff. Do you have time to come inside for a cup of coffee?"

"No. I've got a lot of rounds to make. I'm telling everyone to stay put. Don't go visiting. Don't go to town unless it's absolutely necessary."

"No, we won't. Thanks for stopping by." She started to turn away, then stopped. "How are the rest of the Carmichaels doing? Have any of the other children taken sick?"

"No, none of the other children have shown any symptoms. Doc thinks Mr. Carmichael might pull through."

"That is good news, at least."

"Hold on to it," Jonah said. "It may be the last good news you hear for a while."

"I will try," she said. "I will surely try."

"Well, I'd best be going. The day isn't getting any longer, but the list of things I've got to do sure is." He guided his horse into a wide turn. "I hope I have better news the next time I see you. Good day."

"I hope you do, too. Take care of yourself. We can't do with you coming down sick."

"I'm too ornery to get sick," he said.

"Good-bye, Sheriff."

Susannah went off to find Reed.

Reed penned the last bunch of bawling heifers, then mounted his horse and headed back toward the barn. He'd barely had time to dismount when Susannah came hurrying toward him, a line of clothespins fastened to the bodice of her dress flapping in unison with each military step she took. He could tell by the way she walked that something was wrong. He stood there, watching her until she stopped and put her hand on the horse's rump.

"The sheriff was here. He just left."

"Bad news, I take it."

"Oh, Reed, it's typhoid."

"Damn, damn, damn," he said, and dropped the

reins. He walked a few feet, kicking clods as he went, and stopped. He rammed his hands down into his back pockets, leaned his head back, and closed his eyes. Typhoid. God almighty. He didn't need this. Not here. Not now.

"It's bad, isn't it? Real bad."

"It can't get much worse." He caught the mare by the curb strap under her chin, led her to the fence, and tied her. He stood there for a minute staring down at his hands–the hands that used to heal. He knew what a typhoid epidemic was like. He knew that one doctor in town wouldn't be able to keep up with the number of people falling ill once the epidemic was in full swing. The healer in him called out. The man in him repressed it. He had answered that call once, with his own wife, and paid a dear, dear price. The medical community turned its back on him and stole five years of his life. He didn't owe them a damn thing.

I will use treatment to help the sick according to my ability and judgment, but I will never use it to injure or wrong them. . . . Now if I keep this oath, and break it not, may I enjoy honor, in my life and art, among all men for all time; but if I transgress and forswear myself, may the opposite befall me.

The words of the Hippocratic Oath.

"Reed?"

"What?"

"What are you thinking?"

"Nothing. I'm just feeling sorry for all those poor bastards."

"Do you think we're safe as long as we remain at home?"

He shrugged. "It will definitely decrease your

chances of contracting it, but who knows? You might have come in contact with it before the sheriff came by. Symptoms don't appear until about three weeks later."

"What are the symptoms, besides headache and fever?"

"Coughing, intestinal hemorrhaging, rose-colored spots on the skin."

"Where does it come from?"

"The cause hasn't been discovered yet. It occurs in the majority of cases in youths and in adults, most frequently in late summer and early fall, especially if the summer has been hot and dry."

"How do you know if you've got it?"

"In the beginning there's a feeling of being tired, very tired, which may last for several days. You will get severe headaches and muscular aches, and feel a general dullness and disinclination to do much. You may experience nausea and diarrhea or nasal bleeding, even some deafness. When the fever comes, the symptoms are aggravated, maybe with abdominal tenderness. No two cases are exactly alike. The fever is a continuous one, not periodic. It generally lasts about twenty-one days."

She came to stand beside him and put her hand on his sleeve. "You have to help; you know that, don't you?"

He pulled away from her. "Don't."

"Reed, you're a doctor."

"You gave me your word that you would not mention that fact."

"People are dying. Mrs. Carmichael is practically dead. Her twin sons already are. Those boys were only ten."

"I know what typhoid does."

"Then how can you stand there when people are dying and not lift a finger to help?"

"Because I am not a doctor any longer. There is nothing I can do."

"I don't know how you can sleep at night."

"I am old friends with insomnia."

"I thought I knew you. I thought you were a kind and decent man. I see now that I was wrong."

She turned and he closed his eyes, listening to the sound of her footsteps fading away. She didn't know what she was asking. She did not know that if she asked anything of him, anything that was within his power, he would do it for her.

Anything except this.

Chapter 19

Three weeks later Dr. Bailey died of typhoid, and the town was left in a state of panic.

Jonah stopped by the farm and broke the news late one evening, when everyone was gathered in the parlor.

The moment the words left Jonah's mouth, Reed caught Susannah's quick glance in his direction. He looked off, preferring to stare out the window, where he kept his gaze riveted on the weather vane that whirled on top of the barn, his mind in turmoil.

"What's going to happen now?" Violette asked.

"I don't rightly know," Jonah said. "All we can do is pray."

"That seems the only choice left," Dahlia said.

"The nearest doctor is over a hundred miles away, and new cases are developing daily," Jonah said. "Those who are caring for the sick are overworked to the point of exhaustion. I don't know how much longer we can hold out."

"I suppose we'd better see what we can do," Violette said.

"I appreciate your offer to help," Jonah said, "but I wouldn't feel right about that. The elderly have been especially susceptible."

"There is nothing to worry about on that score," Violette said. "Dally and I had typhoid when we were younger. It hit our entire family. Our baby brother Robert died from it."

"I almost died from it," Dahlia said. "I was near death for two weeks."

"You had the lightest case of all," Violette said, "and you know it."

"That's not the way I remember it," Dahlia said.

"I can help," Susannah offered, leaving her rocking chair.

"I appreciate that, Susannah. I surely do."

"Shall I come into town tomorrow, or do you need me somewhere else?"

"No, town would be a good idea. Doc Bailey's wife and daughter are still caring for all the patients they can. We took out all the pews in the First Methodist Church and made it into a hospital."

"I'll be there early," Susannah said.

"I'll be there early as well," Violette added.

"We'll all be there early," Dahlia chimed in.

Once again Reed did not glance up, but he felt as if every eye in the parlor was staring directly at him. He did not look at anyone as they bid Sheriff Carter goodbye. Immediately, then, Reed made his apologies and left, telling Susannah and her aunts that he still needed to bring the milk cow in from the pasture–a lame excuse, but the only one he could think of.

He did not sleep much that night, and what little sleep came his way was interrupted by the return of the old, haunting dreams that brought back in vivid detail all he had tried to forget–the waxen face of his dead wife, their stillborn child, the insane look of vengeance on the face of Adam Copley . . . the added horror of the aftermath.

When he finally drifted off into a deeper sleep, he

dreamed again, not of the pain of the past, but of Semmelweis and Oliver Wendell Holmes and the devotion to rigid cleanliness and asepsis he had adopted in obstetrical procedures because of their belief in aseptic techniques. When he awoke, the dream was fresh in his mind, but he pushed it aside and dressed. He had chores to do. He had no room for dreams. Not anymore.

Susannah was milking Peony when Reed went into the barn. She didn't say anything.

"Good morning," he said.

She remained silent, but she did nod at him briefly.

"You're up early."

"I want to get an early start," she said, sounding very cool.

"You are still planning to go into town?"

Her hands stilled and she turned the full power of those golden eyes upon him. "On my part, there was never any doubt. I believe you have enough reservations for all of us."

"And your aunts?"

"They are dressed and eating breakfast now."

"Susannah, I don't think this is wise."

"I know you don't, but someone has to help. We can't just turn our backs on the suffering of others, like some people apparently can."

She did not look at him when she spoke this time, but went on with her chore, the sound of the milk hitting the pail somehow a haunting reminder of how empty his life had been since Philippa's death. "I'll hitch up the buggy," he said, and left.

Sometime later, Reed stood in the shadows of the barn and watched Susannah and her aunts climb into the buggy. He saw Susannah guide the mare into a wide turn–saw, too, the long look she gave the barn, as if she knew, somehow, that he was inside watching.

He knew there was no way he could offer to help without revealing his past. It wouldn't take anyone long to realize he had doctoring skills that went far beyond those of a drifter. He would either have to admit his medical background and the reason for abandoning it, or he would have to stand back without lifting a finger and watch people die.

Reed caught his gray mare and rode into town.

As he neared Bluebonnet, he expected to see some changes due to the ravages of the epidemic. But he did not expect to see signs of total deterioration. On the outskirts, he passed garbage scattered among the foul-smelling carcasses of dead animals. He dreaded what he might find at his final destination.

Susannah and her aunts worked until well past the lunch hour. When they finally did stop to eat, Susannah wanted fresh air and a chance to be outside and away from all the sickness more than she wanted food. After washing her hands and face, she unbuttoned the high neck on her dress and splashed water on her throat, then went outside to stand on the wooden walkway that ran along the street. She leaned against a post and listened to Jonah as he talked to a gathering across the way.

He was on the top step that led into Adolph Gunter's drugstore, telling the crowd to be calm. As Susannah listened, her gaze drifted over the various signs that decorated Gunter's drugstore. Behind

Jonah loomed the big sign that proclaimed DRUGS & MEDICINES. Painted on the wall to the left of the door were the words SYRUPS, CORDIALS, ICE, SODA WATER. To the right were the words GENUINE COLOGNE WATER, PERFUMES, TOILET ARTICLES, SPONGES.

Her gaze traveled back to the sheriff as he said, "I sent a telegram to Austin asking for help. I received a reply this morning." As he was taking a yellow piece of paper out of his pocket, Susannah was distracted by the sight of Reed. Her heart began to pound harder and harder while she watched him ride up a short distance away from the crowd and pull his horse to a stop.

Jonah unfolded the telegram. "The governor's office writes that the typhoid epidemic has spread to other towns. The governor won't be sending any help because there isn't any available."

The crowd interrupted with a buzz of discussion among themselves. After a few minutes, John Drysdale asked, "What about a doctor? Will they be sending us a doctor?"

Jonah shook his head. "No. There was a shortage of doctors before the epidemic struck. Now it's even worse."

"We've got to have a doctor," Pearlene Mapes said. "There were sixteen new cases brought into the church this morning. God only knows how many more have taken sick but are too ill to leave home. It's your job, Jonah. You're the sheriff. It's up to you to find us a doctor."

Jonah looked apologetic. "Pearlene, you know I'm doing all I can, but I can't pull a doctor out of a hat."

Everyone began talking, making demands that

Jonah find the town a doctor. Jonah held up his hands. "Don't you think I'd do anything I could to get a doctor if it were possible?"

"We need a doctor and we need one now," Ben Boggs shouted, and the crowd roared agreement.

Jonah took no time in answering, "Just where in tarnation do you think I can find one?"

"Right here," Reed said. "I'm a doctor."

The crowd grew stony as every head turned to stare in the direction of the voice. Susannah held her breath, knowing what those three words cost Reed, how very difficult they were for him to say. His next words, she knew, tore the heart out of him.

"Before you start thinking your prayers have been answered, I think it's only right to tell you why I turned my back on the life I had chosen for myself, why I preferred to be a drifter to healing the sick. Nine years ago, I lost my wife and baby in childbirth. In spite of all my fancy training and knowledge, the simple fact was, I was unable to save them."

Susannah took a quick breath and brought her hand up to spread over her heart, as if this simple gesture could still the erratic pounding that seemed loud enough to be heard across the street. She wondered if those listening would be forgiving and accepting of what Reed offered, or would they be rigid and hard-nosed at the expense of their loved ones?

She looked around her at the pale and weary townsfolk who were showing little reaction. All of them seemed to be wrapped in some kind of spell—an atmosphere Susannah found wholly in keeping with her own present state of exhaustion.

She looked at the sheriff for his reaction, knowing he would be the one to set the tone of things.

Jonah didn't hesitate to express his feelings on the subject. "Thank you for your offer, doctor. I think I speak for everyone here when I say we'd be pleased to have you help."

Irene, the wife of just-deceased Dr. Bailey, who was a gentle, meek soul, spoke up. "I know my husband would want you to use his office for the good of the town."

"That is very generous of you," Reed said. "In view of the situation, I think it best if I take you up on your kind offer."

A step into Dr. Bailey's office was a step back in time for Reed to when his days had been filled with the struggle against gunshot wounds, cholera, scrofula, diphtheria, smallpox, malaria, and yellow fever–all manner of diseases with little more to treat them than many of the patent medicines and cure-alls he saw lining Dr. Bailey's shelves.

He took inventory of the equipment and medicines he had to work with, then headed for the church where the hospital had been set up, knowing it would test the mental and physical stamina of the hardiest to deal with the sick there. However, he still was not prepared for what he found.

The church was stuffy and stifling. The windows were closed, the air warm and heavy with the smell of death and dying. Only a few of the lamps on the walls were lit and not giving off enough light to see to the patients' treatment, yet it was more than enough light to see the gruesomeness of what lay before him. The room was packed with the sick, writhing and moaning, some occupying soiled pallets or small beds, others on the bare floor. Lying among the newly afflicted were the bodies of the dead, ghastly corpses with glazed eyeballs staring up into vacant space, flies swarming around their open mouths.

"Holy mother of God! Why haven't the dead been removed?"

"There aren't enough folks willing to touch them," Violette said. "They are afraid of getting sick."

"You!" Reed said to a young boy of about fifteen who carried a water bucket and a dipper around. "What's your name?"

"Albert Russell, sir."

"Go find Sheriff Carter for me, Albert. Tell him to come on the double."

"Yes, sir." Albert dropped the water bucket and took off running.

Reed turned to Violette. "Where does that water come from?"

"The cistern at the edge of town."

"I don't suppose that water has been boiled."

"No."

Reed shook his head and swore softly. "Take that bucket and dispose of the water. As soon as I can, I'll mix up a solution of carbolic acid. I want that pail and anything that comes in contact with a human to be cleaned before and after contact. All drinking water must be boiled. Where is the closest kitchen?"

"The hotel."

"I'll see if the sheriff can send someone over there to take care of the drinking water. In the meantime, we will have to do without."

A few minutes later Jonah walked in.

"We've got to get these bodies out of here," Reed said. "Find someone to do it, if you have to hold a gun to his head. Get the dead out of here and buried as quickly as possible."

"We've got a shortage of coffins."

"Then bury them without coffins." Reed looked around. "Is there anyone you can enlist to help you?"

"I'll help," Dahlia said.

There were so few willing to work that Jonah took her up on it. Within a few hours, Dahlia had organized the three ministers in town and put them in charge of locating new graveyards, finding materials for coffins, and gathering crews of men to dig graves.

In the meantime, Violette had directed the cleaning of the hospital, and everything was scrubbed down with soap and hot water. As Reed had ordered, anything that the sick or those treating them had come in contact with was cleaned with carbolic acid.

Reed found Susannah in a dusky corner of the church, working quietly to clear a billiard table that had been moved into the back of the room. She was making it into a bed. "Can you come with me?" he asked.

Susannah accompanied Reed as he made the rounds and examined the sick, administering what supplies they had of whiskey, opium, and morphine to ease suffering.

"Isn't there something more we can do for them?" Susannah asked.

"All we can do is make them comfortable. We'll try to hold the fever at bay until the fever stages pass, and hope for the best."

"That doesn't sound like much for such a severe illness."

"It's not, but it's the best we can do. If we only knew the cause, we could treat the problem. That's the dilemma."

Later that evening Reed discovered a large amount of echinacea powder in the drugstore. Immediately he ordered that every patient was to get a dose of echinacea twice a day.

Jefferson Holt, publisher of the *Bluebonnet Weekly* printed out copies of Reed's instructions for sanitation, cleanliness, and boiling water, and the use of echinacea, which Jonah and his deputies circulated. While they did that, Reed instructed Susannah and the ladies of the town on the procedures for using carbolic acid solutions and making powdered echinacea into a liquid to give to the sick.

Once that was done, he again made his way from one makeshift bed to another, ministering to those crying for medical aid until he had worked his way through the growing numbers of the sick. There was two-year-old Melly Brewster, who was delirious with fever and did not look as if she would make it through the night, and Reed remembered the large toll typhoid always took among the young.

He'd examined twenty-year-old William Bell, whom Reed diagnosed as being in the final stages of fever, and looked as if he had a fifty-fifty chance of survival. There was garrulous Mr. McGeary, who enjoyed playing jokes on the children as they frolicked in the churchyard on Sunday mornings.

Then he came to the two young daughters of Joseph Brothers and Reed remembered seeing them with licorice sticks in their hands as their mother shopped in Buck and Smith's a few weeks back. He pulled the sheet over their heads. It was already too late for them.

A week after Reed took charge of managing the epidemic, Tate Trahern was carried into the hospital by two cowboys from the Double T. He was accompanied by his father, Thad Trahern.

"My boy is mighty sick," Thad said. "You pull him through and I'll give you anything you want."

"I'll do what I can for him," Reed said.

"I want my son to be your top priority," Thad said.

"Everyone here is a top priority," Reed said. "Your son will be treated no better and no worse than anyone else."

"I don't think you understand. . . ."

"No, I don't think you understand," Reed said. "Now leave your son and go home."

"It's going to be hard treating him, isn't it?" Susannah asked later, looking at Tate Trahern's pallid face.

Reed lifted Tate's eyelid. "Our differences were put aside the moment he was carried through that door." He unbuttoned Tate's shirt and found the telltale red spots on the trunk of his body.

"Typhoid?" Susannah asked.

"Typho-pneumonia."

"Typho-pneumonia? What is that?"

"Typhoid complicated by pneumonia. He's delirious right now. We've got to get his fever down."

"The drugstore has been out of ice for quite some time. We've only got cistern water to bathe the patients in."

"Just make certain the cistern water is used only for bathing."

A month later the worst of the epidemic seemed to be over. There were fewer cases being diagnosed, and a higher percentage of those already stricken were recovering. Tate Trahern was among those showing signs of recovery, not that Tate appreciated anything Reed and the others did for him. More than once Reed observed him with a resentful look on his face and a caustic remark waiting for the first unsuspecting person who came his way.

Late one afternoon that unsuspecting person turned out to be Susannah. He slapped a bowl out of her hand. It went flying, slinging soup across the sick that lay nearby, and shattered when it hit the floor. "I don't want your watery soup. I don't want your cold rags on my head. I don't want your prayers or your pious attitude of brotherly love. What I want is to get well. Get me some medicine so I can get out of this hellhole."

Susannah remained calm in spite of the fact she wanted to slap him. "There isn't anything that will cure typhoid. We are doing everything we can."

"Ha! I know that bastard who calls himself a doctor wouldn't spit on me if I was on fire. He likes to see me suffer."

"That isn't true!"

"He's found a way to get even, and he'll let me lie here till I rot before he lifts a finger to help me. Not that I expect you to admit anything. It's obvious that he's gotten under your skirts, so naturally you'd defend him."

Susannah stared at him for a moment with wide, astonished eyes. The color left her face. "I . . ." She turned away, obviously unable to say anything, then went to where Dahlia and Hallie Foss were picking up bits of shattered pottery.

"Why don't you go out and get some fresh air," Dahlia said.

"Yes–fresh air. Excuse me," she said. She began threading her way among the pallets on the floor. "I'll get some air. Excuse me, please." She walked until she had cleared those lying on the floor, then began to run.

Reed had seen the whole thing from across the room and tried to reach her, but it was difficult to weave his way among the sick. By the time he got to Tate's bed, Susannah had already reached the door. A moment later he watched her dart through the doorway and out into the churchyard.

Reed paused only a moment beside Tate's bed. His hands curled into fists at his sides, and he knew he could not say anything, for it would be impossible for him to stop with just a few words when he wanted to jerk Tate up and make him regret he had ever heard the name Susannah. Instead he went in the direction she had taken.

He found her standing behind the church. She stared down at the time-washed tombstones, her hands pale, gripping the fence that surrounded the graveyard. The golden glow of lamplight coming through the church windows breathed life into the chestnut braids coiled at the nape of her neck, and he had never wanted to comfort anyone more in his life.

He stepped closer and came up behind her, standing no more than two feet from her now, realizing for the first time just how narrow her shoulders were, how fragile her appearance really was.

"I'm sorry, Susannah."

"I know."

"I would have prevented that if I could."

"It doesn't matter."

"It matters to me." He was conscious of her wounded spirit, her humiliated pride. She had never seemed more vulnerable or remote. He could not leave her here like this, not when he could do something to ease her suffering. He stepped closer and kissed her neck, brushing the soft skin with whispered words as he told her how he hoped he could take the sting of Tate Trahern's hatred away.

Even as his hands reached around her and he took her in his arms, he knew what he was doing was pure insanity. He told himself that he only wanted to hold her. Only hold her. Nothing more.

He might have done just that if she had stayed as she was, with her back to him, but something made her turn toward him and open her mouth, as if she was going to say something.

"Dear God, Susannah! Don't you know what it does to me when you look at me like that?"

Desire washed over him in overlapping waves, each one warmer and more powerful than the one before. "Life is strange. I've thought about having you here with me like this a million times, and now that I do, there is no privacy for us."

"I don't want to think about the past, and I don't

want to worry about the right time or the wrong time. Kiss me, Reed. Kiss me and keep on kissing me until I tell you to stop."

His arms came around her, dragging her against him as he pressed forward, hoping, wanting to absorb every part of her. He could feel her heart beating against his chest, the fine bones of her back through the thin muslin of her dress, the warm softness of her skin beneath. He heard her gasp as his hands dropped lower, over the curve of her waist and down lower to lift her against him.

His breathing was rapid, mingling with hers, and his mouth was desperate to be everywhere, to touch the corners of her mouth, searching, pressing, seeking.

He felt her shudder, and next heard her whispered words punctuated by soft kisses to his throat. "I know what it feels like to be struck by lightning." She pulled back. "Why do the things we want most in life come at the most inopportune times?"

He drew her against him once more and kissed her neck. "I don't know," he said, "but I've never experienced anything more difficult than trying to be magnanimous at an inopportune times."

He released her and took her hand. She looked at him with a surprised, questioning expression. "Come on," he said, and began leading her away.

"Where? Where are you taking me?"

"I'm sending you home. You're tired. You need rest."

"And you need help."

"You're no good to me if you pass out on your feet from exhaustion."

"I've slept as much as you have."

"But I'm the doctor and I'm in charge." He saw

her smile and wondered what she could have found amusing in what he said.

"All right, Doctor," she said, and let him lead her away.

"I had no idea you had such an obedient nature. I thought you'd put up more of a fight. You must really be exhausted."

"No, it's just that I like the sound of that."

"The sound of what?"

"You being in charge."

Chapter 20

Time passed, but the typhoid did not. The few who escaped the dreaded disease worked tirelessly, to the point that Reed was as concerned for their health as those they cared for.

"How much longer do you think it will last, Doc?"

Reed hated to tell Jonah he did not know. "There is no way of telling. We can only hope that the worst is over, that the number of cases will begin to taper off. Only then will we know it is over."

Jonah nodded. "I pray that it will happen soon. Everyone is doing all they can. You look plumb worn out, Doc. Maybe you should get a little rest. If you get sick, I don't know what we'll do."

What he said was true. Every able-bodied person in the community pitched in to assist wherever they could, each of them working long hours with no sleep and little food, but no one seemed to mind. There were precious few families that had not lost a loved one.

Like the sheriff, everyone wondered if the epidemic would ever end.

And then, when suffering, loss, and death had almost become a way of life, the epidemic was over. Suddenly and blessedly over. When he suspected as much, Reed went to find the sheriff.

Jonah was sitting behind his desk when Reed walked in and told him the good news.

"Over?" Jonah asked, as if he could not believe it.

"Over," he repeated time and time again. "I can't believe it's over. Are you certain?"

Reed wearily rubbed the back of his neck praying that what he believed was true "There have been no new cases for over two weeks now. I think we're in the clear."

"My God," Jonah said, then he laid his head down on his desk and cried.

Reed patted him on the back and Jonah raised his head and wiped his eyes on his sleeve. "I feel like a pure-d fool," he said. "Crying like a baby. I don't know what got into me." His voice softened and a sad look came over his face. "There have been so many deaths. So many fine people are gone–a lot of them dear, dear friends. How do you get over something like that, Doc? I don't know if the town will ever recover. I don't know if anyone even wants to try. We've lost so much. How can I encourage folks to go on?

"They eke out a living with no money, they rebuild after a tornado destroys their homes, they replant the crops that have been rained out. They will go on and they will do it surprisingly well."

Jonah stood and pulled his hat off the peg next to his desk. He held the hat in his hands and fiddled with the brim, shaping and reshaping it, as if he were trying to think of what he should do first. "This is sure good news . . . the first *good* news I've had to tell anyone in over three months. It's the best Christmas present I could give."

After his visit with Jonah, Reed went home to find Susannah.

She was sitting at the kitchen table writing something in the family Bible. She glanced up when he entered. "I didn't expect you home for supper."

"I wasn't planning on coming home either, but I had some news . . ."

She paled and he saw the tears come to her eyes. Quickly, then, he said, "It's over, Susannah. Over."

"What's over?"

"The epidemic. The typhoid has run its course."

Her reaction was much like Jonah's. Disbelief at first, followed by tears, then numbness. When she looked at him after a few stunned minutes, Reed saw the dampness on her sleeve where she had laid her head when she cried.

When the shock passed and Susannah regained her composure, she turned to him and said, "I'm sorry. I didn't mean to dissolve like a wet sugar cake. It's just that it's so long overdue. And now, looking back, it all seems like such a terrible, terrible waste."

He wiped the tears from her face with his thumbs. "Don't look back, Susannah. It's over. Look to the future, the joy that will come."

"Joy." She shook her head. "Death has been with us for so long. I cannot remember what joy feels like." She took a long, deep breath and released it slowly. "I cannot conceive what it will feel like to be happy again."

"Only Nature has a right to grieve perpetually. The cold will be gone soon, and the mockingbirds will sing along the creek just as they always have, and the sound of it will be as pleasant as ever."

" 'For God is in His Heaven and all is right with the world.' "

"Or will be for me as soon as I get some sleep."

He kissed her quickly, gently on the nose.

"Why did you do that?"

"Because I wanted to."

"You're a decent man, Reed Garrett. Don't ever let anyone tell you different."

He ruffled her hair. "Like you, I cannot conceive what it would feel like to be happy again."

A week later Reed sent the last patient home from the makeshift hospital, then said to Reverend Pettigrew, "Looks like you can start using it for a church again, Reverend."

After leaving the church, Reed went to Dr. Bailey's office and put things in order there before riding home. He could not remember a time when he had ever been so tired, a time when exhaustion had seeped so deeply into his very bones. He felt like he could sleep for a week.

"He's been sleeping for two days," Susannah said to her aunts after dinner. "Do you think we should check on him?"

"I don't suppose it would hurt to take him a bite to eat," Violette said.

"The chicken and dumplings were especially tasty tonight," Dahlia added. "Why don't you take him a nice bowl of dumplings? They would feel mighty good in a man's insides, I think, on such a cold night."

As if proving Dahlia's point about the weather, a gust of wind whipped around the corner of the house and whistled its way along the eaves, sending a few gusts into the house through the drafty places. Dahlia pulled her wool shawl more tightly about her and said, "Well, I'd best be getting back to work. I've got a lot to do." She went into the storeroom she had cleaned out for her personal use, stopping just long enough to turn around the sign that hung on a nail beside the door so it read, DO NOT DISTURB.

Susannah glanced at Violette and smiled. At some point during the epidemic, Dahlia had found her calling. It happened innocently enough one afternoon when Reed needed more echinacea to be powdered, then mixed into liquid form. Seeing Dahlia standing around looking lost and helpless, he assigned the task to her. And that was when they lost Dahlia to a collection of medicinal herbs.

Now she had herbs growing in pots all over the house and bundles of herbs hanging from every available beam and nail in the kitchen and storeroom. Her days were filled with making frightful-looking concoctions from the plants she collected. Once they were made, she tried to foist them off on anyone who would take them. No one had died from her potions–yet.

"It gives her something to do, something that makes her feel useful," Reed had said, and Susannah supposed that was the most important thing.

Susannah spooned up a tin full of dumplings and put that in a basket along with a jar of fresh milk and half a loaf of bread. As she was about to open the door, Violette walked over and dropped the box of dominoes in the basket. Susannah gave her a puzzled look. "No need to rush back," she said. "If you're going to take the time to walk down there, you might as well stay a spell."

"Dominoes?"

Violette winked. "Or you might find another

game to play," she whispered, and Susannah put her free hand over her mouth to stifle a laugh.

She lifted her cape off the peg by the back door and settled it across her shoulders before adjusting the hood to cover her head. When she had the basket on her arm, she stepped outside and felt a cold draft of wind travel up her skirts.

"Don't rush back," Violette said as she closed the door.

"I won't," Susannah said, and started down the back steps.

She walked toward Reed's house, her step brisk because of the cold. The night was sharp and clear, and the sky was littered with a million stars that seemed delighted to cast their light upon her path. Somewhere, not too far away, a cow bawled and something flapped out of a nearby tree.

When she reached the orchard, she remembered the first time Reed had kissed her and how very long ago that seemed. She paused briefly, trying to make out the tree where he had carved her initials, and found herself tempted to go there, as she often had, merely to put her finger on the letters, as if by doing so she could feel his warmth and strength and love.

She walked past the orchard and continued down the path until she saw the silhouette of his house and saw, too, the dull glow of amber light coming through the window. Her heart skipped a beat.

When she arrived at Reed's door, she knocked twice, but there was no answer. Freezing now, she opened the door and peeked inside. The room was empty, so she entered and shut the door behind her, then carried the basket to the table.

There was a big fire going in the pot-bellied stove,

and the room was overly warm. Her heart hammered in her chest as her first thought was that Reed was ill and running a fever. It made sense that he would build a fire to ward off the alternating chills.

Susannah tossed her cape over a chair and hurried into the back bedroom, expecting to see Reed writhing in pain on the bed. What she found surprised her.

Reed was taking a bath, or rather he was just stepping into the tub to take a bath. He was now standing up in the water with a look on his face that she was certain matched the astonishment on her own.

"Susannah?" was all he managed to say.

Susannah, however, couldn't even muster that much sound from the dry depths of her throat, so surprised was she at the effect his nakedness had on her. It didn't surprise her to see a naked man–God only knew she had seen plenty of those in New Orleans as a child, nor did it surprise her to see that Reed's naked body was basically the same as she remembered a man's body was supposed to be. The surprise came from her reaction and the wild surge of desire she felt for him. She perceived his body not as an instrument of ugly and sordid intentions but as a thing of beauty that she was more than curious to know.

She seemed frozen to the spot, unable to take her eyes off him. How hard and lean he was, how perfectly formed, with a tapered torso and unbelievably long legs. It was what was between those legs that both fascinated her and left her feeling a mixture of fear and awe, for there he was as beautiful as he was everywhere else, and even in the relaxed state, there was a subdued sort of magnificence to him that she saw as both powerful and vulnerable. Never would she have thought she could have looked at a man and felt desire for him, desire that was born of love and tenderness. She realized suddenly that none of the taint, the sordidness had followed her from her childhood, that what she saw was a man, no better, no worse than herself, a man who neither forced himself upon her nor denied his feelings for her.

"Susannah . . . love, what are you doing here this time of night?"

"We were worried about you. I came to see if you were all right. I was afraid you might have a fever. I knew you must be hungry."

"I wanted sleep more than food, but now that I see you, I have a hunger of another sort."

Her gaze dropped down to the proof of what he said, and she heard his laugh, then the splash of water as he lowered himself into the tub. When she looked down at him sitting in the immense tub, she started laughing, for he wasn't sitting in a washtub of the sort she and her aunts used for bathing, but in a watering trough.

"Do you have enough room?"

He chuckled. "For me and Miss Lavender."

"You must have been heating water for hours."

"I have been, but now that I am in here and enjoying the luxury of a bath where my knees aren't sticking out, it was well worth the effort." He fished around in the water and came up with a sponge. He extended it toward her and said, "Wash my back?"

"If you promise not to throw water on me."

"Never."

She came toward him, took the sponge, kneeled beside him, and began scrubbing his back, lathering his skin with the big bar of soap he handed her. When she finished, she said, "All right. You can rinse off now."

After he dunked himself, she lathered his head, then poured fresh water over it from the pail on the floor. She no more than put the pail down when she felt his hand close around her wrist. Before she could think about what he was doing, she found herself yanked into the tub, clothes and all.

She came up sputtering and calling him names, which he soon silenced with a deep and lengthy kiss. "You said you wouldn't do that!"

"No, I didn't. You asked me to promise, and I said, 'Never.' " He kissed her again.

When he released her, he began unlacing her shoes. "We might have a time drying these out, so I'll toss them in the corner."

"You have soaked my clothes."

He threw one shoe into the corner and then the other. "Take them off and I'll hang them in front of the stove. They'll dry in no time."

"It's hot enough in here to scorch them."

He started with the buttons on her dress, and when he had them undone, he said, "You'll have to stand up. I can't get these things off with you sitting down."

"I don't think I can get up, and even if I could, I have no intention of taking anything off. It's one thing to be in here with you with my clothes on, quite another thing entirely to be here with nothing on."

"I didn't ask your opinion. You are in no position to know what's best for you, but as your physician, I can tell you that bathing with your clothes on is not the best medicine."

He stood up and tugged her hand, drawing her up to stand beside him. He pulled her dress over her head.

"Reed, I had a bath this afternoon. I don't need another one."

"That one was for you."

"Who is this one for?"

"This one is for me."

Quickly then he worked on getting her undergarments off. He stepped out of the tub, gathered up her clothing and carried the bundle into the front room to hang by the stove. She sat down in the tub and began washing herself.

"Oh, no, that's my job," he said, coming back into the room. He stepped into the tub and held out his hand. She stood, giving him her back, and felt his hands come around her. They moved over her slowly, agonizingly so, stroking and caressing her until she was desperate to get closer to him, to submit to the warm pressure of his fingers. While he touched her, he began to kiss her neck, her shoulders. She felt her breathing coming in hard gasps; her knees grew weaker with each touch of his lips until she was afraid they'd no longer support her. He turned her around then, kissing her stomach with his hands on her buttocks, drawing her closer against him as his mouth dropped lower.

"Reed, don't . . ."

He did not say anything but grasped her more firmly. His mouth was moving lower and lower still, until he was kissing her where she never thought a man would ever kiss her. She never knew anything could feel so exquisite, or could leave her yearning for more. Of their own accord, her legs moved apart, and she heard him groan and pull her closer. She could feel him more intensely now, and the touch of his mouth on her was insanity. She must be dying. She must. How could she control herself–her breathing that came in painful short gasps? Of its own accord, her body pressed forward, wanting to draw him closer.

"Reed," she whispered hoarsely, "please, I can't stand up any more."

She felt her body shudder with the increased tension that mounted within her. She cried out, overcome with weakness. Just as her knees gave way, she felt his arms come beneath her and he lifted her out of the tub. He laid her on the rug on the floor beside the tub, then covered her with his body. Instinctively her legs opened to him.

"I've wanted you for so long, Susannah. I can't think of a reason why we should wait a minute more."

"Neither can I."

He kissed her and she kissed him back, knowing what was coming next and knowing, too, that it would hurt the first time, that there would be bleeding and that she would be a virgin no longer, not that her virginity was a golden medallion she wanted to wear around her neck for the rest of her life. She had worn it long enough, and the leaden weight of it had grown far heavier than she wanted to endure. She welcomed the feel of him as he pushed against her, welcomed even the sharp stab of pain that followed.

"I love you," he said, and moved inside her.

She had believed she knew all there was to know about the coupling between a man and a woman. Now she learned that she'd known virtually nothing–nothing about this incredible shift from pain one moment to intense pleasure the next.

"I love you, Reed. I love you," she said. She locked her arms fiercely around him, as if by doing so she could prolong this beautiful moment and keep him with her forever. He must have mistaken her tears of joy for something else.

"What's wrong? Are you in pain?"

She placed her hands on each side of his head and drew his face down to kiss him. "No. I have never felt so wonderful or so loved."

His lips moved over the dampness on her cheeks. "Tears come for a reason. Tell me. Why are you crying?"

"I don't know."

He looked so bewildered that she wanted to laugh. "You don't know?"

She shook her head and released a deep breath. "It's a lot of things."

His lips moved in her hair. "Like what?"

"Because . . ." She sniffed and tried again. "Because I'm normal, Reed. I'm normal and it's the first time in my life I've felt this way. I'm normal and I don't know how to tell you how much that means to me. I thought for so very, very long that I would never know what normal felt like."

He smiled and kissed her eyes. "That's only one reason. What else?"

"Because I'm afraid this golden moment will vanish, or I'll awake to find it was only a dream."

"It's no dream. As for the other, only we can do something about that."

Love, warm and enduring, flowed through her. Surely no one had ever been this happy, surely no one deserved to be.

He wrapped his arms around her and Susannah

lay still, her heart thudding against his chest. Was this how two people became one? Each feeling so close to the other that they began to think alike and feel each other's thoughts and pain until at some point in time it was impossible to tell where one began and the other ended?

She lay there listening to the sound of the wind in the bare trees outside, the occasional scrape of branches over the tin roof. The physical existence of the world about her slowly returned: the hard floor and the thinness of the rug beneath her, the heat of the room, the surprising softness of his hair. She wished she were an artist so she could capture this moment, for how could her memory do it justice?

She felt the strokes of his hand in her hair, his hand unsteady and seemingly awkward, and infinitely dear because of it. "Any regrets?"

"None."

"I'm relieved to hear it. I was afraid . . ."

"Except–" She could feel his sudden indrawn breath, the tensing of his muscles. "Except I wish it had happened sooner."

The air rushed out of his lungs with a *whoosh!* She laughed and kissed him, and found renewed contentment lying in his arms, listening to the rhythm of his murmured love words, feeling a deep and profound peace.

She had almost drifted off to sleep when she felt him shift his position, which was followed by a groan. She was reminded of the cold, hard reality of what they were lying on. She rolled forward into a sitting position. He did the same, although he wasn't as quick about it.

"How old are you?"

He scowled and rubbed his back. "It isn't the length of time it takes you to run, but the distance you go."

She wrinkled her nose and looked him over. "You look like you've used up plenty of both."

"Let's boil your hide until it's tender and see how you fare." He went to the stove and brought back a bucket of hot water and poured it into the tub. When he returned, he put the bucket on the floor and scooped Susannah into his arms. He carried her back to the bath, stepped over the side, and stood her on her feet. "You stand there and I'll sit down first."

He had no more than sat down in the water when Susannah grabbed his hand and tugged him upward. "Oh, no," she said. "It's your turn to stand and I'll sit down."

Reed came to his feet and waited for her to sit down, but Susannah did not. Instead she knelt in front of him.

"Dear Mary, Joseph, and the wise men. I'm as weak as a newborn."

And he must have been, Susannah discovered, for he literally slid down into the warm, soapy water.

"Turnabout is fair play," she said. "Now you know what it feels like to stand on legs that don't seem capable of supporting you."

"I think I know," he said, kissing her, "but I'm not certain. Perhaps, if you tried that one more time, I'd know for sure."

"Glutton," she said. She picked up another bucket on the floor beside her and poured the water over his head.

"Yeoooowww!" he said, and sprang to his feet. "That's cold."

She laughed and tossed the last bit of water in the bucket at him.

He flinched.

"You need a little cooling off." She held up her hand and said, "Now, help me up. I've got to feed you and then get back to the house. My aunts are going to be wondering what I've been doing."

"Maybe you should forget about feeding me."

She saw his concerned look. "Why? Are you worried about what they'll do to me?"

"No. It's not you I'm worried about. It's my hide they'll be after."

"I'll tell them to be gentle."

He chuckled, gave her a hand, and pulled her to her feet. He kissed her nose. "I wouldn't worry about what your aunts think. I bet they have a pretty good idea." He picked up a towel from the chair beside the tub.

Susannah waited patiently as he dried her off, luxuriating in the moment, the strong, sure strokes of his hands, the nearness of him, the tenderness she saw he felt for her. "Oh, I'm certain they have more than an idea."

He turned his head to one side as he concentrated on what he was doing. "They've probably gone to bed by now."

"If Aunt Vi could drag Aunt Dally out of the storeroom. She was busy mixing up some potion for me to give to Peony. She said it would make her give more milk."

"Or give her the *hobbledy-trotts*," he said, and they both started laughing.

* * *

While Reed finished eating, Susannah dressed, then loaded the tin back into her basket. He picked up the box he saw lying there and turned toward her. "What's this?" He brought it up to his ear and shook it. "Something else to eat?"

Susannah had forgotten about the dominoes, and when she saw them she started laughing. "Dominoes," she said. "It's a box of dominoes."

"Dominoes? You brought dominoes to a starving man? Why'd you do that?"

She held up her hands in a show of innocence. "It was Aunt Vi's doing, not mine. She put them in the basket as I was leaving. She said I needn't rush back. She suggested I stay for a while and the two of us could play dominoes."

Reed threw back his head and laughed. "Your aunt is a shrewd old woman."

"The shrewdest and the dearest."

"Too bad she didn't send something that would have taken all night," he said. He put his arms around her and drew her against him. "I want to sleep with you beside me–just sleep with you beside me for the rest of my life."

"Just sleep?" She frowned and said irritably, "I don't know. That doesn't sound very appealing."

He took her chin in his hand and lifted her face so she looked at him. "Susannah Jane Dowell, I want you. Now. Tomorrow. Forever. I want to give you everything in the world that you've ever dreamed of having–as well as a few things you've never thought of, and perhaps even a few you may not want. That includes my heart, my love, my name, my children–if we are so blessed–and my solemn pledge to love you until the day I die, and longer if that's possible."

She listened patiently and then agreed–well, not exactly, but she did agree in general. To be precise, what she said was, "I might as well, because my cleverness is no match for your Yankee patience and tenacity. If there is anything I've learned it's that patience and tenacity are worth more than twice their weight of cleverness, and Yankees know just how to use it to their advantage."

He smiled and held her close. "Susannah, will you marry me and sleep beside me for the rest of my life, if I promise to be appealing on occasion?"

"If I can pick the occasions," she said and raised up on her toes to kiss him.

"Is that yes or maybe?"

"It's maybe a lifetime won't be long enough."

"I'm sorry I didn't meet you sooner."

"You wouldn't have liked me sooner."

"How do you know?"

"I wasn't very likable."

"Maybe I could have changed all that."

"Maybe we should be happy with what we've got now."

"Maybe you're right. When are we going to tell your aunts? When do you want to get married?"

"It better be soon on both accounts. I know what it feels like to be illegitimate, Reed. What we did could give me a baby. I want it to be born in wedlock."

"It will be, love. It will be, I promise."

Reed walked her back to the house and kissed her once more. "I'm finding it damnably difficult to let you go. I want to keep on holding you."

"If Aunt Dally hears us, you may find it damnably difficult to hold a cup of coffee . . . after she breaks your arm."

He released her with a soft chuckle and kissed her. "I'll see you in the morning. Now, get inside. It's freezing out here."

He opened the door, and she went inside, bestowing a melting smile on him before she closed the door.

Reed pulled his coat together and buttoned it, then turned the collar up before he shoved his hands deep into his pockets. He walked back to his house, his thoughts on Susannah and what had happened. He was facing the reversal of many of his life's decisions.

In his house he noticed that the light seemed much brighter than it had before. Details seemed to leap out at him. He caught the scent of Susannah lingering in the room, and was aware of the acuteness of his senses all over again.

When he was in bed, he folded his arms behind his head and stared at the faint shadows on the ceiling. He remembered that day when he'd driven Susannah and her aunts to church–the day Violette gave him a Bible and told him to read Job. He remembered, too, how the words had moved him to the point of bringing God back into his life after turning his back on Him during the dark, dark years.

He saw that as a turning point, the beginning of his journey up and out of the valley of the shadow of death he had been in for so long. He had his medical career back, but, more important, he had a woman to love, one who loved him in return.

He had come full circle. His life was good. Susannah would be his wife soon.

What could possibly stand in their way?

Chapter 21

The next day dawned a bit warmer, but the wind was blustery. The trees were bare now, and the leaves were piled against the side of the barn. With each blast of wind, the skeletons of dead plants rattled together while the leaves on the evergreen bush danced and flapped to a tune of their own. Everything looked as gray as the sky overhead, with only a hint of brown that was visible in the dun-colored pastures dotted with stubble from last summer's crops.

Reed was in the tack room working on the worn harness and tracings, replacing the old leather with new. When he finished, he went to the house to get slops for Miss Lavender and her brood. He found Violette in the kitchen, coping with a mountain of vegetables from the root cellar that Susannah had cut up for today's lunch of vegetable stew.

"I'm up to my elbows in here," she said. "It's my job to put these vegetables in the pot. But I'm having a bit of a problem."

It was hard not to smile when he looked around the kitchen and counted seven pots and seven lids lining the counters and kitchen table. "What's the trouble?"

"I can't seem to find the right pot," she said, exasperated. "This one is too little. This one is too big. I'm beginning to feel like Goldilocks."

She turned to face him, and he saw she was truly vexed.

"It's one of the things I hate about getting old. My memory comes and goes. Today it is mostly gone. I can't seem to judge the size of these pots. I pour the stew base in one and it overflows. I pour it in another one and it barely covers the bottom."

He looked the pots over, then went to the table. "Try this one," he said.

She poured the broth from another pot into the larger one he handed her. "So far, so good," she said, and began scraping the vegetables into the lid, which she placed just under the edge of the cabinet. When the lid was full, she dumped the vegetables into the pot. Three lidfuls of vegetables later, she declared the job done.

"A perfect fit," she said. "I don't know what I would have done if you hadn't come along."

"That's the beauty of families," he said. "There is always someone around to help when the going gets tough. I'm an excellent pot sizer-upper. Call on me anytime."

Her eyes were bright and she looked at him with genuine fondness. "I'll do that for certain." She paused. "It is nice to be a part of a family, isn't it? I can't tell you how pleased I am to hear you feel like part of ours."

It struck him that he did feel a part of their family, and he found it strange that it had never occurred to him before. "It's a nice feeling," he said. "I dropped by to see if you needed any help. While I was here, I thought I'd take the slops and feed Miss Lavender for you."

"You just missed Susannah. She took the slops on

her way to feed the chickens. That was a while ago, so she's probably milking Peony by now."

"I'll check there, then."

He found Susannah in the barn. "Good morning," he said, and bent down to kiss her on the top of her head.

"Good morning." She gave him a warm smile and returned to her milking.

Next to her sat a basket of freshly gathered eggs and the empty slops pail. He turned the slops pail over and sat down to wait for her. He didn't say anything but was content to listen to the rhythm of the milk squirting into the bucket as he watched her hands. When she finished milking, he offered to carry the pail.

They didn't mind the cooler weather as they made their way back to the house in silence. He found it interesting that they could enjoy just being together, without the need for conversation. He walked beside her, carrying the bucket of milk. Susannah had the basketful of eggs on her arm.

When they walked into the kitchen, the stew was bubbling on the stove, its fragrant aroma a welcome reminder that there would be something hot and filling for lunch, but mingling with that was a strange, smoky smell. Violette was sitting at the kitchen table watching the leaves blow past the window as she waited for the teakettle to come to a boil. Dahlia was melting paraffin on the stove, a billowing column of smoke rising from the pan.

Reed and Susannah exchanged glances.

Susannah put the eggs down on the cabinet. Reed put the pail of milk beside the eggs. Then they faced her aunts.

"We have something to tell you," she said.

"Last night, I asked Susannah to become my wife."

"And I accepted."

Violette sprang from her chair and rushed over and gave each a kiss. "I knew it was coming," she said. "I just knew it. Of course you have my blessing."

"You have my blessing as well," Dahlia said. "A wedding. How exciting. I think we should get out Mother's silver. The little silver bonbon dish will look lovely on the lace tablecloth, full of sugared pecans. Of course we'll have to use the cut-glass cake plate for the wedding cake." Her hands came up to her face, and she turned toward Violette. "Sister, you don't suppose they are too badly tarnished, do you?"

"A little silver polish should do the trick," Violette said.

"Perhaps I could mix up something that would do a better job," Dahlia said as she turned back to the paraffin, which was smoking profusely by this point. "I think I should like to be in charge of things, Sister. I don't want you overworking yourself. Yes, that is just what I'll do. I'll take care of everything."

Violette was looking at the smoking pan. "Get that pan off the stove. What are you trying to do, Dally? Burn down the house? That stuff smells worse than singed chicken feathers. What are you going to do with it?"

"It's a secret," Dahlia said. She carried the paraffin to the sink and poured it into a copper bowl. On the cabinet beside her were two jars of herbs and a crockery pot full of lavender. Next to that was a bowl of dried dewberries and a bottle of vanilla extract.

"It's either something to drink or rub over your

body," Violette said. "And if it's the former, I, for one, am not going to try it."

Reed noticed that Susannah looked distracted and that surprised him. This should have been the most important day of her life, but she was staring intently at her aunt, her mind obviously a thousand miles off. He looked at Dahlia and realized something about her was different.

"Aunt Dally, what have you done to yourself?" Susannah asked.

Dally looked down at her dress in an absent-minded way. "Done? Whatever do you mean, dear?" She pulled a clove of garlic out of her pocket and began peeling it, dropping the dry peelings into the other pocket of her apron but missing with most of them, which landed on the floor. "You need to start taking garlic," she said. "Both of you. Garlic will keep you from getting sick, and you're going to need your health with the wedding and all." She looked around. "Now, where did I put my mortar and pestle?"

Reed and Susannah watched Dahlia search through the kitchen cabinets, unable to believe their eyes. Where once had been the picture of perfection, now stood a woman who looked as though *she* had dressed in the dark. Gone were the disciplined clothes, the well-matched colors and patterns. Strong blobs of color, none of which went together, adorned her body. Her blouse was an unrecognizable pattern with a black background and splashes of bright green, red, and yellow, to which she had sewn purple braid and gold tassels. Her skirt was a light blue with yellow fleurs-de-lis that looked awfully similar to the pillows she had made last week for the parlor. Come to think of it, they had gold tassels, too. The very idea of turning her loose on the wedding preparations made Reed cringe.

"I think I'll let you ladies work out the plans for the nuptials," Reed said, taking his hat from the peg. "I need to go into town and spend a few hours in the office. I'm sure there will be plenty of coughs and colds and sore throats to see to, and Mary Madison is due to have her baby any day."

"Deserter," Susannah whispered.

Reed laughed and blew her a kiss.

"Oh, I do hope Mary doesn't have her baby during this nasty weather," Dahlia said. "If you'll wait just a minute, I'll send her a tin of that nice sunflower seed salve I made last week."

Reed waited until Dahlia handed him the salve, which he tucked into his coat pocket. "I'll be back in time for supper."

"Say hello to Mary if you see her," Susannah said, and added, "Oh, Reed, it might be a good idea to stop by and see the reverend, so you can tell him about the wedding."

"I'll do that," Reed said. He kissed Susannah on the cheek and departed.

Susannah watched him through the kitchen window. "I do hope he is muffled up and warm enough. I don't want him catching anything."

"He's caught you," Violette said. "That's the most contagious thing he's likely to come in contact with."

"I hope so," Susannah said, "but I can't help worrying. What if something goes wrong? What if we have another epidemic or something and we can't get married?"

"Lord-a-mercy! Listen to you carry on like an old worrywart," Violette said. "Even if he did catch cold, Reed Garrett wouldn't let a thing like that hold him back."

"Yes, I suppose you are right," Susannah said.

"Well, now that we've got that settled, what else can you think of that could possibly happen to prevent the two of you from getting married?"

That afternoon, Tate Trahern went into Buck and Smith's. He noticed Mr. Truesdale standing behind the post office counter, and had a twinge of regret that it wasn't Daisy's cheerful face he saw there. He would have gone to her funeral if he hadn't been so sick with typhoid himself, but by the time he was on his feet again, Daisy had been buried for over a month.

He remembered her telling him that she was the only one working in her family, and wondered what they'd be doing now, not that he was really interested. What he was interested in was seeing if he had any mail.

"I was wondering if you were going to come into town anytime soon," Mr. Truesdale said. "I've had a letter here for you for some time now. Course I knew you'd been sick. It's a good thing that Garrett fellow turned out to be a doctor or you might be out there with all those other poor souls who didn't make it."

"Yeah, Garrett is a regular angel of mercy."

"That's the gospel if I ever heard it," Mr. Truesdale said.

"How about that letter," Tate said. "I've got a lot of business to see to today and I need to get started."

Mr. Truesdale handed him the letter. "It's from

Boston," he said. "At first I thought there was some mistake, since Dr. Garrett is the only one who's been getting mail from Boston, but it's got your name on it, sure as shootin'. That's quite a coincidence, both of you getting mail from Boston."

"Yeah, quite a coincidence."

Tate took the letter and left the store. He stepped over Otis Crowder and Lee Roy Harper, who were sleeping off last night's drinking binge on the boardwalk, before he went across the street to the Roadrunner Saloon. There he ordered a whiskey and carried it to a table in the back of the room, hinting to everyone present that he did not want to be interrupted.

He drank the whiskey, then ordered another. He took one sip and opened the letter from Boston. When he finished reading it, he folded the letter, downed the glass of whiskey, stood, and placed the letter in his pocket.

"Give everyone a round of drinks and put it on my tab," he said to Frank Weatherby, who was tending bar.

Frank nodded and began lining up shot glasses, but Tate did not stay around to watch.

When Muriel Emenhizer heard about Susannah and Reed's engagement, she went to her husband, Loy, and ordered him to drive her out to the Wakefield place immediately. Loy Emenhizer was president of the First National Bank and considered himself to be the busiest man in town, so he didn't take too willingly to his wife's intrusion.

"Honey lamb, I'm busy right now, but I'll drive you out to the Wakefield place after we close."

"Loy Emenhizer, I cannot believe you could be so unappreciative when you know full well that if it hadn't been for that kind and dedicated Dr. Garrett, I wouldn't be standing here this very moment ordering you to do anything."

In the end, Loy drove Muriel out to the Wakefield place and sat patiently in the parlor with his bald pate shining in the lamplight as his rotund wife laid out her plans to give the betrothed couple an engagement party.

"It will be a party the likes of which the people in Bluebonnet have never seen. Loy and I want to show our eternal gratitude for what you did to pull me through that dark and trying time when I was so ill with typhoid."

Muriel added, "I will spare no expense," and there was a sound in the room remarkably like a groan. Susannah and Aunt Vi glanced at Loy, but he was gazing out the window as if he wasn't hearing a word of what was going on.

Muriel went on talking. "I have taken the liberty of speaking with Sam Slater about the use of the Roadrunner Saloon for the affair."

"Muriel, have you taken leave of your senses? You can't expect decent folks–especially women–to go to a party at the Roadrunner Saloon," Loy said. "It will be full of drifters and drunks, and it will certainly not be the kind of place where any self-respecting lady would put in an appearance."

"Loy, if you would listen, I will explain. Sam Slater was kind enough to agree to close the Roadrunner for the night–for a fee, of course. He has assured me that he will see to it that the riffraff are kept away."

"I bet Reverend Pettigrew will order the entire congregation to boycott your party if it's held at the saloon," Loy said.

"I have already spoken with Reverend Pettigrew. He understands my predicament. There isn't another place in town big enough to accommodate everyone I intend to invite. He said as long as the bar was closed and the drunks kept away, he didn't see a thing wrong with using the Roadrunner Saloon."

"Just how many people do you intend to invite, lovey?" Mr. Emenhizer asked.

"Why, the whole town, Loy. The whole town."

The day of the Emenhizers' party, it turned much colder. A northerly wind whipped up the few remaining leaves from the garden and froze the puddles left by the last rain. Everyone in Bluebonnet went about their chores bundled in their heaviest coats and capes, keeping their collars and hoods up and their hands snug and warm in knitted woolen mittens.

Reed stayed a bit longer than usual in the doctor's office, as the cold weather was causing the elderly to have flare-ups of rheumatism and the children to cry with earaches. The druggist across the way was busy mixing up numbing salves and cough syrup, and Dahlia was busily foisting off her own home remedies on anyone willing to give them a try.

Winter, it seemed, had settled in, and everyone in town was looking forward to the grand party the Emenhizers were throwing in the Roadrunner Saloon. Why, word had it that there was even a band coming from as far away as Dallas, and everyone speculated that the rumor must be true, for a group of newcomers had arrived only this morning and checked in to the Peach Orchard Hotel.

When Reed got home, Susannah and her aunts were dressed and waiting for him. He changed quickly, then harnessed the buggy and drove up to the house for the ladies. Susannah, he thought, looked lovelier than ever in a gown of antique gold velvet that set off the color of her eyes and pulled the light from the lamps and settled it in her hair.

Susannah said Violette and Dahlia were like a couple of mismatched bookends, and Reed didn't have any trouble agreeing. Dahlia looked as if she had gotten a good price on a reel of yellow ball fringe and used all of it on her bright red dress. Violette was a bit more subdued–but only a bit–in a wool dress of black-and-white checks trimmed with jet beads. The feathers in her hair bore a remarkable resemblance to those in the feather duster.

When they arrived at the Emenhizer party, no one seemed to notice the outlandish dresses worn by Susannah's aunts, but everyone stared at Susannah as if they had never seen her before. Tate Trahern looked especially green with envy.

The green of Tate's face didn't go at all well with the deep golden velvet gown Susannah wore. But the adoration in Reed's eyes did. He had known her for a beauty, but he had never seen her dressed like this.

"That's because I've never *owned* a dress like this," she told him when he complimented her. "My darling aunts made it for me. It's truly a labor of love."

"And you look like a love in it," he said, kissing her softly. "My love. My one and only true love."

He wished he weren't standing so close to her and found himself envying those who stood farther away, for they had the pleasure of taking in all of her lovely appearance: the way the gown nipped her waist and flared out into a softly bustled train; the intricate embroidery along the hem with gold thread; the neckline that was, Susannah swore, "far lower than anything I have ever worn."

This was the first social gathering since the typhoid epidemic, and everyone seemed to be enjoying themselves more than ever before. When it was apparent that everyone in town had gathered in the Roadrunner, Muriel and Loy Emenhizer stood on the bottom steps of the stairway and called Reed and Susannah to come and stand with them.

"I know everyone in Bluebonnet shares with me a tremendous amount of gratitude for the way Dr. Garrett and Susannah gave so unselfishly of themselves during the late unpleasantness, and I know there are many of you, like myself, who owe their very presence here tonight to Dr. Garrett. It doesn't take a wise man to realize what this town would be like now if we hadn't had the fortune to have a man like Dr. Garrett in our midst."

The people erupted with clapping, whistling, and shouts of "Hear! Hear!"

"For this reason, Loy and I want to extend a personal thank-you on behalf of all the citizens of Bluebonnet," Muriel said, turning to Reed and Susannah, "and as a token of our appreciation, we would like to present you with this." She handed Reed an envelope.

"Go ahead," she said. "Open it."

Reed handed the envelope to Susannah. She opened it and found it full of money.

"A thousand dollars isn't much when you think of how many lives you saved, but it's our way of saying thank you. We hope you will accept this money and use it to refurbish Dr. Bailey's office, which his widow has deeded over to you. It is Mrs. Bailey's wish that you continue the work her husband started here."

Susannah and Reed thanked them but were cut short by Muriel.

"And now, I would like to get on to the real reason I invited everyone here tonight. I have some news that will bring a tear to your eye and a smile of joy to your lips. It is my greatest honor and privilege to tell you that our own beloved Susannah Jane Dowell has agreed to become the wife of our respected and admired Dr. Garrett."

There were catcalls, applause, and general all-around shouts of goodwill, as many of the town's residents crowded forward to congratulate Reed and Susannah. In the midst of all their newfound joy, a shot rang out.

The room grew deathly quiet as everyone turned toward the sound.

Tate Trahern stood on the bar. He waved a six-shooter over his head, his motion awkward and wobbly. It was obvious to one and all that Tate was drunk.

The sight of Tate hit Reed with a dose of apprehension. A sick sort of fear began to build within him. Tate was up to something, something that Reed knew involved him. He tightened his hands into fists and stood immobile, wary of what was happening yet unable to do anything about it.

"I just wanted to get everyone's attention," Tate said, slurring his words. "I want the happy little couple to know how important I think it is that they start out their life together without any secrets between them. For that reason, I want everyone in the room to know that our resident saint, Dr. Reed Alexander Garrett, the third, served five years in Massachusetts State Prison for the murder of his wife and baby."

A horrified gasp went up around the room.

Reed's insides knotted. Anxiety spread through his body, reaching the extremities with a slow, creeping heat that consumed him. While everyone around Reed began to talk, a multitude of memories and feelings wafted through his head.

Tate fired off his pistol once more. "Just in case any of you self-righteous folks don't believe what I say, you might want to look over this letter I received from the *Boston Herald*. They sent me a full accounting and copies of the articles that appeared in the newspaper during his trial."

Reed went stone still. He knew at that moment that he would never be free of the past. It would follow him like a hound, nipping at his heels. A normal life would never be his. The thought of losing Susannah just when he had found her was unbearable. Dear God, would this albatross ever be gone from around his neck? How many times did a man have to pay? He was reminded of a passage in the Bible, one that said it was appointed that man should die only once. And yet he was dying a second time. How ironic that he had served his five years only to find his debt to society was not paid in full. Rage and despair ate away at him. He wanted to throw back his head and howl. He wanted to smash something, to beat his fists against something until he could no longer stand.

But he did not let any of those feelings show. His face an expressionless mask, he thought about what he should do next. He turned to Susannah, knowing she had been standing there, listening with growing dread to the poison being spewed by a snake named Tate Trahern.

She closed her eyes, and when she opened them, he saw the shock, the pain. He knew it was all over. He realized now that there would never be another life for him, that he would never belong. He could not marry Susannah any more than he could expect her to spend her life running from his past.

He watched her standing there, a wild sort of expression on her face as she looked about, like a demented being. She extended her hand as if she was going to touch him, but she must have reconsidered, for she pulled her hand back. Reed was afraid she would turn and run. But it was the clouded look of doubt in her eyes that was his undoing. When she searched his face, pain sliced through his heart.

Oh, Susannah, not you. I could take this from anyone but you. Don't turn away from me now, when I need you most. Of all people, you are the one I thought would stand beside me. . . .

Nothing–not the death of his wife and child, not the five years of his life spent in a horrible prison–had prepared him for this. She was the woman he loved, the one he chose to marry, and she had turned against him just as Philippa had. His life was nothing but one disappointment after another. He shouldn't have been surprised that she doubted him. He felt exhausted, vanquished, wishing now that the court in Boston had sentenced him to death. At least that way it would have been quick, unlike the slow, anguishing death he was experiencing now.

He looked away. It didn't matter. Without Susannah, nothing mattered. He wondered why he thought things would be different. He wasn't a doctor. That had been taken along with the five years of his life. He had been a fool to think he could have it all again–a wife and family, a medical practice, respect.

He was about to turn away and leave when he felt Susannah's slender arm slip through his and her hand give him a reassuring squeeze. The gesture more than suprised him. She started to speak, and he lifted his eyes to search her face for meaning.

"Whatever Tate has found out is old news," Susannah said, her voice dry and scratchy, the words coming out jerky. "My husband-to-be has paid his debt to society twice–once in Massachusetts and again here, in Bluebonnet, when he revealed to everyone that he was a doctor so he could give so unselfishly of his time. As Muriel said, I don't have to tell you how many lives he saved."

As she gazed around the room, her expression belied the confidence of her words. Not that it mattered. Reed was tired. Tired of lying. Tired of running. Tired of trying to be something he wasn't. It was as if that one look from Susannah changed everything. He was not destined to find happiness in this world . . . with Susannah or anyone else.

Susannah may have put on a show of defending him with her words, but Reed saw in her eyes what was in her heart. She was lost to him, and the pain was unbearable. There was no longer a reason to fight. Without a word, he turned and walked out the door.

The sight of his retreating back was like a slap in her face, but it did serve one purpose: It cleared the fog from Susannah's mind. She realized she had made a wretched mistake and done a terrible disservice to the man she loved. She would go to her grave remembering the blank, detached look Reed gave her just before he turned away. She knew what he must be suffering, the desolation and despair he must feel, thinking she had turned her back on him.

Well, blast it, Reed. What do you expect? she argued in her mind. *I was shocked and taken by surprise. It wasn't that I doubted you, not really. I was simply caught off guard for a moment. Damn you! If you'd waited, you would have seen that. Why did you leave? Why did you give up so easily?*

Reed Garrett may have given up easily, but Susannah was not going to. She had something worth fighting for, and she was ready to take on the whole town if need be. She wished Reed had told her about his going to prison. She understood why he would have been reluctant to tell her, but it would have made it easier to defend him if she had known. She took a look at the door where she had last seen Reed, and wished she could go after him and the town be damned. But someone had to say something. Tate couldn't get away with this.

She stiffened her spine and was about to speak when she had the surprise of her life.

"Let me through! Get out of the way! Let me pass!"

Susannah stared open-mouthed as Dahlia made her way through the crowd, rapping those who did not move fast enough with her parasol.

When she made it to the front, Dahlia faced the crowd in a manner that Susannah could only call magnificent. "I am shamed to admit I'm part of this community, a place where the likes of this reptile"–Dahlia pointed a wagging finger at Tate–"can get away with slandering the name of a just and upright man. There isn't a one of you who doesn't owe Reed Garrett a debt of gratitude. You stop and think about that for a minute. Where would you be now if he hadn't stepped forward and bared his soul to us in order to help? He could have left us to face the typhoid epidemic on our own." She turned toward Tate and smacked him across the shin with her parasol. "He saved a lot of people from death, including your own worthless hide."

Jonah stepped forward and silenced the murmuring crowd. "I think a man deserves a chance to defend himself against his accusers. If Reed Garrett went to prison, I think he has a right to explain why."

"He can't explain why," Tate said, "because he's too yellow to face up to what he did."

Dahlia whacked him again. "You say another word against Dr. Garrett and I'll mop the floor with you, you worthless bully! I'm sure Reed has a good explanation for what happened, but I'm not too certain that we need to know, or that we even have the right to ask him to tell us. He has proven himself on the battlefield, and I say that the best thing we can do is to be forgiving and to get on with the living of our lives."

Everyone began to applaud and show their agreement, but Susannah knew this thing would always hang over his head, that there would come a time when first one and then another of these well-meaning folk gathered here would wonder. She knew, too, that the children they would have one day might find themselves on the taunting end of comments and their lives would be tainted by his past. She held up her hand to get their attention and the room grew quiet.

"I appreciate your support and your faith in the man I love as much as I appreciate your willingness to let bygones be bygones, but I know that Reed is not a man to accept a handout. If he went to prison, I am certain there was a reason. I think he has earned our respect. It is time to give him our trust." She glared at Trahern, who tried to get down from the bar, misjudged the distance, and went sprawling.

When he tried to get up, Dally said, "Stay down there in the dirt where you belong, you lily liver!" Then she smacked him on the head. Tate fell back to the floor and lay on his face, spread-eagled.

Susannah was so busy watching Dahlia and trying to decide where this woman had been hiding for so many years that she did not notice Violette had moved to take a place on the stairs.

When the voices in the room suddenly subsided and faded to quiet, Susannah turned in the direction everyone was looking. There stood Violette with her hands raised in the air.

In stunned silence, Susannah listened to her as she began to tell the story of what happened in Dr. Reed Garrett's life during the birth of his child. There wasn't a woman with a dry eye in the room when she spoke of the way Reed's wife turned against her husband in favor of her father and how this tragic decision cost both her life and the baby she carried.

"But the story is far from over. Reed Garrett's father-in-law, Dr. Copley, was naturally grieved over the loss of his daughter and grandchild, but he did not let it end there. Because Dr. Garrett had used the latest methods developed by Dr. Semmelweis in Austria, he was accused of witchcraft, of using procedures that endangered the lives of his wife and child. Two weeks later, Dr. Garrett was charged with murder."

A gasp went around the room.

"Dr. Adam Copley was out to get him, but even now, Reed is the first to say that he sincerely believed it was his grief causing him to strike out. Of course, Reed believed the old man would come to his senses. Even when his own father tried to warn him that his former father-in-law would not stop until he destroyed him, Reed disregarded it. He rejected the offers of help from his father, even the suggestion that he be allowed to hire the best attorney Boston had to offer."

Violette paused a moment and looked out over the crowd. "Have you ever been so consumed with grief that you didn't care what happened to you?"

With the memory of so many deaths on their minds, there wasn't a person in the room who did not understand and nod in agreement.

"Naturally Dr. Garrett was in a stupor. When he was first brought before a judge to hear the accusations against him, he was suffering so much he did not say anything to defend himself. His family tried to make him understand how important it was to get control of himself, but he refused to even let them hire a lawyer. Well into the trial he had still not accepted the death of his wife. He did not lift a finger to defend himself. It took a severe confrontation between his father and himself before he finally realized what was happening . . . what could happen. Only then it was too late."

She paused again and looked over to where Tate was lying on the floor, his head held down by the point of Dahlia's parasol. "You heard Tate mention an article from the *Boston Herald*. Well, it was almost the end of what the *Boston Herald* called 'the most lengthy and notorious trial of the century' before Reed came to terms with his loss and made an attempt to defend himself. He explained how the infection that killed his wife came from her father, and not from him."

She looked around the room. "You can imagine how this shocked the courtroom. They didn't believe him. Even when he explained how Dr. Copley taught medical classes at Harvard, and how he had come straight to his daughter's bedside from an autopsy class that day, and how he readied himself to deliver his grandchild, without sterilizing his hands. Because of Dr. Copley's reputation, the influence he had in the city and at Harvard Medical School, they didn't believe him. Even when his father brought in a well-known lawyer who provided lots of distinguished witnesses attesting to the credibility of the pioneering work done by Semmelweis, no one listened. Their minds were made up long before that moment."

Violette came down off the stairs and walked around. "You are probably asking how anyone could be so ignorant. Well, you have to understand that even after the antiseptic procedures were accepted in Europe, there continued to be debates published in American surgical journals concerning the validity of this new germ theory. There was science and there was medicine. American doctors believed that anything that came out of the laboratory was dubiously influenced by foreign interests. When Lister came to America to give his three-hour talk before the Centennial Medical Commission of Philadelphia, the *Boston Medical and Surgical Journal* gave more recognition and comment about his personality and determination than they did his technique." She stopped walking and began to look people straight in the eye. "My friends, Reed Garrett didn't stand a chance."

She started pacing again. "Of course, to understand why you must consider the fact that Adam Copley was such a powerful and well-respected doctor. Out of devotion and respect for him, the legal and medical community in Boston couldn't put much faith in anything Reed said. That, added to the fact that he waited so long to defend himself, worked against him."

"You don't mean they found him guilty?" someone asked.

"I do."

"What happened? What did they decide?" Loy Emenhizer asked.

"It was the unanimous sentence of the court that Dr. Reed Garrett serve five years in prison for contributing to the death of his wife and stillborn son." Susannah could tell that Violette was doing her best to keep the cynicism out of her voice. She knew it was extremely difficult for her to do so.

"You know, it's strange, but even when Reed

shared his story with me, he said that when he heard the sentence they handed him, he showed little emotion. As far as he was concerned, his life had ended when his wife and child died. He could not help wondering how they could possibly hurt him more than he was hurting already?"

"What happened after he left prison?" Sheriff Carter asked.

"He went home . . . back to Boston. He tried to make a go of it there, but the past was always before him, entering doors ahead of him. He realized after a year or so that his family was suffering because of him. He couldn't watch his mother and father go through it day after day. He left Boston and the practice of medicine for good."

Violette was finished. With her heart in her throat, Susannah waited, wondering how the people of Bluebonnet would react.

Everyone in the room began to clap and crowd forward, surrounding Violette and Susannah, upon whom they lavished good wishes for a long and happy marriage. Susannah looked at Tate lying on the floor, Aunt Dahlia standing guard over him, parasol in hand. "If anyone in this town deserves to be punished and turned away, it's that man," she said, pointing at Tate.

"Lock him up, Sheriff!"

"Run him out of town!"

"The town isn't big enough for a good man like Dr. Garrett and the likes of Trahern!"

As the townsfolk vented their spleens and turned their anger where it rightly belonged, on Tate Trahern, Susannah slipped out of the room.

She hurried home, praying she wouldn't be too

late, for she knew it was Reed's intention to leave, to run from his past as he had been doing when he wandered into all their lives.

When she arrived at Reed's place on a borrowed horse, Susannah met him coming out of the house with his saddlebags slung over his shoulder. "Are you going somewhere?"

He did not look at her but kept on walking. "You might say that."

She stepped in front of him. "But, you asked me to marry you. Have you forgotten about that?"

"No, but apparently you did."

"Reed, I'm sorry. I did not mean for you to think I doubted you, that I did not trust you. You must understand that I was shocked . . . caught off guard. I couldn't hide my surprise. If you had stayed there a bit longer, you would have seen that."

"Then I will never know, will I?" He started around her and Susannah felt a surge of anger and desperation. She couldn't let him leave. She couldn't.

She looked around frantically. Her gaze settled on a block of wood. Without another thought, she picked it up and hit him over the head. With a sense of acute disbelief, she watched him fall forward. She dropped the chunk of wood as if it were glowing hot and stared stupidly down at the man she loved who lay unmoving at her feet.

Terrified, she prayed she hadn't hit him too hard. She was wondering what she should do, when her aunts drove up and pulled the buggy to a halt a few feet away.

"What's going on here?" Violette asked as she approached and looked down at Reed's prone form.

"I'm afraid I've knocked him out."

"I can see that. But what happened to make you take such action? You were always the peaceable type."

"Worms can turn."

Violette smiled. "So I'm told."

"He wouldn't listen to reason, Aunt Vi. He was leaving. I didn't know what else to do. I couldn't let him go. Not like this." Susannah went to Reed and dropped down beside him. She rolled him over until his head rested in her lap. "You don't think I've killed him, do you?"

"No, but you may wish you had when he wakes up with a roaring headache."

"Do you want us to help you?" Dahlia asked. "We could carry him into the house and put him to bed."

"That's a great idea," Susannah said.

The three of them managed to drag Reed into the house. It was impossible to lift him onto the bed, so they made a pallet on the floor and rolled him onto it. "I'll be right back," Susannah said.

A short time later, she returned with a length of rope.

"What are you going to do with that?" Dally asked. "Hang him?"

"First I'll try tying him up."

Delight danced in Dahlia's eyes. "Yes, and keep him tied until he comes to his senses."

Once Reed's hands and feet were secured, Dahlia and Violette went home, but Susannah remained with Reed.

Susannah was sitting beside Reed when he opened his eyes some time later.

"What happened?"

"I hit you."

"What with?" He closed his eyes for a moment, as if trying to push back a sharp pain.

"A block of wood."

"Why?"

"I had to. Reed, you were being foolish and pig-headed. I couldn't let you leave."

He looked down at the ropes that bound him. "How long do you plan to keep me tied?"

"For as long as it takes," she said, filling her voice with as much firm resolve as she could muster. "I've gone this far, I might as well see this thing through to the end."

"And if I don't change my mind? What will you do then? Keep me here like this until I'm an old man?"

She threw up her hands. "You are impossible! I swear you'd find a loophole in the Ten Commandments!"

"Untie me."

She narrowed her eyes. "Are you going to listen to reason?"

"Untie me and I'll tell you."

She frowned at him. "I don't trust you, Reed Garrett, any further than I can throw you."

"Ha! You're asking me to understand you, to trust you, and yet you don't trust me?"

"Sometimes I hate being a woman. Why is it that we always have to lose? I get very tired of that. Once in a while I think we should be allowed to win."

"Then do something about it."

"Like what?"

"Untie me and I'll show you."

"Are we back to that again?"

"Susannah . . ."

"I'm sorry you didn't stay in town. You would have been proud of Dally."

He gave her a surprised look and finally asked, "Okay, what did she do?"

"She lit into Tate Trahern with her parasol. Last I saw of him he was sprawled, facedown, on the floor."

Reed chuckled at that.

"Aunt Vi told them what happened."

"Who?"

"The folks in town. She told them the reason you went to prison and how–"

"She told them that?"

"Yes."

"Are you angry at me for telling Violette and not you?"

"I was at first, but now I understand why you did it."

"And why is that?"

"Because you love me and wanted to protect me from all the painful details." She paused a moment. "Of course, it could have been because you were afraid you would lose me." She paused once more. "On the other hand, it could be because–"

"Susannah, my love, will you shut up and untie me?"

"Why? So you can be on your way?"

"So I can tell you properly how much I love you."

"Well, why didn't you say that to begin with?"

She untied his feet, then his hands, and stood up, placing her hands on her hips. "Okay. Talk!"

He laughed and stood up, then his arms came around her and he kissed her mouth softly. When he drew back and looked down into her face, he shook his head and said, "For this, I gave up a perfectly good rib?"

Susannah and Reed used the gift of their wedding money to fix up Dr. Bailey's old office, and they bought a small farm that adjoined Violette's land. Although there was a house on the property, it was in disrepair, so they spent most of their spare time getting their future home in order.

A week before their wedding, the house was ready, and Susannah took her aunts over to help her with the finishing touches by hanging the curtains over the shiny new glass-paned windows. Two days before the wedding Reed and Susannah moved their clothes. That evening, Reed said he would sleep in the barn to keep an eye on things.

"You can't sleep in the barn," Susannah said. "That's ridiculous. Sleep in the house. There are sheets on the bed. Everything is ready."

"Love, I wouldn't dream of sleeping in our bed or our house without you. I'll sleep in the barn until we are married, and then wild horses won't be able to drag me out of that bed."

"I wish your parents could be here for our wedding," she said.

"I do, too, but my father isn't up to the trip. My mother is afraid it would be too exhausting for him."

"Do you think we could go to Boston to visit them afterward?"

"I don't see why not. If there's anything I'd like to do, it's show off my beautiful wife. My parents will adore you, by the way."

"I know I'll love them."

"How do you know?"

She stood on the tips of her toes and put her arms around his neck. "Because they raised you and helped to make you what you are, so I give them credit for all your *good* qualities."

"And my bad ones?"

"I'm afraid you will have to take credit for those yourself."

"I love you. Do you know that?"

"Yes, and in case you're interested, I love you, too."

They were married in the First Methodist Church by the Reverend Pettigrew, who announced to the congregation, "I think it is only fitting that these two be joined in holy matrimony in the very building where they both worked so tirelessly to save so many lives. It was here that they began to fall in love, so that makes this place even more special. So, it is with much pleasure that I pronounce them man and wife."

"Well, it certainly took him long enough to move in for the kill," Dahlia said to Violette, in tones that were whispered a bit too loudly. This sent everyone in the congregation into peals of laughter. And why not? Laughter was not a bad way to begin a marriage.

The newlyweds settled into their new home, and

Reed, true to his word, did not spend another night in the barn. Everyone in town talked about how happy they seemed, but no one had any way of knowing that their newfound happiness wasn't destined to last.

Chapter 22

They had been married two blissful months when Susannah became concerned. There was something wrong, something that made her wonder if Reed regretted taking her for his wife. She did not know exactly what the problem was, but something bothered Reed–something that made him troubled and distant after they made love.

This particularly fine morning, when the weather was clear and surprisingly warm, Susannah watched Reed leave for town after breakfast, then she busied herself with cleaning the house and putting everything in apple pie order.

She was attacking the furniture in the parlor with the feather duster. *Reed might be sorry he married me. Reed might not find me desirable. Reed might not want to make love. Reed might not be able to make love. It's been so long, Reed may have forgotten* how *to make love.*

She shook her head and slapped the lamp with the duster. None of those were the problem. She decided the problem with their lovemaking might be because Reed was tired when he came home at night. And that gave her an idea.

It was almost time for him to come home for lunch. Perhaps if they made love earlier in the day–say, after lunch, things might be different.

Different or not, Susannah decided as she set the table, it was worth a try.

She cooked Reed's favorite, fried chicken, and served him a big helping along with collard greens and mashed potatoes. Her sourdough bread was piping hot, and the butter was the freshest Peony had to offer.

Reed ate as if he had been starved for a week. When he pushed back from the table and rubbed his stomach and groaned, Susannah sat on his lap and kissed him on the mouth. "You didn't eat that much, Reed Garrett, so stop your groaning."

He kissed her nose. "You're going to make me as fat as Miss Lavender, if you aren't careful. How come you feed me so well? You keep that up and you won't be able to get me out of the kitchen."

"You know what they say about the way to a man's heart being through his stomach."

He kissed her, a long and lingering kiss. "Is that what they say?"

"Yes, and do you know what they say is the best way to a woman's heart?"

"No, what is the best way to a woman's heart?"

Susannah stood and pulled him to his feet. "To get her *out* of the kitchen."

She led a laughing Reed out of the kitchen and into the bedroom.

As Susannah began removing his clothes, he said, "What do you call this?"

"Dessert." She finished taking off his clothes, shoved him into the bed, removed her own clothes, and joined him there. She rolled over on top of him and kissed him soundly. "I've decided to take matters into my own hands," she said. "Don't even think about putting up a show of resistance."

"I would never be so vile."

She straddled him and he moaned.

"Love, I think I'd better take matters into my own hands on such a full stomach," and he rolled her over and put her beneath him. Susannah did not argue but welcomed him as he came hard against her. A moment later she felt him enter her, and she did not think about anything else, save the way she felt each time he did this, as if it was the first time.

She moved with him, knowing when he was coming close to losing control, and she prayed that it would be different this time, that he would not withdraw and spill his seed on her stomach.

She wanted a child. His child. Their child.

The sadness she felt must have reached out to him for he asked, "Susannah? Sweet love, what is it?"

"Oh, Reed," she said, and threw her arms around his neck.

"Honey, what's wrong?"

"I know, Reed. I realized it a moment ago." She could feel her eyes filling with more tears with each word she spoke. Soon, it would be impossible to hold them back, and in all honesty she wasn't certain she wanted to.

"What do you know, love? What did you realize that is making you so upset?"

"I know what you think, even though you don't believe I know. I do know, Reed. I truly know."

"What? Tell me, Susannah. What is it?"

"I know you don't want me to have a baby because you feel you can never replace the one you lost, that I'm not capable of giving you a child you could love. Is it because you loved your first wife so much, or because of my past?"

At first, he looked dumbfounded, but then his eyes began to twinkle with humor.

Susannah felt no such humor, however. *If he laughs, I'll choke him.*

"Oh sweetheart, it's neither of those reasons, believe me." He kissed her face, her neck, her eyes. "I love you, Susannah. Only you. The rest is in the past. You are my present, my reality, my life. You're all I think about, all I want."

"Then why do you pull away before you can give me a baby? What's wrong with me?"

He released a long and heavy sigh. "It isn't you, Susannah. It's me."

"What is it?"

"I'm afraid."

"Afraid? Of what?"

"I lost a wife in childbirth once. I cannot bear to lose you. I won't risk it. Not even for children. You are my life. I couldn't go on without you."

Susannah started crying again. "Oh Reed, you aren't going to lose me, because I'm not going to turn away from you the way Philippa did. I want you to deliver our child . . . all of our children, and I know whatever you decide to do when the time comes will be the best decision that could be made. I trust you."

"I don't deserve you," he said, kissing her again. "And you don't deserve the cruel way I've treated you."

"I know, but that's a whole new discussion and I want to stay on this one for a bit longer."

She ignored the fact that he was limp with laughter and poked him in the chest. "You don't deserve the cruel thing I'm going to do to you if you stop before we finish this time. It's showdown time, Reed."

Reed was laughing so hard Susannah wondered if he would be able to finish what he had started. She needn't have worried. Her husband, she learned, never left anything undone. This time, when Reed made love to her, he stayed with her, and when he came inside her, Susannah knew, somehow, that Reed had given her the greatest gift of all, his child.

"That isn't fair," Susannah said.

"What isn't fair?"

"That you should know before I do."

"The important thing isn't who knew first, but the fact that we're going to have a baby."

At the sound of those words, a dozen different emotions jammed in her throat. But of all the things she felt, the one that touched her the most was the sorrow that her mother wasn't there to see the happy ending. When she told Reed how she felt, he put his arms around her. "I have a feeling she knows," he said.

"Do you really think so?"

"Believe me, she knows."

And, oddly enough, Susannah knew that Reed was right.

She sat back with a satisfied sigh and thought about her mother. Like a snake that sheds its skin and emerges a different color and texture, she was a new being. She opened her heart to the woman who had gone before her and marveled at the power of healing.

When he first discovered Susannah was going to have a baby, Reed was elated, but that night, when the dreams of Philippa and their dead child came back to haunt him, he awoke in a cold sweat. No matter how hard he tried, he could not shake the memory of what had happened. He could not forget the sight of his first wife's dead face, or the weight of the stillborn son he held in his arms for such a brief time. The dreams continued.

It was Susannah who held him after he woke until he could fall asleep again. Susannah was the one who showed the strength now, but not even she could totally erase the fear of the past.

One afternoon, after Reed finished seeing patients in town, he stopped by Buck and Smith's to pick up the mail. Mr. Truesdale handed him a few letters and said, "Hold on a minute there, Reed. I recollect there was a package in the back that I forgot to give you last week."

Reed took the package home and opened it. When he saw that it was from Dr. Ledbetter in Boston, he remembered writing a long letter to his father after his talk with Violette about Susannah's mother. So much had happened since then, he'd almost forgotten about it.

When he opened the package, he found the personal belongings of Captain J. D. Carpenter, CSN, a Bible, some military medals, and a few old letters. There was also a letter from Dr. Ledbetter.

Dear Reed,

Imagine my surprise when I opened the letter from you, surprise that doubled when I read your inquiry about Captain Carpenter. Although it has been a long time since the war, I am happy to report that I do, indeed, remember Captain Carpenter quite vividly.

I have enclosed the personal effects that were in Captain Carpenter's possession when he died. Shortly before his death, he asked me to see that his things reached his wife. I cannot tell you how happy I am to forward these items to you and to put this longing to do the thing I promised behind me. I must tell you that after so many years, I feared the worst when I did not hear a reply to any of the letters I wrote to Captain Carpenter's wife, Rachel. During the war, I normally did not have, nor did I take, the time to show such a personal interest in the life of a soldier, and certainly not a Confederate one, but Captain Carpenter saved my life and lost his own life in the doing of it. After his death, I felt I owed it to his family to do the right thing and honor his wishes to see that his personal effects reached them. Even when I did not hear from his wife, I was reluctant to dispose of Captain Carpenter's belongings, so I kept them with me throughout the war. When it was over, I carried them back to Boston with me. I had forgotten all about them, I must confess, until I received your letter.

Captain Carpenter took a bullet that was meant for me. He died from infection when gangrene set in. During the time it took him to die from the infection, we had the opportunity to become quite good friends. When J.D. realized he was dying, he told me all about his young wife and the child they were expecting. He also told me of his fears for her safety, for he knew if anything happened to him, that his younger brother, who was "a greedy bastard named Warren," would stop at nothing to get the family plantation and the vast inheritance that went with it. The problem lay in the fact that his wife and child were his legal heirs, and they would stand in the way of Warren having all that he wanted.

Captain Carpenter told me he was from a wealthy Mississippi family. At his parents' deaths he was made the sole heir because his father considered his brother to be unfit. Warren evidently contested the will, but it held up in court. Not long after that, J.D. filed a will of his own, leaving everything to his wife and any unborn heirs, then left for the war. Just before J.D. left, his brother had become furious and said he would get the plantation if he had to kill the entire family to do it. Many was the time that J.D. expressed a fear that his brother would do exactly as he'd threatened.

I do hope the things I have told you are of some value to you and will help you in your quest. I see your family often and have kept in touch with your whereabouts through them. I know you will be pleased to hear that the tide is turning here in the medical community in Boston. Men of esteem who hold the same beliefs that you and Oliver Wendell Holmes held are growing in numbers. It is, I think, only a matter of time until you can return to Boston and the promising life you had when tragedy struck.

I trust this letter finds you in good health.

I am, as always, your friend,

John Ledbetter

Reed put the letter down and picked up the Bible. He opened it and turned to the page where family events were recorded. There he found the record of the marriage of Rachel Jane Bradford to James Dowell Carpenter.

Dowell . . . Now he realized where Susannah's mother got the name she had given to her daughter.

Reed closed the Bible and picked up the letters from Rachel to her husband. He read through three of them, finding the usual things a wife would write to her husband. But the fourth letter was significant, for in it Rachel revealed that she carried his child.

Reed looked at the date on the letter and compared it with the date of Susannah's birth. There was no doubt that Susannah was the legitimate issue of James Dowell Carpenter. He also understood that out of fear for the safety of herself and her unborn child, Rachel had gone to New Orleans.

After reading Dr. Ledbetter's letter again, Reed went to find Susannah. She was sitting in the parlor stitching a sampler for the baby's room.

"Sweetheart, I have something here that I think you ought to see."

She looked up. "What is it?"

He took a seat next to her. "Put your sewing away, because I don't think you are going to feel like sewing after I show you this."

Susannah put the sewing on the table next to her. "All right. Show me what you have in the package that has you acting so suspicious."

He handed her Dr. Ledbetter's letter and watched her face as she read. A few minutes later, he took out his handkerchief and began blotting the huge tears that rolled down her cheeks.

When she finished reading, Susannah put the letter down. "Carpenter. Do you think my father was J. D. Carpenter?"

"I am certain of it. If you look at the date of the letter and count a few months forward you will end up at your birthday."

Reed showed her the other letters and the Bible. Then they settled into a discussion of the possibilities of what might have happened, considering the events that would have prompted her mother to do what she did. He told her about her father's brother and how he had come to Bluebonnet after her father's death, looking for her mother.

"You think she was afraid of him, afraid for us?"

"I am sure that's what she thought, and apparently for good reason. I doubt your uncle was looking for her to console her."

"She went to New Orleans out of fear for both of our lives," Susannah said. "It makes perfect sense. I think she was afraid to go back home to Mississippi, because she was afraid of what Warren might do."

"So she lost herself and her soul in a bordello in New Orleans, knowing he would never dream of her doing so, that he wouldn't think of looking for her there."

"Oh, Reed, she did love me."

"She must have loved you very much to do what she did."

The discovery made Susannah cry. It did not undo the awful years she and her mother had endured, but it made them more understandable. "I realize now," she sobbed, "that I can forgive her. I can finally forgive my mother. I feel so sorry that

I didn't know, that I carried this grudge against her for so long."

"Sorry? Why should you feel sorry? You didn't know the truth."

"Don't you see, Reed? The woman I have always accused of having never done anything for me actually went to great lengths to protect me."

Reed put his arms around her. "Don't cry overmuch, sweetheart."

"Oh, Reed, how can I ever thank you? You have given me my past."

"Maybe I can give you even more," he said. "I'll see the judge in town tomorrow. I want to check things out. I want to find out about this plantation and your uncle Warren Carpenter."

Susannah looked pensive for a moment. Then she said, "I don't want you to do that, Reed. I have what I need most, and that is the knowledge that J. D. Carpenter was my father and that I'm legitimate. I have proof now that my mother loved me more than herself. The rest is part of the past. Let's leave it there."

"Don't you want to know? Don't you wonder why your mother chose a life of prostitution over being a maid or a shop clerk?"

"There was a time when I wondered about all that, but not anymore. I don't want to spend the rest of my life trying to find answers to those old questions. My mother did what she did because she felt it was the only way, or the best way. I have to trust her judgment. I want us to go forward, not back into the past."

"You aren't even curious?"

"No. We can speculate all we want, but we'll just have to accept the fact that we won't ever know why my mother was so desperate that her only option was a bordello."

"If you're certain that's what you want . . ."

"I am. You are my future." She put her hand on her stomach. "You and our baby." She reached out, took his hand. "I am content to leave it at that."

"Without a doubt?"

"Without any doubt whatsoever. I know the best years of our lives lie ahead of us."

Chapter 23

As the time of her travail drew near, Reed lived with the consuming fear that something would happen to Susannah. He was not a born pessimist, but experience had taught him to expect the worst. And the worst was that there would be complications when it came time for Susannah to give birth. He could not go through that again. He could not lose Susannah. He could not face life without her.

It wasn't his intent to worry her, but he could not help himself. He became withdrawn. It was only her infinite patience and compassion that enabled him to face each morning knowing this might be the day, only her love and depth of understanding that comforted him each night when he fell asleep with a prayer of thanks on his lips–thanks that he had made it through another day without being called to face the most difficult moment in his life.

Susannah, ever the optimist, obviously understood this and said to him more than once, "Reed, there is nothing to worry about. Everything will be fine. I feel it in my very bones. Nothing is going to happen to me . . . or to our child."

He had always been told that optimism was contagious. He earnestly wished that were true, but no matter how much he wished it upon himself, her jubilant optimism never rubbed off on him.

He wanted to believe her. Desperately. But the question lingered: What if . . . ?

The answer arrived with Susannah's first moan of pain.

For the past week Susannah had been feeling restless. One morning she awoke and said, "I feel lightheaded and shaky. Do you think it's the baby's time?"

Reed was jolted awake by her words. According to his calculations, the baby was not due for another three or four weeks. He did not tell her that. Instead, he leaned over and gave her a kiss and said, "Only time will answer that. Babies do not always adhere to the doctor's schedule."

She placed her hands on her enormous stomach and spoke loudly. "Well, I for one am ready for this birth."

"Who are you talking to–me, or the folks in town?"

"I'm speaking to our son."

"Oh, and how do you know it's a boy?"

"I know. Call it woman's intuition."

Thankfully, Susannah did not give birth and Reed closed his eyes that night with yet another prayer of thanks. A few hours later, he realized his gratitude had been a bit premature.

It was half past three in the morning when Reed awoke to Susannah's discomfort. The moment he heard her first moan, his thoughts were on her and the child she was bringing into the world.

After a particularly vicious spasm gripped her, Reed assured Susannah, reminding her that he would be there with her. A short time later, he slipped out of their bedroom and went upstairs to wake her aunts, who had been staying with them for the past week, so they would be on hand at this moment. They were there to comfort Susannah, but to Reed's surprise, their presence was a comfort to him as well.

"Is the baby coming?" Violette asked the moment she opened her bedroom door, her long gray braid hanging over her left shoulder, her eyes remarkably bright and alert for one just yanked from the depths of sleep.

"Yes, but it will be a while yet."

"We'll be right down," she said.

Reed went back to Susannah, unable to believe the day they had waited so long for had finally arrived. Susannah's pains were coming closer together. Soon she would be well into her labor.

Reed was there with her, never leaving her side for a moment, but after several hours of painful contractions, he gave her another examination. The baby was turned, with one foot in the birth canal. He realized that what he had feared the most was happening. No matter how many contractions she had or how long she stayed in labor, Susannah would not have a normal delivery. The only chance to save her and the baby was to deliver their child by cesarean.

The old memories came rushing back and he saw himself cutting into the flesh of a woman he loved. His hands began to perspire and his heartbeat escalated, in spite of all he did to remain calm. The simple fact was, he would have to remove his child from Susannah through an abdominal incision.

Could he do it? *No! Please God! Not again!*

Memories of Philippa flashed through his mind.

It's too much, too similar to the time before, he thought. *I can't do it. I can't risk losing Susannah. I could not live with her blood on my hands.*

He looked down at Susannah's pale face, her beautiful features distorted with pain.

"What's wrong?" Dahlia asked.

"The baby is coming out wrong . . . feet first." His hands trembled. Fear gripped him.

"Can you turn it?" Violette asked.

"I've tried."

Susannah moaned and began to thrash about in the bed. "Please . . . please . . . Help me, Reed. It hurts so."

He would withstand the horrors of hell, the agony of torture for her. He would die for her. Anything but this. He felt nauseated. His hands were shaking so badly now that he doubted he could even deliver a baby the normal way.

"She is depending on you," Dahlia said. "We're all depending on you."

"I can't."

Susannah was panting and thrashing about more than before. When she rolled to her side, he saw the bright red blood beneath her. He rolled her over and examined her again.

God . . . No . . . Please, no. Not this. Not this time. Not again. Don't ask this of me.

"You can't let her die," Violette said coldly.

"Oh, God!" Dahlia said. "Not this way."

The words ripped him apart. The reality that he was losing Susannah was as effective as a slap in his face. Her pain tore into him. The baby was breech and Susannah was bleeding to death. He knew she would die if he didn't act soon. He looked at his medical bag, then at the instruments on the tray beside the bed. *God, give me the courage. I can't let her die without trying. Help me. Give me the courage . . . please.*

The courage came at last, and when it did, it came to him through Susannah.

Weak and in pain though she was, she must have realized what he was feeling, for at that moment she put her pale, trembling hand on his arm and whispered weakly, "You must do what you know is best. Don't think about what happened before. I love you. I know it will be different this time. I trust you, Reed. I know you will do the right thing."

He looked at Dahlia. "Hand me that can of ether and some cotton."

Dahlia handed it to him, and Reed doused the cotton and put it over Susannah's nose.

Susannah lay still, her thrashing and moaning ceased. Reed stared down at her. Remembering her words of love and trust, he picked up the knife. After a few agonizing moments, he cut into the flesh of the woman he loved more than life. He knew that if anything happened to her, he would join her in death. He would not, could not live without her. It was her love that guided him now, her faith that gave him the courage to go on.

Fifteen minutes later, Reed triumphantly delivered a live and kicking baby boy.

He held the baby in his arms and turned to hand him to Violette. But Violette wasn't there.

"Here, I'll take him," Dahlia said, coming quickly to take the baby.

"Where's Vi?"

Dahlia indicated with a nod of her head.

Violette was stretched out on the floor, flat on her back. "What happened?"

"Ether."

Reed saw a wad of cotton lying in her limp hand. "Curiosity got the best of her?"

"Nope, it wasn't that," Dally said. "She couldn't bear the sight of all that blood."

When Susannah woke up, Reed made certain he was the first thing she saw. "I love you," he said.

"I told you," she responded weakly.

He leaned down closer and asked, "You told me what?"

"That everything would be all right. You should have trusted me."

He kissed her. "Next time, I will."

Dahlia came to stand beside him with their son in her arms. "I suppose you want to hold your baby."

Susannah's face was radiant. "Yes," she said. "Oh, yes!"

Reed took his son and handed him to her. Susannah kissed his soft, downy head, then looked from Reed to her aunts, who stood proudly beside him.

"At last," she said. "I have a real family." Tears rolled down her face. "After all this time, I finally have a family."

Reed smiled. "You have the *beginnings* of a family. There is more to come."

"I'll do my part," she said.

He laughed. "So will I." He placed his hand on her forehead. "How do you feel?"

"Like a mother."

He sat down next to her.

"We need to think of a name."

"You did all the work bringing him into the world," he said, and kissed her softly. "I think it only fair that you should name him."

"Well, we could name him after you or your father. Or we could name him after my father." Susannah smiled and Reed could tell by the light in her eyes that she had come up with a name.

Suddenly he had a horrible thought. She wouldn't dare . . . Or would she?

He studied his wife's face, remembering this was the woman who conked him over the head and tied him up. She would. God help him, she would.

"Susannah," he said like a warning.

She smiled at him sweetly. "Yes, love?"

"Not a flower," he said, praying.

She nodded. "But, it's a family tradition."

"I know, but–"

"Reed Garrett! Are you going back on your word? You said I could name him."

Reed gulped. He was trapped. All he could do was nod. He closed his eyes against the horror of hearing his son had been named Weed or Dandelion.

"How about Sweet William?" Violette said. "It has a nice ring to it."

Reed groaned. She couldn't stick their son with a first name like Sweet could she? And come to think on it, wasn't that what she named one of those piglets? *Please God. Please don't let her name our son after a pig.*

Susannah smiled and kissed her son's tiny fingers. "Sweet William. I like that."

"I prefer Johnny Jump-up," Dahlia said.

Susannah nodded and said, "Johnny Jump-up."

Reed wasn't too enamored with that name either, but it was infinitely better than naming his son after a pig, so he nodded enthusiastically.

"I don't know," Susannah said. "Johnny Jump-up is nice, but I really do like Sweet William."

Reed was about to reach for the ether when Susannah looked at him. She must have found something amusing in his expression, for she laughed and said, "I like both names. How about we call him John William?"

"Yes!" Reed let out a relieved sigh. There was a benevolent God. "Yes . . . yes . . . yes . . ." In his enthusiasm he was a bit loud and John William began to cry.

Violette took the baby and rocked him in her arms until he quieted. Then she and Dahlia put him in the crib next to the bed. The two of them looked back at Reed and Susannah, nodded, and went quietly from the room.

Reed heard the door click as they shut it behind them. He looked down at his sleeping son. Happiness washed over him. He reached for Susannah's hand and kissed it as he told her how much he loved her, how very happy she had made him. "I have loved you all my life, it seems, but never more than I love you right now."

"When did you know?" she asked. "When did you know you loved me?"

He kissed each of her fingers. "I can't remember. It wasn't something that happened all of a sudden. It was a gradual thing."

He saw the disappointment on her face and realized how important it was to her. He thought back. "I think the first inkling I had was a time when I watched you when you were unaware. I remember thinking that I could overcome my past and find the courage to face the future, to start over, if only I had . . ."

". . . someone like you," she whispered.

Reed took her in his arms. Suddenly his attention was distracted by the sound of Daffodil's frenzied honking.

John William began to cry again.

"I know your aunts meant well, but sometimes I wish they hadn't been so charitable as to give us Daffy for a wedding present." He reached into the crib and picked up his crying son and handed him to his mother.

"But she's such a lovable goose. I'm sure our son will love her as much as I do."

"That's what I'm afraid of," he said and kissed her soundly. "Thank you," he whispered. "Thank you for giving me my life back, for more happiness than I deserve."

Susannah kissed the baby's head and began to soothe him. John William grew quiet.

"A mother's touch."

"And a father's love." She reached for his hand and there, in the presence of their slumbering son, two people who had been nothing more than two empty halves, laughed, realizing they were now whole.

Outside the sun was setting and the rooster crowed. They could hear the mighty flapping of wings, then a blaring honk followed by a loud crash, then a series of dazed honks.

Susannah and Reed laughed.

ABOUT THE AUTHOR

ELAINE COFFMAN is the award-winning author of several bestsellers, including the *New York Times* bestseller *If You Love Me*, *Angel in Marble*, *For All the Right Reasons*, *Somewhere Along the Way*, *So This Is Love*, *Heaven Knows*, and *A Time For Roses*. A native Texan and former elementary-school teacher, she is the mother of three children.

She lives in Washington, D.C.